THE WALKIN' TRILOGY

'JUST AS GRIPPING AND COMPELLING AS
YOUR BROTHER'S BLOOD
... VERY MUCH WORTH YOUR TIME'
A FANTASTICAL LIBRARIAN

BEAUTIFULLY WRITTEN,
LITERARY HORROR AT ITS BEST ... AN
INTENSE AND TIMELESS
TALE OF FAMILY AND LOVE
.. A WONDERFUL INTRODUCTION TO AN
EXTREMELY TALENTED NEW VOICE'
READERDAD

SURPRISED ME WITH ITS ORIGINALITY.
DIFFERENT & RESONANT'
BIBLIOSANCTUM

VERY WELL WRITTEN TALE ABOUT FAITH
AND WHAT THAT EMOTION CAN DO TO A MAN.
NOT YOUR AVERAGE ZOMBIE
NOVEL. IT'S WAY BETTER.
A REAL PAGE TURNER'
FANTASTICAL IMAGINATIONS

YOUR SERVANTS AND YOUR PEOPLE

David Towsey

JF

Jo Fletcher

BOOKS

First published in Great Britain in 2014 by Jo Fletcher Books
This edition published in 2015 by

Jo Fletcher Books
an imprint of
Quercus Publishing Ltd
Carmelite House
50 Victoria Embankment
London EC4Y 0DZ

An Hachette UK company

A CIP catalogue record for this book is available
from the British Library

PB ISBN 978 1 78206 439 8
EBOOK ISBN 978 1 78206 438 1

10 9 8 7 6 5 4 3 2 1

Typeset by Jouve (UK), Milton Keynes

Printed and bound in Great Britain by Clays Ltd, St Ives plc

For Kath

PROLOGUE

The Pastor adjusted his cassock. It was hot and itchy under the noonday sun. He knocked on the door again, harder this time. It was no surprise they hadn't heard him, with all that was going on inside. He would wait before knocking once more.

His shaggie was tethered to a rail that ran the length of the house. There was a trough that the animal was drinking from. The sky was clear today, but Pine Ridge got more rain than Barkley. The house was on the outskirts of town. Half a mile or more between neighbours – a good, discreet distance. He pulled at his collar. He'd like to take it off but the Good Lord was watching. Always watching.

The Good Book felt heavy in the Pastor's hand. He knocked again.

This time he heard movement from inside. Boards creaked and the door swung open. A large woman grimaced at him. She was sweating. Not just from her brow, but her arms were slick all the way from her rolled-up sleeves to her wrists. The sister.

1

'You've got some nerve,' she said.

'I'm here to see Josie.'

'I know why you're here. Come to see if it's got hooves?'

'That's—'

'You're not coming in. She doesn't want you here.'

'You can't stop me,' he said.

'Oh yes I can.' She planted a meaty fist on the doorframe. Her fingers were stained with blood.

'If you insist on being unreasonable.' He drew out a little pistol from his pocket.

She looked from the gun to his face. She went to shut the door, but he wedged his foot in the gap.

'Go away!' she bawled.

He pressed the pistol into her gut. Her eyes were as big as hay bales. If he fired, would she even feel it? He should have brought a shotgun.

She stepped back and let him in.

'Carry both on you, do you?' she said, nodding to the Good Book.

'When necessary. Where is she?'

'Upstairs.'

He got a foot on the first step before she pushed him out of the way. He followed her immense backside. A low moaning drifted down the stairs. The banister was broken. The wood had snapped there, and it bulged outwards in places. One of the uprights had broken off too. Looking at Josie's sister ahead of him, it wasn't difficult to imagine what had happened.

At the bedroom door she stopped. She opened her mouth. He still had the pistol and the Good Book in his hands. One or perhaps both made her keep her silence. She led him into the room.

'Josie, girl, he's here,' she said.

Josie was lying in bed, the sheets pulled down below her knees. Her thin nightdress was coloured grey with sweat. It was damp against her; she was a slight girl. She looked up. Her cheeks puffed out and she growled at him.

He put the pistol in his pocket and went to her. He held out a hand, but she slapped it away.

'You shouldn't be here,' Josie said. She panted between each word, dealing with the heat like a wool-wrangler.

'I had to come.'

She stopped focusing on him. Her eyes glazed over and she cried out.

The sister huffed and puffed. She put a large pan of water on the bed. 'If you got to be here, stay out the way,' she said. She shooed him into a chair in the corner. It had one leg shorter than the rest, which caught him unawares every few minutes. He opened the Good Book. It was difficult to see the words in the gloom. The curtains were drawn, bathing the room in dull red light.

'"Shall I bring to the birth, and not cause to—"'

'You can stop that right now!' the sister said. 'Last thing this room needs is more hot air.'

He forgave her her blasphemous words. There was no helping a soul such as hers. Josie had liked it when he read.

3

She would close her eyes with her head resting on the pillow. He could tell from her breathing that she wasn't asleep. But Josie didn't seem to be hearing him right now.

He skipped back a verse. It took all his concentration to focus on the words and not the noises around him. *Who hath heard such a thing? Who hath seen such things?* A high-pitched scream made him look. Josie's knees were hitched up. Her sister was attending, making soft sounds that weren't words at all. Josie wailed again and he went back to the Good Book. *Shall the earth be made to bring forth in one day? or shall a nation be born at once? for as soon as Zion travailed, she brought forth her children.* Children. He hadn't thought on twins. Josie was too small for that, surely? The Good Lord had blessed him in so many other ways it wasn't inconceivable. *Shall I bring to the birth, and not cause to bring forth? saith the Lord: shall I cause to bring forth, and shut the womb? saith thy God.*

He closed the Good Book, his thumb marking his place. Perhaps he'd chosen the wrong chapter? Talk of shutting the womb was not appropriate. He took his thumb out of the book. He mopped his brow with the cuff of his cassock.

The heat was unworldly. With the light and the animal-grunting the room seemed to spin. He held his head in his hands, but it didn't stop. The noises became worse: guttural curses, heavy moans. The Pastor tried to block them out. He curled in on himself, the Good Book wedged hard against his chest. This was a vision of his judgement. He should have known there would be no forgiveness for what he'd done. Condemned for a fiery eternity. Words he'd spoken so often in church were now his own fate. He begged for the Good Lord's mercy. He was met with screams.

Piercing, hungry screams. He risked a glance. The sister was holding the child, smeared in blood, its little legs and arms flailing. She wrapped it in cloth and passed it to Josie, who smiled weakly down at her baby. He fell off the chair onto his knees. He clutched the Good Book between his hands and shuffled to the bedside.

'I knew it would be a boy,' Josie said. She ran a finger gently across his forehead and down his nose.

'A boy,' he said.

Her hair was flattened by sweat, the normal bounce of her dark waves gone. She looked beyond him. Her smile was not for him, or anyone.

The sister opened the curtains. Bright sunlight blinded him. Tears came but he didn't weep as the Good Lord washed hotly over him. He'd been saved by his son.

'He shall be called Obadiah,' he said.

The sister snorted. 'He'll be called no such thing.'

'Call him what you will, wench. Before the Good Lord, his name will be Obadiah. His servant.'

BOOK 1

BOOK I

1 : 1

Bryn watched the other wagon crawl along the track. He was squinting, but he couldn't see the driver, not properly. It didn't get closer and it didn't get further away. It stayed the same size. The roof canvas blurred into the ground as the yellow earth rose to the horizon. Bryn licked his lips and tasted salt. A speck settled on his hand, then circled, like it was searching for a good spot to sit. Won't find one out here. Not here. Not in this wagon. That one over there, maybe.

He didn't swat at the speck. He only had to wait, and not long. The wheel he was sitting over hit a rock and everything bounced. The speck flew out beyond the canvas curtain. Bryn went back to watching the other wagon.

'There's women,' John said. 'Two of them. Isn't that something?'

It was, but it didn't need saying. Saying it made it somehow less true. But John was staring at him. 'Two of them?' Bryn said.

'Two.'

There were four of them sitting on crates in his wagon:

9

Bryn, John, Silas and George. Four men, and two women in the other wagon. Bryn took a slug from his water-skin. The feel of it in his mouth quickly became a memory. He plugged the top, pushing until his fingertips turned white. John was still staring.

'You're married?' Bryn said.

John's face screwed up all sour. 'Why'd you have to say a thing like that?' He sat back, resting his head against the canvas. It stretched behind him, changing colour, making a dark halo. Saint John. He belched under his breath and loosened one of the buttons around his gut.

The other wagon disappeared as they went around a bluff. Bryn counted the seconds. At seventeen he could see their animal and at nineteen he saw the full wagon. The sun was sharp and his eyes started to water. The spring air was so thin the light cut right through, but he still looked out. He was bored of John's face and his large gut, bored of the profiles of Silas and George, the patchy royal blue of their jackets, the tapping of their boots on the wooden boards.

For something else to count he marked the bushes they passed. Short and full of thorns, they seemed angry at being alive. They covered the ground in muted explosions, not the full covering of grass in a field. Bryn struggled to picture grass or ground that was anything other than yellowed and cracked; it stretched out for miles. The bushes were everywhere. When the land fell away from the track, so did the bushes. They clung to the bluffs, so high it hurt Bryn's neck to count them, but he did. He was peering up, the count at ninety-two, when the Lieutenant pulled up behind the wagon on his courser, his pistol drawn.

'Gentlemen, you are all dead,' he said.

Bryn blinked. John didn't move.

'About time,' Silas said.

'If even a speck farts his way across this verandah of yours, I expect four trained muzzles on it. Clear?'

'Yes, Lieutenant,' they said.

'Bryn, give me your water-skin.'

'Lieutenant?'

'Your water-skin, boy. Think of this as a hold-up.' The Lieutenant grinned at his own joke. He tipped his hat up with his pistol, in the style of a bandit. Bryn didn't grin. He handed over his water, suddenly thirsty. The Lieutenant turned his courser and headed down the track towards the other wagon. The courser's shiny, taut rump became smaller and smaller.

Bryn picked up his rifle. The others didn't. That was fine by him. If a muzzle did go poking out of the wagon it would be his and he wouldn't be rubbing down the Lieutenant's courser that night or any other for a while. That animal was a biter.

He had to roll up his sleeves – his uniform was too big. His cuffs had to be folded over three times before he could see his wrists. The jacket bulged down his body but not in the way John's did. It was heavy, but Bryn didn't get so hot. George had stitched up the hem on Bryn's trousers for him. He had tripped in front of the Lieutenant when they were loading the wagon. The others didn't laugh. They didn't help him up either. The Lieutenant gave the order in between questioning the space left in the wagon and chivvying John to haul quicker: 'Stitch those hems, George.' Bryn couldn't meet George's eye when he handed the trousers over. Not trusted to stitch his own hems. Bryn returned to his bush-counting, this time ready for any ambush.

'You know the best part about this posting?' Silas said. He crouched between Bryn and John and draped his arms out the back of the wagon. 'We won't see another gun-toting prick the whole eight months.'

'Just you pricks,' John said.

'Just you pricks,' Silas said. 'And it's no great surprise. Who, being in charge of his faculties, would want to come out here?'

'Someone must do, otherwise there wouldn't be a garrison,' Bryn said.

Silas scratched at his stubble. Everyone else had stubble and everyone else scratched their faces a lot. 'Not true. Fort Wilson, if I can call it by its *proper* title, is pre–emp–tor–ary.'

'Where'd you overhear that?' John said.

Silas spat out the back. 'When we was loading. We're there in case something worth being there for turns up.' Silas spat again. How did he have that much spare? 'Which suits me. I've been doing just that my whole life.'

Bryn didn't understand, but the wagon went quiet after that so it must have meant something. Three of them stared out the back as the sun went down. The land turned pale, almost white, and the stars came out. The Lieutenant appeared in the dusk a few hundred yards away. He took his time coming up to the wagon. Bryn let him get to within ten feet before thrusting his rifle forward. The Lieutenant came closer. Shaking his head, he tossed Bryn's water-skin in the back and then rode ahead.

Their wagon stopped. Bryn rubbed his numb backside. Another day on the crate and there would be nothing but bone.

John woke up and stretched. 'Think there'll be a bar this stop?' he said.

Silas whistled. 'This ain't no one-bar town. You got your pick. How do you like them, Bryn? Buxom? Blonde? Or like I do – cheap?'

John put his hand daintily over his heart. 'Bryn Marvington is not the kind of fellow to frequent a bawdy tavern. He has a preference for farming stock. Isn't that right, Marvington?'

The others laughed. Bryn was ready to punch John's wobbling face, but instead he just said, 'That's right.'

It was his fault for telling John about Gloria. He and Bryn had shared a tent during their last posting and one night John had wanted to talk. Normally he fell asleep with his boots still on, but he'd started sharing and didn't want to stop. All kinds of things about his wife and the women he'd bought and the places he'd drunk and the men he'd killed. John only remembered two men – both because they had red hair. 'Do you think that's unlucky?' he'd said. Bryn hadn't known. He'd felt John squirming beside him. It seemed to matter a lot to the burly soldier. John had been in battles. Bryn hadn't.

'All out!' the Lieutenant called. They all stepped down gingerly. Bryn's legs were so stiff his knees felt locked straight. The wind pushed his baggy uniform tight against his shins and ribs. The air was fresh, like ice in his lungs after the fuzz of riding under canvas with three other men. He gulped at it until he felt cold from the inside out. They were high up on a bluff looking out over miles of pearly scrubland. The track they'd climbed wound gradually down and out of sight. Bryn couldn't recall going up. His head felt heavy and his eyes were gritty. He had to turn away from the view. He wasn't good with heights.

'Tents up,' the Lieutenant said. 'Bryn, take Lester.' He handed Bryn the courser's reins.

'But I—'

The Lieutenant was already walking away. Bryn yanked hard on the bridle, which Lester didn't like. The courser stamped at the ground and flicked his head, wrenching Bryn's arm. He almost lost his grip. He glared right into the beast's big black eye. He led Lester away from the tents and dropped the reins. Someone had already unloaded the hobbling posts, so Bryn picked them up. Lester twitched with the urge to bolt. He was struggling against years of training; dropped reins meant a Lester-statue. No other option. Somewhere in that long head of his he knew he should be half a mile away.

'Can't do much about that, can we?' Bryn said. Lester nipped at him, but it was half-hearted. If the courser had really wanted to, he could have taken a few fingers. Bryn dug two holes in the hard-packed dirt, drove in the hobbling posts, then looped Lester's reins over. He went back to the wagon for the feed and the brush. The tents were up and a fire going. The breeze cooled the sweat on his forehead and he shivered. He busied himself brushing whilst Lester ate from the nosebag.

The man who drove the wagon, Travis, came over, leading their shaggie. He was shorter than Bryn but twice as broad. It was all muscle by the looks of it. Travis hobbled the shaggie and strapped on a nosebag.

Bryn was rubbing down Lester's back legs when the courser decided to shit. The sound of it hitting the ground was like a series of quick slaps. He waited for Travis to make a joke, but the squat man just patted the shaggie and went over to the fire. Bryn finished up and followed him.

There was a pot over the fire with beans in it. Dried meat was passed around. Everyone except John and the Lieutenant were sitting as close as they could. It got cold out here, much colder than at home. Gloria would be at a hearth with her four brothers – her mother was bedridden. She would be warm. There'd be conversation and smiles and games. Bryn chewed his meat and took his bowl of beans without a word. George handed him an extra bowl and motioned to John. Another chore. Just because he was the youngest. Just because he didn't sigh when he sat down or rub his back when he stood or complain about his knees. He took the bowl over, pretending that someone would do the same for him if he wanted to waste time staring at nothing. There was nothing to see but scrub and dirt and stars. And a camp.

Bryn passed John the food and stared down at the small orange light of the other wagon's fire. His stomach suddenly dropped to somewhere around his ankles. He took a step back.

'Long way down, isn't it?' John said. He hadn't touched his beans.

'Three paces and you're gone.'

'Easy as that.'

'That's what bothers me,' Bryn said.

'Still, two women.'

Bryn left him to whatever thoughts those women were conjuring. The others were rolling tobacco. Bryn didn't smoke, but he joined them. He liked the smell.

'Does this farm-girl have a name?' George said.

'She does.'

George laughed. Smoke came out of his nose.

'Tell us about her,' Travis said. Bryn looked at each of them, trying to find a smirk. But they were calm by the fire, loose faces and tired eyes. Even Silas was still. They just wanted a story. So Bryn told them about Gloria. Her brothers.

Her sick mother. Her father, with his hands the size of spades and just as rough. Their farm.

'What do they keep?' Travis said.

'Woollies mostly. And some neats for milk.'

Travis nodded.

Bryn explained what they grew. What was good and what was bad. How Gloria had a good eye for the weather. She was good with shaggies – they didn't need a courser, though she'd always wanted to ride one. If he became an officer he would take a courser back and let her. No one laughed at the idea. They nodded as if that was a sensible thing to do. He described their house: big, with a lot of bedrooms. But it would never be his and Gloria's – not whilst her brothers were still around. No, he wanted to build a house for them. And their children.

'Where do they go, those dreams?' Silas said.

The fire was going out, but only Bryn seemed to notice. He put on one of the logs from the pile, which scattered some of the embers. They watched it take, then blacken, then crumble. No one said a word the whole time. Bryn's story was enough.

Bryn shared a tent with George and John. He slept in his uniform, pulling the thin sackcloth blanket high over his face. It smelled of damp cellar. The ground beneath him was cold and relentless. He tossed and turned, trying to get comfortable.

'You get used to it,' George said.

John was still outside, staring down the bluff.

17

'I don't want to.'

'Better hope they have feather mattresses at Wilson then.'

'I'll build them if not.'

'I'll take a double,' George said. He got ready to bed down. He was older, but it was difficult to say how much. His skin was dry from too much sun and there were lines near his eyes. His teeth were yellow but not rotting. He couldn't be that old.

'Do you have a wife?'

'Never did own a woman. Didn't want them owning me, either,' George said.

'John has a wife.'

'Lucky John.'

'I think so,' Bryn said.

1:2

They broke camp. Travis took his seat, the Lieutenant mounted on Lester and the rest of them climbed into the wagon. They were rolling down the track before the sun was fully up. Bryn rubbed his arms and legs, trying to get some warmth in them. This early he was glad of the closeness beneath the canvas. He'd be cursing it before midday.

They passed the other wagon. John leaned out the back, desperate to see the women. The others were curious too but all they saw was canvas and a free-grazing shaggie. John waited longer than the others; he was sitting on the edge of his crate. Bryn hadn't heard him come into the tent the night before. He had black rings under his eyes.

'Ladies do like their beauty sleep,' John said.

Silas snickered. Then he started laughing, a braying noise that shook him, and he didn't stop until he was almost crying. John watched the track. He was leaning on his rifle, his chin resting on his hand. He looked six years old.

It took most of the morning for the other wagon to catch up. John kept his vigil the whole time. Silas needled him in the ribs, but he didn't respond and Silas grew bored. At midday they stopped and got out and without a word headed in different directions. Bryn put a large bush between him and the wagon. He unbuttoned. There was a hole in the ground a few feet ahead of him. He toyed with the idea of pissing in it. But it was likely a husht hole and he didn't like the notion of angering a husht. That must be bad luck. Instead, he was careful to relieve himself a good distance from the hole. He had to stand with his feet wide apart because of his baggy trousers. The thick string he used as a belt was slipping. He grabbed at it, though his other hand was still on his prick. He shook, then managed to sort out the string before it came undone. He tried to ignore the two little blotches on his trousers. No one would notice, but he knew and that was worse.

On his way back to the wagon he stretched his legs. His buttocks were sore already. He hoped Fort Wilson was close. But it was supposed to be in the mountains and he couldn't see mountains. The horizon was as flat as a tablecloth. His neck was starting to get hot. His skin burned quickly – though at home that was only in the summer. Here he would burn all year round. He stood in the thin shadow cast by the wagon. Travis was tending the shaggie. It needed a lot of water in this kind of heat and no wonder: shaggies were like coursers wrapped in winter blankets.

In the wagon they passed around dried meat. Bryn's jaw ached after the first mouthful. It was like gnawing on a log and his teeth seemed to rattle in his gums. But his stomach welcomed it.

Silas pulled out his pack of cards. George groaned. 'I'm not losing any more smoke,' he said.

Bryn felt the wad of tobacco in his jacket pocket. He didn't mind losing. Even though he didn't smoke, the others had insisted he buy in with it. He liked cards. It passed the time better than counting scrub or staring at the other wagon. They all took it more seriously than he did. Bryn didn't really understand the rules. Sometimes you picked up cards from the wagon bed, other times you put them down, but Bryn rarely knew the difference. Occasionally he won, though he didn't understand how. Silas wasn't happy when Bryn won.

Silas dealt out the cards. It was good to have numbers that went together. Bryn was glad the numbers didn't go too high. His hand seemed fine. George was leaning back against the canvas, watching. Bryn showed him.

'Hey! No helpin',' Silas said.

George just shrugged. Tobacco wads were placed in the middle. Bryn let the others go first – it helped him remember what to do. Silas put down a three and a four and a five, all different colours. So they were putting *down*. Bryn followed with an eight and a nine. They went round and more cards were added. The wagon lurched and some of the cards slipped. John looked at him. It was his job to set it all right. He leaned over and knocked the deck.

'Damn it, boy, be careful!' Silas said, cuffing him round

the ear. It made a hollow sound, like a drum was hit very close to him. He righted the deck and straightened the other cards. John was staring intently at his hand. George had his eyes closed. It was Bryn's turn. He put down a seven next to his eight.

'Don't do that,' John said.

'He already has.' Silas leaned forward.

'Pick it up, Bryn.'

'Like hell! He's already gone,' Silas said.

Bryn looked from one to the other.

'Pick it up.'

'Don't you touch that card.'

Bryn reached out. Silas took out his knife and slammed it into the seven. George was awake now. The knife handle quivered. No one said anything as Silas laid down his six, stealing everyone else's runs. The knife stayed there the whole game.

Bryn woke. His mouth was dry. He'd dozed off with his head against the canvas. The sound of heavy hoofbeats had woken him. John and the others were looking forward, though they couldn't see what was going on. But they could hear.

'Off the track,' the Lieutenant said.

'Sir?' Travis said.

'Get off the track.' There was a pause. 'There, over that ridge. And quickly!' The Lieutenant thundered past the wagon. 'Red-coats,' he called. Then he got smaller very fast. He was pushing Lester hard.

Everyone picked up their rifles. Bryn and John peered out the back, though that was no help. The wagon swung round and headed towards the ridge. Travis hurried the shaggie as best he could, but the going was rough. Bryn bounced on the crates, jolting his back.

'Out,' Travis yelled. They didn't argue. They followed beside the wagon and pushed when it would help. Bryn couldn't see anything ahead but the other wagon was getting closer. It left the track and angled towards the ridge. Bryn still couldn't see the red-coats. The ground started to rise. The shaggie slowed; Travis flicked the reins. It wasn't a mountain, but Bryn wasn't hauling those crates. One of the wheels caught on a rock. John called them over.

'Ready and . . . *lift*.' The four of them managed an inch, which was enough.

Bryn had to move quickly to get out of the way. His trousers caught under his feet and he fell. George helped him up. Bryn could see brown smoke far ahead of them on the track, as if it was on fire. That's what it looked like: smoke. But it wasn't. It was dust. A lot of red-coats made that kind of dust.

He scrambled up the rise. 'We have to go faster,' he said.

'There is no faster,' Travis said, though he flicked the reins again.

The other wagon was starting on the rise. The Lieutenant was already at the top, his eyeglass trained on the cloud of red-coats. Bryn couldn't make out individual riders yet. They still had some time. He ran towards the other wagon. He heard his name called, but no one followed him, not even John. He skidded down the scree, his arms flailing for balance. Thorny bushes snagged his trousers. He was breathing hard and his legs wobbled when he reached the wagon.

'Faster,' Bryn said between gulps of air. The driver turned to him. It was a woman.

'You don't say?' she snapped. She was older – maybe the same age as his mother. Her hair was a mess, tumbling about her face. She spat and focused on the reins. Their shaggie was bigger, but that wasn't necessarily a good thing. Its teeth were bared; its nostrils flared and then shrank and then flared again.

'Where's your rifle, soldier?' the Lieutenant said. Bryn looked back at their wagon. 'And what good are you without it?'

'I came to help,' he said.

'Take this and count off the riders you see.' The Lieutenant handed him the eyeglass.

Bryn ran up the ridge. John and the others were now at the top. He covered one eye. He hadn't used an eyeglass before. His father had one, but it wasn't for Bryn to play with. It wasn't a toy. He moved it too quickly and the earth became a blur. His hand shook. The Lieutenant was doing his best to encourage the shaggie up the slope. The woman swore at him. Bryn blinked. His eye stung. He managed to find the track and steadying his hand, he lifted the glass until he saw the riders.

24

'Five,' he shouted.

'First rank. Call when you see the second.'

Bryn focused on not moving his arm. He tensed every muscle. He wanted to see how the wagons were doing, both of them, but he waited. He wasn't going to foul this up too. Forgetting his rifle – what kind of soldier did that?

'Ten!'

He could make out faces now. Not clearly; they were pale drops on top of red coats. He didn't want to see details. Beards. Different coloured eyes. Tired faces covered in dirt that branched in wrinkles. He'd rather close his eye than see that.

'Fifteen.'

And there were more coming. A lot more. He kept his hand as still as he could and risked a glance at the Lieutenant who was pulling at the shaggie. They were almost at the top. Travis was easing their wagon down the other side. A little further and they would be hidden from the track.

'Twenty-five!'

'What happened to twenty?' the Lieutenant said. Bryn handed back the eyeglass. 'Guide this shaggie downhill.'

Bryn made a grab for the bit, but the shaggie was quicker. It nipped at his fingers and caught his pinkie. He cried out at the pain, balling his fist. He readied to hit the damn animal.

'Don't you dare!' the woman said.

He pulled the shaggie towards where the bushes cleared.

Behind him he could hear the gnashing of teeth – the animal had a taste for him.

'Who would hit a poor defenceless animal like that?'

'Defenceless?' he said. He wrenched at the bit and the shaggie shook its head.

There was a loud crack, like gunfire. He looked up, thinking the red-coats had caught them. But it was the wagon: something had broken. It pitched at an angle and the woman screamed as she was thrown from the seat. He saw a flash of her white petticoats. The wagon lurched. It hung for a moment, then crashed down on its side. There were cries from beneath the canvas. The shaggie buckled.

Bryn heard two snaps, like twigs. The animal whinnied as it went down. Bryn stared at its watery eye. It thrashed its front legs and gave a low moaning sound. Bryn was vaguely aware of the Lieutenant rushing down the slope. At the edge of his vision he saw people climbing out of the wagon. He couldn't look away from the animal. It was dying. Its long lashes blinked as it tried to focus. Bryn felt a hand on his shoulder. He looked up at the Lieutenant.

'Step away now, Bryn.'

The shaggie moaned again, louder this time. As the Lieutenant pulled him away he saw the shaggie's back legs. They were a mess of bone and blood and splintered wood.

'You'll need to do it quickly. They'll hear,' the Lieutenant said.

There were three people – a man and two women: the older woman who had sworn at the Lieutenant, and a younger one. She could have been Bryn's age. She didn't look at him or the shaggie but off towards the ridge. The shaggie's noise didn't seem to bother her. Bryn jumped every time it moaned. The man was very pale. His skin looked like paper and in places it was scarred and cracked. Half his face was missing.

Bryn tried to turn away, but the Lieutenant stopped him.

'Just a Walkin'', the Lieutenant whispered.

Bryn looked up at the officer. His jaw was set, his eyes forward. He didn't like it either, Bryn could tell: a Walkin' alone with two women.

The Walkin' stepped forward. 'Shouldn't be me. I just scare the animal.' It had the voice of a man; maybe a little flat.

'No time to argue it,' the Lieutenant said. He handed the Walkin' his knife. The older woman looked away, her hand to her mouth. She didn't have to worry about the young girl, who didn't even flinch when the shaggie moaned in pain. Bryn didn't like the way she was staring at nothing in particular.

The Walkin' edged towards the shaggie and the animal started to thrash, its head smacking against the ground. A wet sound. All the while its eye stared right at the Walkin'.

'I'm sorry, Betsy,' the Walkin' said. He knelt beside the shaggie's long neck. Its hooves flailed in the air and then it was still. Blood seeped past the Walkin', slow as a lazy river.

'Stay with them, Bryn.' The Lieutenant picked his way

back up the ridge. He hunkered down behind some bushes and then Bryn couldn't see him. The girl stared at the dead shaggie. The toe of her shoe was just touching the blood. The Walkin' and the older woman went to the back of the ruined wagon.

'Wait,' Bryn said. 'Don't do anything. They might hear.'

'I'm Thomas. This is my wife, Sarah.'

Bryn looked from one to the other. 'Wife'. The Walkin' said 'wife'. Bryn didn't think that was allowed. And how would it work? Surely they didn't . . . It wouldn't . . . It would be disgusting.

'Not many married Walkin' where you're from?' Sarah said.

'No.'

'Us neither, but there it is. Better get used to it.'

'And the girl?' he said.

'Our daughter, Mary.'

He stared at Thomas, wondering how it was possible. 'There's six of us,' he blurted. 'Travis, Silas, John, George, me, and the Lieutenant. Some are married.'

The woman dragged a crate from the wagon and sat on it. There were markings on the side, the same markings on the crates Bryn had been sitting on the last few days. He looked inside the canvas. It was much the same as the soldiers' wagon: crates lining the floor, pots hanging at the far end, a hook in the top ring for a lamp – though no lamp hung there. But these three weren't in the army. He'd expected to see pillows and blankets and candles and incense. That was how a woman was supposed to travel – if she travelled at all.

The Lieutenant had said to stay with them; that meant keeping his eye on all three. He wished he had his rifle. He checked back on the daughter, Mary. She hadn't moved. He knew he should go over and talk to her. A dead shaggie was not right for a girl to see.

'That's not good,' Thomas said.

'What?'

'Blightbirds.'

Bryn squinted; he had no talent for spotting birds. People would point and say 'look' and by the time Bryn was looking the birds were gone. But blightbirds were big and black and where there was one there was usually a dozen. He couldn't count them this far off, but a dozen was a good guess.

'Blightbirds are everywhere out here,' Bryn said.

'But when they're curious, people get curious.'

The Lieutenant was still hidden on the ridge. The redcoats hadn't passed, so maybe they would see the blightbirds, like the Walkin' said.

'Do you have a faith, Bryn?' Sarah said.

He shook his head.

Thomas knelt down in front of her. They put their hands together and prayed. Sarah's mouth moved, but Bryn couldn't hear the words. Maybe they weren't for his ears – the ears of a man without a faith. Secret words. Mary didn't join them.

He looked over at the other wagon. The four soldiers stood

in a line, rifles ready. Four against hundreds – they should be running. Leave the wagons, let the shaggies go and run as fast and as far as they could. But there was open scrubland all around – how far would they get, a mile? The coursers would catch them.

Bryn dropped to his knees. He put his hands together and he asked that the red-coats would keep riding. He didn't know who he was asking – anyone that would hear him. He didn't have any special words or secret ways of saying something.

'Please, let them keep going. Let me and these people and John and the others live. Let me see Gloria again,' he whispered. He said it over and over, the words changing sometimes but the message the same.

'There's no point,' Mary said. He hadn't heard her come close. When he looked up she didn't meet his eye. She was staring at his chest. Right at his heart. He turned away, but she didn't move.

'Your parents are praying,' he said.

'He won't hear you. Or them. He doesn't listen.'

The girl walked past him, heading towards the ridge. She wasn't even ducking or using the bushes or anything.

1 : 3

'Thomas? Sarah?' Bryn said. But they didn't stop their prayer. He ran after her. Mary was halfway there. She was going to get them killed. He didn't care that she was a girl; he was going to stop her. He plunged through bushes, their thorns snagging at his trousers and stinging his legs. He was getting close. And then his footing went.

His ankle turned and he cried out. It felt like something big had just bitten his ankle and wouldn't let go. He hit the ground hard, landing on his shoulder. He looked down and couldn't see anything attacking him but there were husht holes everywhere and their bite was bad. He should have pissed in them all. He grabbed at his ankle and pain ran up his leg. He pulled up his trousers. The skin was already bruising, but he couldn't see any bite marks. He slumped back down. Mary was just nearing the top of the ridge. He called out, but she didn't turn. She towered above the bushes. The red-coats couldn't miss her.

Just as she reached the top, the Lieutenant stood up. He was going to shoot her – it was the only thing he could do. It

31

wouldn't stop the red-coats, but it would be a mercy. Red-coats took women, everyone knew that, though Bryn hadn't seen it himself. He couldn't see the pistol. He waited for the shot, focusing on the Lieutenant rather than his ankle. Instead, the Lieutenant waved. The other soldiers raised their rifles and hooted. Mary was standing at the top of the ridge, shielding her eyes. Bryn struggled to stand. He tried his foot. He winced from the pain and fought to keep his balance. He called out to the Lieutenant, but his voice was small. There were clouds now; his head felt hazy.

'Give me your arm.'

Bryn turned his head to see the Walkin' behind him. Thomas held out his hand. He was missing a finger. His skin was blackened and broken.

Bryn tried to swallow, but his mouth was dry. He pointed up the ridge at Mary. 'How did she know they were gone?' he said.

'I used to ask those kinds of questions. Back when she prayed, I thought maybe He spoke to her. Maybe He still does.'

Bryn stared at the white of Thomas' shirt. It was thick, and looked itchy. He let the Walkin' help him, putting as much weight as he dared on Thomas' bony shoulder. They shuffled towards the soldiers' wagon, the going slow as they had to get around every bush. Bryn was breathing heavily, but when he glanced over at Thomas, the Walkin's chest didn't move. His mouth was closed. His nose was silent; it had so many holes that Bryn was sure it would make all kinds of noise if Thomas had been breathing. He hadn't been this close to a Walkin' before. He expected them to smell – they looked like they would smell. But he became more aware of his own sweaty, unwashed body. He felt he should apologise, but he wasn't sure the Walkin' had a sense of smell. He should know more about the Walkin'. They were one of the reasons there was a war. There were other reasons, but Bryn didn't know much about them either.

'There's red under your shirt,' he said.

'It's burned on.'

'From before?'

Thomas nodded.

'Best not let the others see,' Bryn said, as they came near the wagon.

Thomas stopped. None of the soldiers came to help Bryn. Once Bryn could stand on his own the Walkin' moved a few paces away. Everyone watched Thomas. They still had their rifles in their hands.

'You're with the other wagon?' John said.

'Thomas McDermott.'

'And the women, are they Walkin' too?'

'No,' Thomas said. 'I'm the only one.'

'One's enough,' Silas said. He raised his rifle and took aim. Bryn tried to step between them and his ankle flared hotter than a campfire. The Walkin' didn't move. He stared down the barrel like it was as common as the night sky.

'Silas, lower your gun,' the Lieutenant said. 'Or maybe you're wearing the wrong colours?'

Silas spat from the side of his mouth. 'Don't need to be a red to shoot.'

'You don't know who you're aiming at.'

'A bag o' bones, that's who.'

'General Turner himself signed the escort papers,' the Lieutenant said. 'Until Fort Wilson, we're to protect this family.'

'Turner is a bone-loving dried-up prick.'

'Your gun, Silas. That's an order.' The Lieutenant drew his pistol. 'I won't ask again. I think Mr McDermott takes a ball better than you.'

Silas took a moment and then eased his rifle back to his side. 'I won't ride in the same wagon as it.'

'You'll sit with Travis then. Or walk.'

'They're riding in with us?' John said.

The Lieutenant nodded. 'Get the wagon over there and help them load up.' He mounted Lester and went back up the ridge. The sunlight caught on his eyeglass.

Thomas McDermott was already on his way back to his family. Bryn hobbled over to the wagon.

'We saw you fall,' George said. 'Was waiting for the sound of the shot that felled you.'

'I didn't see the hole.'

'No one does.'

George helped him up into the back of the wagon. He stretched out his leg as best he could. It throbbed, nagging at him, demanding his attention. He winced as John got in. John had a smile an acre wide.

'You saw them, right?' John said.

'Saw who?'

'Were they pretty? Young? Blonde?'

Bryn shook his head.

John tried to get him to talk more. He didn't want to disappoint John – it seemed to mean a lot to him. At home Bryn only had eyes for Gloria; how was he to know if they were pretty? They were pretty compared to John. Mrs McDermott looked to be about the same age, and she was blonde. He tried to picture the daughter, Mary, but the bouncing of the wagon and his aching ankle didn't help. She had darker hair. He couldn't really remember how she looked, just the way her eyes had focused on anything but him. Brown eyes. Gloria had blue eyes and she looked you right in the face.

The wagon stopped and John and George got out. Bryn shifted to the far end. Travis' back was close enough to poke, even through the canvas. He could smell the man too; a heavy sweat mixed with shaggie. And they were bringing women in here. Silas was next to him. Neither of them helped load the wagon.

'Don't worry yourself, ladies, I'll take that,' John said, loud enough for the whole range to hear. Bryn had no doubt he was sucking in his gut and puffing out his chest. He was the first to appear at the back of the wagon. He had three crates piled one on top of the other, his arms stretched around them. The veins in his neck were bulging.

'Shuffle up and grab one of these, quick now,' John whispered.

Bryn caught the top crate just as it was falling off. He started a second floor, putting the crate next to where George had been. He hoped there weren't too many, else they'd have no room to sit – they'd have to lie down the whole way to Fort Wilson. Maybe that was why John was grinning.

But it didn't take John long to load up. There was room for everyone to sit, though you couldn't pass a blade of grass between them. The three soldiers sat on one side, the McDermotts on the other. The Walkin' was at one end, as far from the shaggie as he could get. Mary was between her parents. She was staring at Bryn's ankle. It felt like she could see through the rolls of cloth right to his swelling purple skin. John bounced his leg. Bryn had seen pups with that kind of energy, a restlessness. Gloria's family always had pups coming and going.

As the wagon climbed back over the ridge, the blightbirds descended. The sound was like a hundred rugs being beaten on washday. They fought amongst themselves, single feathers spiralling into the air and then lost in the frenzy. Everyone looked away, except Mary; she kept watching until the birds were out of sight. Her mother didn't even try to stop her. The girl's face didn't change. She stared blankly as their shaggie was torn into little beak-sized strips.

1 : 4

The men stank. It wasn't their fault. It was hot in this kind of country, even in spring. But in their weeks of travelling, Mary had somehow forgotten what a man smelled like. And perhaps she and her mother weren't as fresh as the new day, but that was different. There was something about men that made their smell stronger. Her father didn't stink.

The young one had hurt himself. His ankle wasn't broken or he'd be making a lot more noise. But it was swelling and he'd find it hard to walk for some days. Impossible to run.

'Come on now, you don't want to see a thing like that,' one of the soldiers said. It was the one who kept staring at her like she was a bottle of whiskey and he hadn't had a drink since the war began.

'Don't I?' she said, not meeting his eye. He was looking at her breasts anyway.

'It's not the kind of thing a young girl should take notice of.'

'You can't hide from the suffering in this world,' her mother said. 'No matter how young you are.'

37

'That's a grim way of seeing it.'

'Any other way is deluded,' Mary said.

The soldier frowned. He tried to say something, but stopped.

The wagon was back on the track and the going had become easier. Mary had grown used to the motion, to the jarring collision of spine and crate – but would a cushion have been so difficult for the army to acquire? They had managed pots and pans and saws and nails: everything her father needed to build them a new home. A home that might not burn down this time. A home they might not be chased from. Their new neighbours were sitting right here – except the ones who wouldn't sit with Thomas. And there it was. It was already beginning. Mary was not surprised.

The soldier was staring at her chest again. She folded her arms beneath her breasts and pushed them up. He almost fell forward.

It must have been midday because the wagon stopped. John rushed out to help the women. George helped himself. Bryn tried to stand, but his ankle was too painful. He sank back against the canvas. The sweat on his neck made his skin stick to the material. He felt uncomfortable all over. The Walkin' was still with him.

'Not going out? We only get one rest until we make camp,' Bryn said.

'I don't need to stretch these legs.' Thomas smiled, which

pulled his torn cheek closer together. The patches of skin were close to touching.

'Did you really know General Turner?'

'I knew a few answers to some of his questions,' Thomas said. 'He was a difficult man to know.'

'How long have you been a Walkin'? If you don't mind me asking?'

'Seven years, give or take.'

'That's a long time,' Bryn said.

'Apparently not.'

But it was, whatever the Walkin' said. Bryn thought back to what he was doing seven years ago: playing in the yard with their wrangler, avoiding chores. Hoping there would be a dessert at dinner each night. All before his father sold the farm.

'A lot's happened to me in seven years,' Bryn said.

'I'm sure.'

'But you've not changed at all? Since the day you died?'

The Walkin' glanced down at his lap and then out at his family. 'I wouldn't say that.' He held up his hand. 'I died with all my fingers.'

Bryn forced himself to look at Thomas' missing finger. To turn away would have been rude.

'Did it hurt?'

'No,' Thomas said.

'My ankle hurts.'

The Lieutenant was standing at the back of the wagon,

shielding his eyes from the sun. 'Bryn, why didn't you fall out with the rest of them?'

Bryn reached for his rifle, but it was under his legs and it hurt to move. 'I'm wounded, Lieutenant.'

Thomas laughed.

'Wounded how?' the Lieutenant said.

Bryn told him about the girl and her likely giving them all away and his attempt to stop her. He explained that he thought it was a husht bite at first, as there were so many in these parts, but he couldn't find the marks on his purple skin.

'If anyone is going to take my foot off, I want it to be you, Lieutenant.'

'Blood and bones, boy.' The Lieutenant climbed into the wagon and rolled up Bryn's trouser leg. He poked and squeezed Bryn's ankle. 'This hurt?'

Bryn nodded. He was biting his lip. He didn't want to cry out in front of the Lieutenant.

'I don't see a husht bite. And it isn't broken. You'll be all right in a day or two. I can't fault the act, just the execution.'

'I'm sorry my daughter caused you trouble,' Thomas said. 'She can be difficult.'

The Lieutenant shuffled back out of the wagon. 'There's a crutch somewhere in here, Bryn. Find it when we make camp,' he said.

Bryn waited a while, then said, 'He's a good officer. If I make Lieutenant I want to be like him.'

'All the Lieutenants I've met were in charge of a lot more than five men,' Thomas said.

'So?'

The Walkin' shrugged.

The others got back in the wagon, John again helping the women.

'I'd manage on my own if someone moved that knife,' Mrs McDermott said. But Silas' knife, and the seven of hearts beneath it, stayed right where they were.

Mary sat at the campfire with the young injured soldier. His name was Bryn. It sounded provincial – but then, he hadn't chosen it. It was just another thing parents inflicted on their children. The second thing – right after the world.

The others were all busy putting up tents, looking after the shaggie and courser or hacking away at scrub for kindling. Bryn seemed very happy not to be one of them. His smile was as vacant as a woollie.

'Do you miss your father?' he said.

She had ignored his previous attempts at conversation: remarks on the coldness of the night air and the chances of rain in this part of the world.

'My father is right there.' She pulled her cardigan tight.

'But do you miss him from before?'

'Do you miss *your* father?' she said.

'Yes, but he didn't come back when he . . .'

The simpleton was close to tears – he was so quick to change his feelings. She could let him cry; it might even do him some good. But that would mean questions from her parents. She moved closer and put her hand on his arm.

'I do miss him. I was a child then, and everyone misses that time.'

Bryn wiped at his eyes. 'I do.'

The other soldiers joined them one at a time, when their tasks were finished, except for Lieutenant Matthews. He had his own tent with a brazier. The soldiers passed around sticks of dried meat and Bryn offered her some.

'No, thank you. I don't eat meat.'

They all stopped chewing.

'It's good,' Bryn said, pushing it at her again.

'I don't eat meat.'

'What you mean?' the one called Silas said. The one who had left his knife in the wagon.

'Do I need to say it again?' she said.

'Maybe you do, because what I heard was that you don't eat meat.'

'You heard right.'

'We'll just have some beans, thank you,' her mother said. 'We have more in the wagon, which we'll share.'

'I'm guessin' you don't eat meat neither, Bones?' Silas said.

'I don't eat anything,' Thomas said.

'Good. I'd hate to see that half-face of yours chewing.'

The dried meat finally shut Silas up. The beans were undercooked and hard and she chewed and swallowed as quickly as she could. She didn't eat much. Her mother put more into her bowl, but she didn't finish them.

Their tent was just big enough for the two of them and they slept under the same blanket. Mary wore a nightdress that came down to her shins. It was thin, but surprisingly warm. It had buttons up the front that pressed into her whenever she lay on her stomach. Her mother was asleep, her hair loose over the pillow, some of it covering her face. It made her look younger, how Mary remembered her from Barkley. She snored, and Mary nudged her. She rolled over. There were a few minutes of quiet and then she started snoring again.

Mary curled herself into a ball and tried to rub her feet warm. She caught a finger on one of her toenails – they were long enough to cut holes in her shoes. She was looking forward to having a new home, however long it lasted this time.

The top fastening on the tent popped undone, and the next. Mary closed her eyes. If it was one of the soldiers, who would they take first? Her mother would fight and scratch and curse. But she knew it wasn't a soldier – she would have been able to smell his sweet dirt. So it was her father, checking on them. She could feel him watching her. She took slow, deep breaths. The hairs on her arms and legs were up and it was hard not to rub at them. He might see. She shivered, and focused on breathing, on being asleep. Finally, she heard the canvas of the tent rustle. She opened an eye. Her father sat down in the same spot every night. He was like a stone gargoyle, reminding them of the bad spirits outside the tent. She could see his shadow on the tent wall as he settled his shoulders, put away his wings and then was still.

They were different people out here – some more different than others. He was mostly the same. She wasn't the girl who had lived in Barkley. She hadn't crossed the Redlands. She hadn't broken hearts in Marsdenville. Her house hadn't burned down. Not Mary's.

She lay awake wishing she had a light to read by. And a book. Her things – the few she was allowed to bring, mostly clothes and books – were in the crates in the wagon. If she had had her way, it would have been all books and she would just wash the same dress. They were going to the mountains: evening dresses seemed unnecessary. 'Who knows where we'll be next spring,' her mother had said, checking her father wasn't around. No matter how often they moved, Thomas thought this would be the last time. They knew better. But it didn't stop them trying: one day he might be right. So she packed a dress that she wouldn't wear for a year, maybe more – but likely less.

She needed to pee. She didn't want to; it was cold outside and it would mean opening the tent, whispering to her father and waking her mother. Sarah could sleep through a whole herd of shaggies thumping past the tent, but leave the blanket and she was awake at once. She would bolt upright and reach, grasping, for something with both hands, until she properly woke. Mary wondered what she was trying to hold, but she didn't think it right to ask. Her mother might not even know. The need to pee didn't go away but built like a river, starting as a small spring and gathering into a stream, and the longer it went, the bigger it got.

She started at the fastenings as her mother reached for something neither of them could name.

'Just need to pee,' Mary said, loud enough for both her parents to hear. Sarah dropped back on her pillow. Thomas helped her with the last pegs.

'Want me to come with you?' he whispered.

She checked his face, the missing cheek, the scars and the blackened skin. He wasn't joking.

'No,' she said.

It had taken her a while to see the quirks of his face when he was trying to be funny: the slight upturn of the left corner of his lips – the right side was too burnt to move properly. The way his eyes pinched in a little, unless he was trying to arch an eyebrow, which must take some effort but was rarely successful.

She put on her shoes and headed off behind the tent. She hugged herself against the cold. The sky was clear; the stars and a fat moon made it as light as day. As she picked her way between bushes a breeze caught her nightdress and it snagged on a thorn. She unhooked herself carefully, but there was a hole nonetheless. As she straightened, she remembered a dream she had had a lot when she was younger. She was running through bushes, their thorns cutting through her nightdress, stinging her skin. There was a glassy river ahead of her. She was running away from

45

someone, someone big, but she couldn't see who, just that he was behind her. There were shadows everywhere that twisted like hands trying to catch her. She always woke up before she got to the river.

They had camped high on a plateau. The soldiers preferred this kind of camp, Bryn had told her. She stared out over miles and miles of rolling earth. It felt good to breathe up here. She hoped it would be the same in the mountains. She liked having space around her. It wasn't complicated and it was honest.

She squatted down and pulled her nightdress up over her knees. Her thighs were as white as clean sheets – in Marsdenville, women painted their faces to get that colour. She had to shift so her stream didn't touch her shoe. Not for the first time she wished she could pee standing up like a man. They seemed to enjoy it. It was the kind of thing Mary would have liked to enjoy. Men's sounded different, too. It was one long note, while hers came in stops and starts. Obviously there was a reason, but Mary didn't know why they should be different. She stood and let her nightdress roll down her legs.

'Hello.'

1 : 5

The voice was behind her. She didn't look round. She started walking back to the tent. She had taken two steps when he caught her arm. She didn't fight him.

'Not so fast,' John said, coming to stand in front of her. 'Wouldn't want you wandering off alone out here.'

She didn't look at him. She stared down at the ground, away to the side, her head tilted. She could feel his smile.

'It's dangerous.' He pulled up her chin with his hand. She kept looking down. 'Don't speak much on your own? That's okay.' He undid a button on her nightdress and grabbed her breast. His hand was warm against her nipple. She didn't move. She didn't punch or kick or scratch him. He wasn't smiling now. His fat brow was low over his eyes.

'Mary?' her father called. The whole camp would be awake.

John took his hand away and did up the button. She walked past him. Her father waved, but she didn't bother to wave back.

*

Bryn noticed the landscape change, even from the far end of the wagon. His view was framed on one side by John's profile – the man was fat in his face too; his nose was rounded, like a vegetable. On the other side was the Walkin', Mr McDermott. His dryness suited the scrubland of the last few weeks, but when the ground changed to green he looked out of place. It was a relief to see grass again, even if it looked washed-out and faded. It would make for thin neats and scraggly woollies. Mr McDermott was planning on having some stock on whatever patch of land he claimed as his own. Bryn hoped for his sake that land was better closer to the mountains. Mountains might be good for farming, though he didn't know – his father's farm had been in a wide valley with a river running through it. And Gloria and her folks at the other end. Couldn't get a better spot.

John was asleep. His head kept rocking back and forth and he would snort and wake up then go back to sleep. He had woken them all last night. He came into the tent and stomped around; did it on purpose, Bryn was sure. He looked close to tears, and kept clenching his hands into fists.

'What's wrong?' Bryn said.

'It wasn't supposed to be like that. They're supposed to get angry.'

'Who?'

'Just shut your mouth,' John said. He was shaking.

That was it. He wouldn't ask John again, no matter how upset he got over something. Bryn only needed to be told once. He might be furthest from the opening, but when the

Lieutenant – or anyone, for that matter – came by he had his
rifle in hand and ready to fire.

Next to his rifle he kept his crutch. It was plain, sturdy, a
pale wood. Whoever made it knew what they were doing.
The joints were smooth. Bryn liked to run his thumb over
them and imagine the carpenter-soldier in his workshop.
They did that, the army, they made use of skills you had
before you became a soldier. Bryn had listed what he was
good at when he joined up and the clerk wrote it all down.
He smirked when Bryn said he was good at milking neats,
looked bored by shearing woollies and nodded at handling
wranglers. 'Farm lad then?' the clerk had said. When Bryn
said yes he laughed – Bryn didn't know why. There wasn't
anything funny about being brought up on a farm.

John's head fell onto Bryn's shoulder and somehow he
stayed asleep. Bryn left him there, but if he saw any dribble
he was going to shrug hard. The McDermott girl, Mary, was
smiling at him – the kind of smile that was laughing really,
but without making the noise. It probably looked funny to
her; a man using another as a pillow. He saw that all the
time. You got your sleep when you could. Blankets, pillows,
tents even – they were all luxuries. The wagon bounced and
the two of them bounced together. John barely stirred.
Mary's grin was even bigger. He smiled back and then she
stopped looking.

They were going uphill now and the shaggie was slower.
The grass sloped away, though Bryn could still see the
scrubland in the distance. What would he count now? He

tried clouds, but it was a grey day and it was difficult to make out where one cloud stopped and another started. The grass wasn't very high here, well below the knee – another sign that Mr McDermott would have to work real hard. When they didn't graze or plough a field on his father's farm the grass grew shoulder-high. Though Bryn was a lot smaller back then.

'Travis,' Bryn said through the canvas, 'can you see mountains?'

'Nothing but,' Travis said.

'Are they big?'

'How should I know?'

'There's white on their tops,' Silas said.

White-topped mountains. Gloria would never believe it. One winter they'd had a kind of icy rain. They knew what snow was – it was in the books that her family read around the fire. Wesley, one of her brothers, he said that snow came down from the sky all at once, like a big blanket, that's how it covered things like mountains. 'What if you're under it?' Bryn had said. Wes ran his hand across his throat and made a noise.

'We're not going to the top, are we?' Bryn said.

'*We're* not. Might send you up to check for Southerners and were-winks,' Silas said.

Travis and Silas had a good laugh at that. *Were-winks*. They thought he was seven. He knew there was no such thing.

John was dribbling on him. He jerked his shoulder and John came half-to, pulling himself upright. He made a noise, like something was stuck in his throat. He didn't seem to breathe for a long moment. Could you choke in your sleep? On your own bile? No one else was concerned. Bryn watched him closely. If he did choke that would be one less person in their tent – but they were close to Fort Wilson now and he didn't think they'd be in tents once they were there. Were there other good reasons for John to choke? He smelled bad, but they all did, except for the McDermotts. He was fat – but that wasn't a reason he should die. He did tell Bryn to shut up.

John snorted and started breathing again, loud enough for everyone to hear. Bryn should have felt relieved, but he didn't.

The wagon stopped and they got out. This time Bryn made the effort. He wanted to see the mountains and breathe something that wasn't a combination of his and other peoples' stink. He shuffled over the crates, his crutch balanced on his lap. He left his rifle, like the others did. George helped him down. His ankle still throbbed. He wasn't really in pain, but he leaned on the crutch as he made his way around the wagon.

Bryn got his first look at mountains. They were real, close-up mountains. It was as if someone had pulled up the ground and blocked out half the sky with it. They weren't like the big bluffs they'd travelled through; these went on as far as he could see in both directions. Some peaks were round, some sharp-looking, and there were more behind each one until they faded so they didn't even look solid.

Ghost mountains. There were trees too, and forests on some of the slopes, though not all. The ones without looked bare, naked, lurid, even.

'Never seen a mountain before?' Mr McDermott said, and Bryn flinched. He'd been smiling so hard his mouth was starting to hurt.

'I've seen pictures, but everything looks small on a page.'

'Something, aren't they?'

'I thought they'd just be big hills,' Bryn said.

Mr McDermott squatted down and pulled up a handful of grass. It was brittle, and came away easily.

'That doesn't look good,' Bryn said. The Walkin' glanced up at him. 'My father was a farmer.'

'How does it feel to you?' He passed the handful up to Bryn as if it were too precious to take any more. Bryn rolled the grass between his fingers. It split almost straight away. It was a pale green, barely more than a yellow.

'Don't expect a lot of milk,' he said.

'We won't need a lot.'

'You'll need a big plot.'

Mr McDermott spread his arms wide. 'You see anyone else?'

'You'll make out okay,' Bryn said. 'You'd have to ask the Lieutenant, but if you needed help I would be glad to.'

'Thanks.' The Walkin' put his hand on Bryn's arm – it felt bumpy, even through Bryn's jacket. Mr McDermott went over to his family.

Bryn looked back at the mountains. He took a deep breath.

It was like someone was pressing little needles inside him – not to hurt, but to clear out all the nasty stuff that hid between his bones. The air filled all of him, head to toe. He'd never thought air could be *better*. He knew it could be worse – milking neats and sleeping in a tent with George and John had proved that – but when nothing was making it bad, air was just air. In and out, sometimes cold, rarely hot, but just air. This was different. He was cleaner for it.

'Wait till you feel the water,' George said. He was getting his fill of the air too. 'Clear enough to cut you, it is.'

'Have you been here before?'

'Bit further south, I—' George stopped.

John was shouting.

They turned to see him poking a finger at Mr McDermott's chest. Bryn winced; John's finger might go right through the skin and touch whatever was left inside.

'. . . and we've been riding in the same bloody wagon all this time?'

'It was a long time ago,' Mr McDermott said.

'Still wearing it, though, aren't you!' John said.

'It's burned on.'

The Lieutenant came back to see what the fuss was. He pulled Lester up a few yards from the McDermotts. 'Step back, John,' he said.

'This bag o' bones has a red coat on under that shirt of his.'

'Don't make me draw my pistol.'

'Did you know?' John said, still not moving.

The Lieutenant reached for his gun. John made to move, but it looked to Bryn like he was building up to punch the Walkin'. Like that would do much good – might as well punch a tree, as Bryn understood it. The Lieutenant must have seen it the same way. He shot the ground by John. It made a funny sound: a little pop, as if it was swallowed by the sheer space around them.

John had ducked at the shot. He eased himself up.

'He's a Southerner.'

'*Was*,' the Lieutenant said. 'Mr McDermott has been more important to the Northern Army than you'll ever be.'

John sneered at the Walkin'. 'I won't ride the same wagon as a red-coat. Or a turncoat.'

The other soldiers were nodding, and Bryn found himself nodding too, though Mr McDermott seemed a normal sort. For a Walkin'. Bryn respected anyone who wanted to turn their hand to farming – that showed character.

The Lieutenant took off his hat and scratched the back of his head. His blond hair was greasy and wet. 'We're only a couple miles off Fort Wilson,' he said to Mr McDermott. 'Wherever you're settling, take what you can carry.'

'And the rest?' Mrs McDermott said.

'Will be delivered once we're in position.'

She wanted to argue it: she had set her jaw and the way she looked at the Lieutenant impressed Bryn. He would have struggled, but the Lieutenant didn't seem bothered. It was the look a lot of women her age could manage – especially if they were mothers.

Mr McDermott pulled out the crates with no help from the soldiers. He looked them over, choosing what he needed to keep his family going for a few days. He carried three himself, his arms stretched wide, but making less work of it than John did when he was showing off. John had been sweating right away, but Walkin' didn't sweat. In some places they burned Walkin' as a way to get rid of them; it was odd to think they wouldn't sweat even when tied to a stake. The women managed two crates between them, carrying a handle each. Seeing Mary struggle made Bryn wish he hadn't hurt his ankle. John didn't seem too happy about the girl lifting either.

They got back into the wagon and this time Bryn took his old station. It was better being able to see out and get a bit of the clean air. John closed his eyes, but Bryn could tell he wasn't asleep; he just didn't want to talk about what happened. None of the others had spoken up for Mr McDermott, not even George, so Bryn supposed they'd done the right thing.

The wagon started moving again. Bryn noticed the track: two lines of dry dirt, the grass worn away but trying to grow back. He was surprised enough wagons came out this far to keep it clear.

The Lieutenant was with the McDermotts, letting Lester take it leisurely and graze some along the way. He went quite a distance with them. They were talking – the Lieutenant would be apologising, no doubt. Yes, they were in the army, yes, there was a war going on, but it didn't mean people couldn't be civil. He'd be using words like that, like 'civil'. That was why he was an officer and Bryn wasn't.

Bryn leaned closer to George. 'Mr McDermott was a red-coat *before* he died,' he said, quiet, so John wouldn't hear.

'Think that makes a difference?'

'Doesn't it?'

'Hell if I know,' George said.

'But his uniform was burned on. He can't even take it off.'

'Some things stick, eh?' George sniggered at his own joke.

1 : 6

Thomas watched the wagon make its way up the mountain. For a while he could still make out the shapes of the men inside. Some of them were angry at him. The boy who had hurt himself just seemed confused; that was understandable.

'You wish you were going with them,' Sarah said. She shielded her eyes against the low sun.

'Silly, isn't it?'

'It's only a small part of you, from a long time ago. I can forgive that.'

He put his arm around her waist and they watched together. Mary was sitting on one of the crates pulling apart stalks of long grass. She was more interested in the view down the mountain.

'Have you ever seen anywhere so open and private?' Sarah said.

'Yes. But there wasn't any grass there.'

Sarah rubbed her nose against his shoulder. 'Are all mountains like this?'

'I wouldn't know. If I was guessing, I'd say they were just as quiet.'

'Was Black Mountain like this?'

'No.' He looked down at her. 'There were more trees,' he said, hoping that would be enough. But she waited for more. 'You know I never saw Black Mountain – not the Black Mountain you mean.'

'There must be a lot of places like that – places with no people and only Walkin'.'

'I don't know. Seeing so much open space here makes you wonder,' he said.

'Don't you want to go back?'

'They wouldn't let us in.'

She smiled.

'What?' he said.

'We'll make a home here. It's quiet, and there's no one to bother us.'

'Almost no one.' The wagon was tiny in the distance. He couldn't see the shapes of men any more – it could have been empty.

They were getting higher. Bryn could still see the dry scrub, but it was far below them now. He leaned out but couldn't see far. They were threading their way between mountains.

Then the wagon turned. Bryn wasn't ready for it; he had to cling to his crate and put his good foot out so he didn't slip. The going became steep. Bryn managed to keep his grip. George was almost on top of him.

'Climbing that mountain, just like you wanted,' John said.

'Wait till I tell Gloria,' George said.

'*You* tell Gloria? But you won't—'

They burst out laughing. Bryn managed to stop himself saying anything else stupid. They came out onto flat ground again and Bryn gave George a shove. Then instead of blank horizons of grass or scrub, he saw buildings, one on either side. They loomed in on him, even though deep down he knew they were only two storeys high. Their lines felt wrong, as if they would topple over at any minute. He pinched his eyes. How long had he been sitting in this wagon?

It stopped and they got out. Bryn looked around. 'Where's the fort?'

'This is the fort,' the Lieutenant said.

'But it's just a few houses.'

'Rundown houses at that,' Silas said.

He was right: they looked awful. The biggest one was still smaller than Gloria's farmhouse. It had what looked like a single room on the top floor. Some of the windows were missing, the front door was off its hinges, one of the walls had slipped, who knew how long ago, and there was a gap big enough to put your hand through. The smaller buildings were worse, little more than sheds, and all badly put together. Not a single wall was straight or a joint well done. There was a poor excuse for something standing at each corner of the square, with a cleared patch of ground in between, where they were standing.

'Lot of work to be done,' the Lieutenant said.

Travis whistled long and low and it echoed like Fort Wilson agreed.

'Aren't we supposed to be relieving this garrison?' Silas said.

The Lieutenant got off his courser and dropped the reins. Bryn could almost see Lester's disappointment. The Lieutenant struggled with the door until it came completely off. It was funny, but the others weren't laughing so Bryn didn't either.

'Hello?' The Lieutenant's voice rang throughout the building.

They tracked his progress through the broken windows, but no one made a move to join him. It didn't look safe in there. The roof looked older than Bryn. He hefted his rifle, though it was difficult to keep it ready and lean on the crutch at the same time. John blew into his hands.

The Lieutenant appeared in the doorway. 'Nothing,' he said. 'Check the other buildings. Travis, help me put this door back on.'

Bryn followed George to one of the rickety sheds, the biggest of the three: almost a single-storey house. He didn't think George would need the help, but he wasn't going to stay by the wagon alone. He pulled his jacket tighter. George stopped a few paces from the door and looked up. On the roof, watching them, were two hoods, all black: eyes and beak and feathers.

'You know what they mean?' George said.

'No.'

'Me neither. My mother would know, but I never listened.'

George went slowly to the door. The hoods didn't move, not even when he wrenched it open. As Bryn passed under them he took their silence as their blessing. It was dark inside. He waited a while, keeping as quiet as the birds, until he could make out shapes. The centre of the room was clear; everything had been pushed to the corners. There were crates – the same as the ones in their wagon – and when they opened one they found tools, hammers and saws and files. The metal caught the small light from the doorway; a saw glowed a cold blue in George's hand. Between the crates there were stacks of wood already worked into long planks, enough to build a proper house.

'It's all so tidy,' Bryn said. George mumbled a response. He was opening more crates, picking tools out of every one. Enough for a whole battalion to be put to work. 'Why are there so many?'

George put down a hammer. 'Why did we bring more?'

There was another door at the back. Bryn barely touched the handle before it swung open. There was a little cleared patch behind the shed where thin work stands had been neatly stacked in either corner. They reminded Bryn of Lester: four legs and the impression they shouldn't be so good at what they did. Hoods sat on each one, so many that they were jostling for room. They were all looking at him.

'George?'

'What?'

'You should see this,' Bryn said, inching away from the door. 'You know what that means?'

George stood very still, then shook his head. 'My mother couldn't count that high.' He closed the door as softly as he could.

They were the last ones back to the wagon. No one looked happy, the Lieutenant least of all.

'All right, sound off,' he said.

'I found food, lots of it,' John said. 'All gone bad, some got at by longtails or whatnot.'

'Lead shot and cannonballs. No cannon, though.' Silas cleared his throat, then spat yellow onto the ground.

'Tools and wood,' George said. He explained the amounts of both, but he didn't mention the hoods.

'Bedrolls,' the Lieutenant said, 'packed away in the top there. Had to dust them off to see what they were.'

'But where are the soldiers?' Bryn said.

The Lieutenant sniffed. 'Might as well unload like-for-like. Bryn: stand watch at the gate.'

The others started moving. 'What gate?' Bryn said, but the Lieutenant was already walking back to the big house. If Bryn were to put up a gate, it would be where they had rolled in. He hobbled over and leaned his crutch against the wall, then leaned there himself. He clutched his rifle in his hands. He couldn't get rid of the feeling that a hundred hoods were staring at him, as if they knew what was coming.

The track ran higher into the mountains and he followed

it as far as he could see. Most of the way it was rough grass and rock. He shifted against the wall and raised his hand against the slanting sun. There was something: a line of black. He put his hand back on his rifle and squinted. But the line didn't get bigger – so it wasn't a line of red-coats. How far did the track go? He didn't know – he didn't think anyone did. On the maps the Lieutenant had these mountains marked one of the edges. Those maps said there was nothing beyond, but that didn't make sense. There had to be something – more mountains, or an ocean. Or maybe you came back on the other side of the map. There might be people beyond the mountains ¬ wild tribes like there used to be, with their mechaniks and other magics. He peered up the track again, hoping to see a glimpse of something from the past. But nothing, not the grass or the black line, was moving. It was easy to be distracted by the grunts and shuffling of the others unloading the wagon.

He caught Silas glaring at him and he went back to his duty as watchman. He hoped his ankle was better soon.

When they were done, Bryn was called back. The Lieutenant had set up camp inside the main building. He had claimed the top-floor room as his own, as was proper. Downstairs, the bedrolls had been rolled out along the wall, a modest gap between each. It would be good to sleep without John almost on top of him. At the other end was a table big enough for them all to sit around, and ten stools. One or two weren't in any shape to be sat on, but there were more than enough for them.

John produced dried meat and some raw vegetables. 'Someone will have to get to cooking tomorrow,' he said. 'I've passed enough dry meat to last a lifetime.'

They laughed, even the Lieutenant, who ate this meal with them. Maybe he didn't want to eat alone upstairs. Or maybe the room was full of hoods that would want a share.

As the light faded, Travis lit some candles that looked new. Bryn had grown used to making his way by moonlight and now it was as if Travis held the sun in his hands. Like he'd stolen it. But Bryn did enjoy how the wax dripped. Each drop cooled and left something for the next one to build on. It lived a little as it moved and then went back to how it started.

'This time last year I was in Peachdon,' Silas said. 'With finer company than you.'

They listened to Silas' story of Peachdon. It was a new one, though he had a habit of repeating stories like he had only just then remembered. He'd been cheated at cards but he couldn't call them out on it because his sleeves were loaded too. And it was a woman. John leaned forward, his elbows on the table. She didn't dress like a woman; she was in trousers and a waistcoat. She had pistols at her slender hips. He didn't like to be out-cheated by a woman. So he figured he'd out-shoot her. He went for his first, while she was scooping up her winnings, but before he even had his pistol above the table she had fired. He started falling to one side and his shot sailed high, chipping one of the ceiling beams. He fell on the floor, hard. She'd shot out one of his chair legs.

'Best woman I ever rubbed sheets with,' Silas said. They thumped the table and John called for beer. Everyone went quiet at that. They didn't have any beer.

They'd been carrying the crates for at least two miles and
Mary couldn't see the track or the wagon or the soldiers
behind them. She wanted to be away from them as much as
her mother and father, but her arm felt hot and started to
tremble.

'Can we rest yet?' she said. She didn't mean to sound so
whiny; it just came out that way because she was tired. Her
father hadn't heard, but her mother stopped. They both
dropped the crates and sat on them. They watched him carry
on across the hillside. He could carry that kind of load from
here to Marsdenville without resting; he wouldn't tire or
complain or need to sleep. If the Good Lord struck down
every shaggie in the land, Thomas would be the best courier
you could buy. There were some jobs Walkin' were just more
suited to. It made a kind of sense: in the North her father
and those like him had been put to work instead of tied to
the stake. And she would be too, one day.

'I don't know why he's going so far,' Sarah said.

'He's scared the soldiers will come after me.'

Her mother picked at a thread on her dress. 'Why would you say that?'

'Because it's true,' Mary said.

'You didn't have to come with us.'

It wasn't the first time her mother had said that. The words had become common after Mary turned sixteen. Sometimes she'd complained – about what, didn't matter – and she was reminded that the choice was hers to make. And that she kept on making it. Her parents didn't ask her why, but she had wondered. If she was being generous to herself, she'd consider the time her father had been away. That split the family once. To leave them would break the family again. The small smile on Sarah's face each time Mary agreed to be a part of the next move was a kind of reward. How easy it was to stay with them was harder to admit.

They had been skirting the base of a large hill. Thomas was nearly halfway around.

'He'll be thinking on seeds. Or woollies. Or neat milk,' her mother said. He hadn't noticed them before he went out of sight.

'Can you imagine him with a hoe? Raking at weeds?'

'Won't have to imagine soon enough. We need to go. We'll lose him otherwise,' Sarah said. But she didn't get up straight away.

Why was it so difficult to picture her father as a farmer? He'd worked lots of jobs since he died, and before then he *had* been a farmer. But now, coaxing things to grow out of the soil – *living* things – she couldn't believe he'd be able to do that. If there was a purpose to the Walkin' being here she didn't think it was growing food – food they themselves didn't eat. Though it did sound like the Good Book: plant a seed, then nurture it, then give it to another.

The rest hadn't helped. Her arm was burning again after three steps. If he wanted these tools, he could drag them over the hills himself. But she didn't stop. She brushed her slick hair out of her eyes and as they rounded the hill they saw him in the distance. She could tell he hadn't looked back, not once. Her mother was making noises under her breath; Mary couldn't hear, but she made out a few choice words. They weren't catching up with Thomas and they wouldn't, not until he stopped. How many hills would be enough to put between John and her breast? She had marks where his fingers had been. They were beginning to fade.

Her arm went, her hand let go and her mother grunted as the bottom crate hit the ground. The top one tilted and then came at Mary. She tried to get out of the way, but it clipped her thigh. She cried out.

Then the crate was tumbling down the hill and the lid came off. Dull metal tools flashed like water and then were gone. The crate kept going, but it didn't look the same any more: it had lost its corners and become a ball of wood and metal and grass. It was hard not to watch it, but her mother was talking to her.

'—can you hear me? Are you all right?'

69

'I'm fine,' she said, though she was bleeding on her dress. Blood was difficult to get rid of.

'Thomas!' her mother shouted and waved, and he started to head back to them. He was still carrying the crates.

'What happened?' he said.

'It was too much for Mary.'

'I'll come back for them later,' he said. 'Can you carry one a little further? Just to the next hill?'

She nodded, though the next hill was not a small one. Neither was the hill after that. But one crate was a lot easier, and she and her mother switched sides often to rest their arms. It was getting dark when Thomas finally stopped. He looked like a statue, the crates at his feet like a plinth. They got closer and he still didn't move – thinking on seeds, most likely – but he looked even more striking close up. The dying light caught the bone of his cheek. His teeth glowed. One eye was normal, the other floated free. Mary could see it spin up and sideways when he noticed them.

'Flat ground – almost – and good distance from the trees,' he said. Good distance from any living soul, too.

'Fine.' Sarah dropped the crate.

Mary wasn't going to argue. Their previous few houses had been far from permanent. Any house her father built would probably be even less so. While Thomas took the lids off the crates Mary was happy to join her mother in just sitting for a moment.

'What's this?' Sarah said, pointing to the red patch on Mary's dress.

'Nothing.'

'Let me see.'

It would be more effort to resist, so she rolled up her dress. She didn't look at it herself.

'"Nothing?"' Her mother tutted. 'Thomas, tell me there's water and bandages amongst these toys of yours.'

Thomas looked up from a crate. He was almost sitting inside it. 'Bandages?'

'Your daughter is hurt.'

He came over and pressed her leg. 'It's not deep.' He tore an arm of his shirt off and handed it to her mother. 'There's water in this one.'

'And how many shirts do you have?' Sarah said.

'How many do I need?' He spread his arms wide.

Sarah got the water and cleaned Mary's leg. It was cold and numbed her thigh. Her mother wrapped the shirt around twice and tied it off. 'That will do for now,' she said.

'Aha!' Thomas said. He stood up, a large saw in his hands. He started towards the woods.

'Thomas?'

He stopped and turned around. 'Yes?'

'Where *are* you going?'

'To get started.' He motioned to the trees.

'Could we eat first? And maybe have somewhere to sleep?' Sarah said.

He looked up at the sky and seemed surprised to see stars. 'I'll put up the tent,' he said. He sounded disappointed. 'There's food in that one.'

Sarah busied herself sorting their provisions. She took everything out and then piled them into a system.

'We're not planning on selling them,' Mary said. She limped over to her father to ask if he needed any help. The bandage was tight and she had to roll her hip to walk. He was banging wooden pegs into the ground: as her parents were busy being useful the best thing she could do would be to stay out of the way. She looked over the open crates. There were things she recognised and things she didn't: tools to make a house with, to start a farm, to keep surviving. Though she didn't see a cooking pot – there was a metal bucket, but no pot. And nothing for frying. Plenty of knives, but the kind you cut rope with, not vegetables. No forks. She waited for her mother to notice. It didn't take long.

'Thomas, where are the things for cooking?' she said.

Her father stood up carefully.

'The what?'

'A pot. A frying pan. A chopping board.' She counted them off on her fingers.

'Not here?' he said, waving his hammer at the crates.

'No.'

'We'll manage,' he said.

'No, *we'll* manage.' Her mother turned her back on them both and that was the end of it.

He smiled weakly at Mary as Sarah collected enough stones to build a firepit before laying out a cooking fire a few paces away. They at least had flint and kindling. Thomas had finished putting up the tent, but he clearly knew better than to say anything. When the wood finally caught, she went over to one of the crates and picked out a short-handled shovel.

'I'm using this,' she said, daring Thomas to challenge her, but he held up his hands. She used the stones to balance the shovel over the fire. When it was hot enough she cracked eggs onto it. They slid a little, and Mary imagined the explosion if they went straight into the fire – but they didn't. She was surprised they even had eggs. They must have been in one of the crates her father had carried.

'Who's hungry?' Sarah said, apparently pleased with the eggs. Thomas and Mary joined her at the fire. They held hands, closed their eyes and prayed silently. This was how they prayed at meal times now – or how her parents did. Mary just waited. She preferred it this way, not having to listen to the words. Pretending was easier for everyone; she'd broken plates before to cover the sound.

There was bread and cheese, both of which were hard. For a treat they had under-ripe apricots. Her mother shovelled eggs onto torn slices of bread. Mary pierced the yokes, which made the bread bearable.

Thomas watched them eat. He tried not to, Mary knew, but he couldn't help it. He looked away, to the trees, to the hills, towards the track, and then he was drawn back to the food, following it from their hands to their mouths. He stared as she chewed – and she took her time chewing.

She ate everything she was given, which wasn't a lot. Her mother had said it would be difficult: that they didn't know where the next meal was coming from. That they would have to wait for her father to grow food and get stock. She had listened silently; her mother had expected a fight, or at least a reaction, but Mary didn't care. It was just food. She had been hungry before.

74

1 : 8

Bryn woke at the first bugle blast. The second and the third weren't needed. But in his experience that was how the army did things: once was never enough. Fire the rifle, stab with the bayonet, pull your knife. Men walk away from a single lead ball.

He took a swig from his canteen as the others stirred. There was a lot to be said for being under a roof again. His mouth was sleep-dry. His head was heavy; he couldn't remember the last time he had slept so well, which was something, considering the hard floor. He could see daylight through the gap between the floor and the wall.

The Lieutenant was standing at the end of the room, bugle in hand. Judging by how light it was outside, he had let them sleep longer than normal. And perhaps they deserved it. They'd managed to not kill each other when they'd been cramped together in a single wagon or sleeping three to a tent. And then there was the McDermotts: a Walkin' red-coat and a young girl. A few extra hours under the blankets was a fair reward.

Bryn stretched. The ghost of the wagon's bumping was still in his muscles, but his ankle felt better today. He tried putting some weight on it. There was a twinge, but not the sharp pain he'd felt yesterday.

'How is the foot?' the Lieutenant said. He spoke quietly.

'Better today. Walking tomorrow,' Bryn whispered.

The Lieutenant went back to the end of the room. He didn't check on anyone else. 'By nightfall I want a section of wall up. I know some of you have done that before and others haven't. Those who haven't will do as they're told. Those who have will be patient.'

'I'm not a bloody carpenter,' Silas said.

'No, you're a soldier.'

A clanking sound, a spoon hitting the side of a pot, reminded them all they were soldiers: breakfast was ready. Oatmeal, plain as sawdust – at least it would be warm. They shuffled to the table and Travis thumped out lumps of oatmeal onto plates. It settled like manure. Bryn used the side of his spoon to cut it, like he would a cake. He could remember the last cake he'd had. It was an orange sponge with icing. It was Wesley's birthday and Bryn's whole family had been invited, in spite of everything, but his father was too ill to go. Bryn pretended he was eating cake, imagined the tang of fruit alongside the doughy texture that left clumps on his teeth.

Silas pulled his knife. He'd finally yanked it out of the wagon-bed last night. He pricked the end of his finger and a drop of blood appeared. The others either didn't notice or care, but Bryn was transfixed. The blood pooled for a long time at the end of Silas' finger. When it eventually went, it was like a cannonball. Bryn waited for craters in the oatmeal. Silas stopped at five drops. He stirred them in, sucked at his finger and grinned at Bryn. His teeth were lined red. Bryn focused on his own breakfast, but he couldn't conjure the taste of oranges.

Bryn was told to follow George to the woodshed. George didn't complain. He just shrugged and said, 'We'll make slow progress.'

That was good enough for the Lieutenant.

'Shouldn't we be considerin' why there was no one here to greet us?' Silas said.

'The new walls are the only thing in need of your consideration,' the Lieutenant said. 'We're here now; that's what matters.'

The air was cold and the sky was a tight blue. They all tramped over to the woodshed, rubbing hands and breathing into them. Bryn's fingers soon went numb around the handle of his crutch. He hoped the sun would wake up some and warm them. It wouldn't get as hot in the mountains as it did down in the scrubland, but he didn't miss that dusty heat. They'd wash their uniforms soon. You couldn't have a fort without water – even Bryn knew that; it was the same as you couldn't have a farm. Mr McDermott would know that too. He wouldn't be too far.

Bryn was relieved to see the roof of the woodshed was

empty of hoods. He looked around and couldn't see any in the fort. It was the same story out the back.

'What does that mean?' he said to George, keeping the joke running, but George didn't laugh.

'You can still use your arms, right?' George said. He handed Bryn a saw. 'It's simple: follow the lines. No line, no cut. Got it?'

'I'm not simple,' he said.

Bryn took great care making sure the saw was definitely on the line. He pushed the plank hard onto the support, so it wouldn't move. He didn't rush. George didn't say a word the whole time; he just picked up the new-sawn plank and went out through the shed. Silence was the best Bryn was going to get.

He spent the whole morning sawing wood. They brought him planks, slapping them down on the thin-legged supports. The planks had a funny way of wobbling. The hardest ones were when the line was very close to the end, with only a little bit of wood to come off. He had to go extra slow then, and then the others tutted and swore and said the sun was quicker about its business. But he was making sure he did it properly. The rest of Fort Wilson was badly built and he didn't want a hand in anything that wasn't done right. He couldn't actually *see* the wall they were building but he knew he'd done his part. By midday both his arms were like walnuts, his muscles shrivelled and hard.

They stopped work for lunch. George came to fetch him, and he limped his way back across the yard. His back was knotted in places he hadn't felt before; his knuckles were raw and he could still smell the burn of the saw on the wood. They passed the wall. It was taller than he had imagined; he couldn't see over it. It covered roughly a quarter of the ground between two of the sheds. It already looked darker there. The sheds were bleak enough on their own, but they'd be working in gloom the whole day when it was done.

Lunch was a broth. He didn't ask what was in it.

'I've been thinking,' Silas said as he sat at the table. He didn't add anything of his own to the bowl this time. 'That rotting food shed doesn't make sense to me.'

'Things go bad,' Travis said.

'But if I turned deserter I'd take the meat at least. So why's it still hanging there?'

'Maybe those before us didn't run off?' John said.

'Then where are they?' Silas waved his spoon to the fort.

'Dead?'

'And the bodies?'

'Buried?' John said.

'I don't see any graves.'

'Maybe there weren't any bodies,' Travis said.

'Walkin'. They wouldn't need the meat.' Silas slurped his broth.

'Time to wake up, Mary. We need water.'

Mary screwed up her eyes. Her mother was letting in a beam of sunlight that fell directly on her face. On purpose.

'I'll get dressed,' she said.

'Thank you.'

The tent flap closed and Mary squirmed under the warm blankets. She could feel the cold outside weighing heavily on the tent. She dressed under the blankets, which wasn't easy with her thigh still bandaged. She wore a plain dress – not Barkley plain, but not something she would have worn in public in Marsdenville. One of the two she had brought with her.

'You'll need a wash too,' Sarah said from outside. 'And best scrub that dress. Don't worry if you don't get all the blood out.'

Perhaps she should just put that dress back on and wade into whatever river or stream was nearby. It might feel nice to have her clothes weightless around her as she sank into the water. Though they'd feel wretchedly cold when she got out.

She stepped out into ordered chaos. Four crates of items had been sorted and sat in a circle around the tent. She stood on the handle of a hammer just trying to get to her mother.

'Your father has almost found everything from the crate we dropped. We're getting there,' she said. She took hold of Mary's shoulders and turned her around. 'If you go that way, around that hill there, you'll come to a stream. It's a busy one. Follow it up into the trees and it pools. The water there is fine.'

Sarah's hair was wet and she didn't smell of dust. That would be a good feeling. Her mother handed her the canteens and a bucket. They were light enough now, but she would work up a sweat carrying the water back. There was no 'clean', not since Marsdenville. She headed off in the direction of the river.

She'd liked rivers as a little girl. They were places you could be naughty and no one would see. She could draw pictures in the sand and they would be gone before an adult could see and rap her knuckles and call her a heathen. She wasn't a heathen then; she was just curious. And angry. There was little to be curious about now.

The makeshift bandage had loosened overnight so she was able to walk without any trouble. She shifted the bucket to her other hand and glanced back at the tent and a lot of mess. The great new start for the McDermotts. She laughed as she skirted the hill. It felt good to laugh alone.

She found the 'stream': it was actually as wide as a wagon and ten times as loud. Her mother had called it 'busy', but Mary would have used other words. It crashed into the rocks that for some reason had congregated there. She didn't understand why; when she looked around the hills it was all grass – she couldn't see a single rock – so why was the river full of them? It was as if they wanted a continual beating; that was their lot in life and they took it with dignity. Rocks in rivers: that was right. She followed them into the trees.

The ground was spongy and her shoes sank in, the moss rolling over their tops. It made for hard going. The trees were old, old even for trees. Seeing them close it was even less likely that there would ever be a real house for her here.

What walls could be built from gnarled trees? Some were big enough, but there was a hollowness to them, and holes large enough to fit her head in. Others had split open completely. She stood inside one as if she was wearing it like a long coat. A solitary wood-y-peg ambled up to her shoe and then turned around. She looked up through the trunk to the sky. The sound of the river was faint from inside, more like a lot of people clapping a few streets over, at the theatre, or an event maybe. She closed her eyes and tried to remember the city, but it was difficult surrounded by the smells of soggy wood and moss and the sound of fresh running water. And she couldn't escape the memory of smoke. So much smoke she'd wept black tears and it burned to breathe. She left the tree.

The pool stopped her for a moment. It was large, and a waterfall curtained the back in a tumble of white ruffles. The water at the edges was clear enough to reflect individual trees. It shifted through greens she didn't have names for until the middle was so dark it was almost black. She un-buttoned her dress, unwound her bandage and stepped naked into the water. It was painfully cold. Her skin was no longer there; her muscles, the fat and finally the bones, they were all gone. She dipped her head, then surfaced and floated on her back. Her nipples burned white like embers. Her skin was blue where the soldier had touched her. She pressed her fingers onto the marks, but she couldn't feel her own hand touching her. Her father said he felt like that all the time.

82

Her thigh was stinging and threads of her blood spiralled in the water. The ragged lines of the cut looked like the peaks around her. She pushed those lines together, stretching the skin, trying to make herself whole again. But it didn't last. She had to wait for it to heal naturally, like every one else. And as she waited it hurt. That was how real pain worked: it lasted. Longer than a bayonet in the stomach. Longer than a cut on her thigh.

There was someone watching her. She lifted her head to see better, water running out of her ears and down her neck. There was a face in the bushes – a man. A man was watching her. His face was smooth; she could tell he didn't shave even from twenty paces away. He had curly brown hair that framed his eyes. She couldn't tell if he was younger or older than her.

He didn't look away, and his cheeks stayed the same pale colour. She swam to the edge of the pond, towards him and towards her clothes, staring at him the whole time. She stepped out of the water. A sheen of water pooled on her skin. Her veins were like rivers, her skin made thin by the cold. She stood for him to see. She waited, counting heart-beats. She gave him ten, and then knelt down to wash her bloodied dress. The stain wouldn't quite come out, though she scrubbed hard enough to bring up the fibres of the cloth. Her mother would be pleased enough with the effort. By the time she was finished, the man was gone.

Mary put on her other dress. She wasn't completely dry and it clung to her in places. She liked the way it felt.

As she followed the river back, she looked between the trees for him: the man with the boy's face. He was definitely a man, the way he looked at her, his eyes lingering but not bulging, not stealing embarrassed glances. It was a tired way of watching a woman. Young men didn't have that; they were eager. Some older men, like the soldier who had touched her, they were hungry.

It was how Walkin' men looked at her.

She stopped and held her breath, trying to hear anything but the river. She turned a full circle, but there was nothing but old trees and stringy bushes. It didn't make sense. Walkin' didn't have smooth skin. She knew her father's skin well enough; she knew how it felt. How it looked. Not every Walkin' had clawed their way out of a pyre-pit, but their skin was always dry. Every one she'd ever met: every one a desert.

She waited for him, longer than she should have. But he didn't come. Now the morning was gone. She wanted to feel as if she was being watched, but she wasn't. The trees weren't interested.

1 : 9

The saw was stuck again. This was the first tree and Thomas had already lost count of the number of times he'd had to stop and pull the blade free. But he was getting somewhere now. An inch more, maybe, and it would be ready to fall.

He stayed close to the edge of the forest, where he found plenty of sizeable trees. He'd paced around the trunk of this one, trying to work out how many floorboards it would make, how many foundation posts he could whittle from it, how many trees he would have to fell for a roof.

He wiped his forehead – not because it was necessary, but because it seemed the right thing to do – and set to with the saw again. He'd taken his shirt off earlier and was bare-chested, except for the remnants of his red jacket. He couldn't fault the quality of the Protectorate's uniforms; the strips of fabric had lasted the years. They were smoother now than when he was a young man. He'd used to think the men of Barkley wore coarse, itchy clothes until he joined the army.

Something snapped – it had to be the tree, but it didn't

sound like it had come from the leaning trunk. It wasn't the kind of noise a tree should make. He quickly pulled away the saw and placed it on the ground. He pushed against the tree, which resisted for a moment, then went. He stumbled with it. The top branches raked at the trees nearby as if reaching out in one last effort. The tree landed without the thunder he'd been expecting; the ground didn't shake. He wasn't sure how many more he'd have to cut down, but this first one was a big moment. He patted the trunk as a 'thank you'.

He dangled a bit of string from the top of his head to the ground. He cut it with his knife and then fixed one end to the base of the felled tree. The posts would be as tall as he was. That felt right: that his own height would be how the first house he built would be measured. He pulled the string taut and made a mark with his knife. He measured two more before the tree became too thin. Half the foundations for his family's home were lying in front of him. He just had to cut off what wasn't needed. That was something the McDermotts had done time and time again.

The forest was silent around him. He was used to that now: the kind of loneliness that comes with being what he was. He wanted to apologise to the birds that had to abandon their nests, to the insects that fled their holes, but they didn't stay around long enough. The noise of his saw was all he heard so he focused on that: on his foundations.

It took him all day to fashion three posts from the tree. He cut their lengths, then sawed away the sides until he turned curves into straight lines, as straight as he could make them. Then finally he cut away at one end of each post, making three huge stakes. He stood upright when the last was done, his hands naturally going to the base of his spine, stretching muscles that didn't need it. He laughed at himself. All these years as a Walkin' and he still had old habits. He hadn't always laughed at those moments. He'd learned to.

The sky was as black as a blightbird. He had no idea how late it was, but he got the impression it was cold. The air seemed crisp – parts of him could feel it, but it was more like being told it was cold. It didn't bother him. He picked up his tools and started home.

'You've missed supper,' Sarah said.

He sat down. 'I'm sorry. I lost track of the day.'

'You weren't the only one,' she said, motioning towards the tent. 'She's spent all day washing one dress and now she's not feeling well.'

'Is it serious?' he said.

Sarah shook her head.

'Then what's the problem? She was probably exploring.'

'She shouldn't go too far. How well do we really know this place?'

'We didn't know Leigh Creek before we moved there,' he said.

'That was different.'

'Exactly. She's safer here.'

'I hope so,' Sarah said. 'Go and see her.'

He pulled Sarah close. 'This house will be for all of us. You can stop worrying.'

He left her by the fire. He opened the tent flap and checked on Mary. She was tightly bundled in blankets, but he could see her shivering. He knelt down by her head. It was slick with sweat.

'Oh, darlin',' he said, brushing her hair away from her face. She whimpered, half asleep, and he pulled the last blanket over her, then re-fastened the tent flap.

'Mary has a fever,' he said.

'I'm doing what I can,' Sarah said.

'How can I help?'

'I wish I knew.'

He looked from his wife to the tent. 'Please.'

'Give her a proper home.'

He picked up his tools and headed back to the forest.

Bryn was awake before the others. Their breathing was deep and together, but at different pitches, like a choir. He was warm, despite the draught from under the wall, and his blanket felt thicker that morning. His own warmth had built up over the few hours he had managed to sleep. His legs tingled. The feeling didn't go, even when he stretched, but his ankle was much better. He was sure he'd be walking again today. He wouldn't have to stand behind the shed working his arms until they were ready to fall off. They could use him on the wall. Building things was a special kind of job: putting something on the landscape, changing it, leaving a little of yourself behind when you're gone. That was worth putting effort into. He couldn't understand why these buildings had been so badly done. Were the soldiers before them lazy? Did they have no pride? Couldn't have done, otherwise they wouldn't have left.

But sometimes you have to leave places, even when you didn't want to. Like leaving Wesley and Gloria, or when his father sold the farm. What else could Bryn have done? No one needed the labour. He'd tried every farm he could walk to. Gloria's parents had been kind, given him a day or two, but they didn't need him and he knew it. He was a burden: that was the word his sister had used as she put a cloth to their father's brow.

Bryn listened for the sounds of the Lieutenant above them, his light steps on the floorboards, but the Lieutenant wasn't up yet. He was normally the first awake and up and doing – that was part of being an officer, or so Bryn assumed. He wouldn't find that part difficult: on a farm you were always up early. Not like Silas or John, card players or roughs. He wanted to know what else made a man an officer. Knowing now would help him in the future, when he was an officer and in charge of roughs himself. He watched the Lieutenant closely, that was the thing to do, taking in everything he said, and how he said it. But Mr McDermott had said something that confused Bryn: that other Lieutenants were in charge of more men. He thought five was enough, especially if they were like Silas and John. A hundred of those kind of men would be impossible to keep in line.

There was scratching outside. He looked through the gap between wall and floor: two little paws and a round body. The paws were rolling something back and forth like they were shaping it. A little snout came down for a nibble and then was gone again. A grain-thief – the smallest grain-thief he'd ever seen. It couldn't be easy out here for his kind. He was probably very glad to see the fort being built. There'd be plenty of crumbs to be had, stores to steal into. Maybe life was easier now – but why so thin? Bryn pushed his finger through the gap. The grain-thief froze – and then it was gone. He shouldn't have reached out for it. That was stupid. Of course it would be scared. Tomorrow he'd make sure he had some food to push under the wall.

The Lieutenant came down the stairs. He looked very clean. His jacket wasn't dusty, his boots shone and he had put something in his hair that made it stay still. He blew the bugle. Travis was the first out of his blankets and headed straight towards the cooking pot. There were plenty of grumbles and moans, and Bryn stretched and yawned like the rest of them. Better they didn't think he'd been awake. It was bad enough being the youngest and coming from a farm.

They all shuffled over to the table and slumped onto the chairs. Bryn tried to sit up straight, but he was soon slouching like the rest of them. The Lieutenant stood at the head of the table.

'Good start on the wall yesterday,' he said. 'More today –

except for you, Bryn. You'll come with me. We're taking the McDermotts their luggage.'

'Back home they'd never let a Walkin' wander around as it pleased,' John said to no one in particular. 'Let alone let it build its own house. Makes you wonder what's going to happen when all the fighting stops.'

'When I was growing up they weren't allowed in the town square. Now one of them is standing for mayor,' Silas said.

'You kept them out of the town square?' George said.

'Too right we did.'

'With rifles, or were clubs enough?'

'Don't remember any trouble like that. They just knew not to,' Silas said.

'Sounds like a lovely town.'

'It was. And if you keep smirking I'll cut it right off your face.'

John turned to glare at Bryn. He was going to see the women again; that was what John didn't like. He would have to find a way to make it up to the big man or there would be trouble. Give John some of his meat, maybe – though he'd go hungry if he started giving all his food away. He didn't care about seeing the women again, but he would like to see how Mr McDermott was getting on. He might need more of his advice. Bryn tried hard not to look too pleased. He focused on the oatmeal, which helped.

The McDermotts' crates were still in the wagon: five normal-shaped boxes with the army's stamp on them and another, a big square one. Bryn was walking without the crutch but the Lieutenant didn't ask him about it. He just knew. Knowing the health of your men: that was another sign of an officer. Bryn would remember that one; he could just think about the time he hurt his ankle.

The Lieutenant drove the wagon and Bryn sat alongside him. They passed where Lester was hitched. Bryn stuck his tongue out at the courser. He was getting out, away from the close air of the fort, into the hills. He wasn't exactly running free, but it was more than the courser had right then. Lester just stared at them.

The seat was narrow so Bryn couldn't sit normally; he had to lean forward to stop his bony behind from feeling every bump and hole the wagon went over. The Lieutenant managed to perch somehow, his back straight, his hands almost dainty on the reins. The shaggie didn't need much guiding. It certainly wasn't going anywhere in a hurry.

'Do you know where the McDermotts are?' Bryn said.

'There's a river not too far from here. They'll be near that. I hope they had the sense to keep this side of it.'

'Is that where we get our water from?' Bryn hadn't thought about water; it just appeared in big metal jugs at breakfast and super, rather than being rationed in a waterskin.

'No, there's a well behind the food shed. Though it could be tapping the same source.'

Bryn didn't know what that meant but he nodded anyway. There was water and that was good; that was all he needed.

'Some view, isn't it?' the Lieutenant said.

They could see a long way today. It was clear and the air was so thin as to be not there. When he'd been at market, the air had been thick with people and animals and food.

'You could see to the end of the world,' Bryn said. His cheeks burned – that was a silly thing to say – but the Lieutenant smiled.

'I hope all the world doesn't look so empty.'

Empty was the right word. The hills were just grass, like an unset table – all cloth and no cutlery nor plates nor people. The scrubland beyond was no better. But empty didn't mean horrible. There was a cleanness to it. Fort Wilson wasn't so clean, but it was a small part of a very big picture. He still thought it was a good thing to build. Maybe one day, long ago, there had been lots of buildings covering the empty places. Gloria's father used to talk about things that happened years and years ago. He said it was important, but Bryn preferred to think about what was happening now. That way you didn't miss anything. It would be some time before there were buildings on these hills – more buildings than the McDermotts', anyway. Were they the start? Bryn hoped not. It was good to have empty places in the world.

'Bryn?'

He blinked at his name. The Lieutenant was looking at him. 'Yes?'

'You think a lot, don't you?'

Bryn shrugged. What was 'a lot'? You had to think; that was how things made sense, how you put things in order.

'It's no bad thing,' the Lieutenant said, 'as long as you don't get lost.'

But thinking was one way not to get lost.

The Lieutenant turned the wagon off the track onto a flat shelf of a hill. The shaggie slowed a little, pulling towards the grass. When the Lieutenant flicked the reins, it snorted and stayed at the same pace.

'Might as well be hurrying a woman,' the Lieutenant said. Bryn laughed.

It wasn't so bumpy now so he could sit back a little. Wind ran through the gaps in the hills, causing the canvas to whip against its frame. The first few times Bryn flinched as if he'd been slapped, but the Lieutenant didn't comment. Bryn was glad. John would have found it hilarious.

Coming around the third hill, he saw the tent. The McDermotts had been busy. There were all kinds of things littering the ground, and the blackened stones of a cooking fire. A little way off, Mr McDermott was hammering a post into the ground. It looked big: as tall as a man and as thick as a tree. But Mr McDermott kept swinging his hammer and the post shuddered and down it went, an inch at a time.

The Lieutenant stopped the wagon a little way from the tent. Mrs McDermott had seen them and was coming over. She didn't wave.

'I was wondering when we'd see you,' she said.

'Apologies, Mrs McDermott. But Fort Wilson was not in the condition I'd been expecting.'

'Nothing ever is.' She stood with her arms folded across her chest.

'We'll get your luggage unloaded and leave you in peace,' the Lieutenant said.

'You might get Thomas to help,' she said.

The Lieutenant eased himself off the seat.

Bryn followed him round to the back. 'She doesn't like us, does she?' he said.

'Coming to this place can't be easy for her.' The Lieutenant motioned for him to get into the wagon and he passed out the crates, one at a time, to the Lieutenant, who stacked them on the ground.

The square box was too heavy for him to lift by himself. 'Has he got a cannon in here?' Bryn said. That was the only thing he'd known to weigh so much and be that small.

'Something more useful, I hope,' Mr McDermott said. He wasn't wearing a shirt. His chest was covered in burn-marks and holes. Before, Bryn had been able to focus on the white, clean cloth and avoid the exposed cheek and eye that swivelled on its own. The streaks of red that had angered John were smaller than Bryn remembered. Perhaps he'd been peeling them off – or maybe they came away with time. Bryn realised he'd been staring and went back to the square box.

It took all three of them to pull it to the edge of the wagon-bed. Then Bryn and Mr McDermott got out and took the weight.

'Easy now,' Mr McDermott said.

Afterwards, the Lieutenant and Bryn stood there panting. Mr McDermott waited a moment before prising off the lid. He made a satisfied noise and Bryn glanced at the black metal box inside the box. It looked expensive. His father had cooked their food in a pot hung over stones, same as Gloria's mother. They hadn't had a stove.

Mr McDermott was beaming.

'But your kind don't even eat,' Bryn said.

The Lieutenant coughed.

'True. But my family does, and I know it will make a difference to them.' Mr McDermott placed a hand on Bryn's shoulder. 'Some things are worth more than they appear at first.'

'So speaks a married man,' the Lieutenant said.

The two men were smiling. So it was about being married – no wonder it was lost on him. But one day he wouldn't even need this kind of thing explained, he'd just know and smile and nod along. There was a lot to take in, and at moments like this he wondered if he would manage it all. But then he remembered Wesley: only a couple of years older, but so sure of himself.

Bryn looked at the post Mr McDermott had been hammering into the ground. 'Are you building a fence?' he said.

Mr McDermott raised an eyebrow. It pulled his free eye up even more. The muscles flexed. 'Foundations,' he said. 'Come and see.'

He led them over. Two posts were already in place, pounded

down so that they stood only a couple of feet above ground. Bryn couldn't believe Mr McDermott had been able to drive such big pieces of wood that far down and he said as much.

'You can do anything with enough time,' Mr McDermott said.

Bryn wasn't the only one impressed. 'You've cut and placed these in the time since we left you? Alone?' the Lieutenant said.

The Walkin' nodded, and the Lieutenant stared at the posts. It was his turn to get lost in his thoughts.

'How long before it's finished?' Bryn said.

'A week? Maybe more. This is the first house I've ever built.'

'First and last?' the Lieutenant said.

Mr McDermott looked over at his wife. She was inspecting the stove, running her hand along the metal. 'I hope so.'

1 : 10

They are your servants and your people,
whom you redeemed by your
great strength and your mighty hand.

Nehemiah

BOOK 2

BOOK 2

2 : 1

The Lieutenant was in a hurry to get back to the fort. But the shaggie was stolid. The lighter load made no difference. It shrugged off the whip-crack of the reins. Bryn's experience of shaggies was the same: they'd work all day, all year, but at their own pace. Like the seasons.

As they entered Fort Wilson, it became obvious why the Lieutenant was worried. Silas, John, and Travis were all sitting on upturned crates smoking. They looked like they'd been there long enough to be growing moss around their boots. It was in their ease; that they'd taken the time to find the most comfortable spot for every muscle. The Lieutenant drove the wagon right up to them, the shaggie close enough to breathe on John's balding head.

'One side done,' Travis said.

'And the other three building themselves?' the Lieutenant said.

'Could be.' Travis blew out a cloud of smoke.

Bryn followed the Lieutenant to the finished wall. His ankle gave a twinge. He was aware of it every few steps but

103

he made sure it didn't show. The Lieutenant thought he was better so he was better.

The wall was even taller than he remembered. It was much higher than the sheds; big enough for two whole storeys. There was a gangway running between the buildings; a man could stand at the wall and you'd only see his head and shoulders from the other side. It was quite a sight. Bryn touched the planks he'd cut and felt the joints that one of the others had smoothed. This wall would be here when he was gone. It might even be here when he was dead: a source of shelter for other young men.

'Idle, but they know their business,' the Lieutenant muttered. Bryn didn't think he was supposed to hear. He stepped back a few paces. It was strange how the wall changed the horizon of the fort. Before, the sheds had been like hills, and the gap in between the view. Now the gap was gone and a mountain stood between the hills. It cast a long shadow. When it was his turn, he would take a lantern, placing his foot deliberately on each of the steps up to the gangway. And then wait with the patience of a shaggie and the eyes of a red-wink. He could be relied upon. The Lieutenant knew that. He'd know danger when he saw it.

'What was she wearing?' John said, so only Bryn could hear.

'Who?'

'The girl. Blood and bones, the girl.'

'I didn't see her,' Bryn said.

'What do you mean?'

'She wasn't there.'

'Where was she?' John growled.

'Why would I know?'

John walked away. It was a good thing Bryn hadn't seen Mary; it meant John wouldn't have seen her either. Bryn might not need to give him some meat after all. If John saw it that way.

Bryn was assigned to the food shed for the day. Someone else had to cut the planks of wood. As the Lieutenant gave out instructions at breakfast, Bryn rubbed his arms, glad of the rest. Travis smirked at him. When he woke that morning, Bryn pushed some cheese under the wall and waited. The grain-thief didn't show but the cheese wouldn't be there when he went to sleep. He knew it wouldn't. But he was looking forward to getting into his blankets that night and checking.

Opening the door to the shed, he was hit by a burning sweetness that brought the oatmeal up from the bottom of his stomach. He vomited against the wall like a blood splatter. The oatmeal was watery and shone in the early morning light. He rubbed at his lips to get rid of the taste. His finger was speckled with flakes. He pinched his nose but the smell from the shed wouldn't go away. He gagged again, but nothing came. Waiting outside, leaning against the wall, he tried to get his breath. Big gulps didn't sit well; he struggled to keep them down. Someone was laughing back in the main building – laughing at him, he was sure. He wouldn't give them the pleasure. When he went back into the shed he left the door open.

It was difficult to move for all the specks. They were like rain. They weren't interested in him; he was in the way. There was a back door and he rushed over and wrestled with the handle. It wouldn't turn. His nostrils itched; he was breathing out instead of in. He kicked the bottom of the door and wrenched at the handle and it opened. He fell out into a little clear patch of grass. The tree-line was ten feet away. He sucked hard at the clean air, quickly, before it went rotten as well. What could possibly go that bad? And how did Travis manage it every morning? The little man had a stomach made of rocks – it was the only way. 'Clear it out,' the Lieutenant had said. Simple. It sounded like a quick job, a morning at most. But the Lieutenant insisted he take the day. Take his time.

He held his hand to his mouth. He thought he was going to be sick again. His stomach cramped instead. The grass was softer than a mattress. He eased himself down and shook his head. The sound of laughing carried to him. He looked around. Travis, or whoever it was, couldn't see him from there.

It took him a while but eventually Bryn got up. Holding his nostrils pressed closed he went inside the shed. The open doors let light in to the walls opposite. He squinted. There were sacks, loose and blotchy. Crates that seemed to have bled – where the wood was cracked there were patchy stains. Meat hooks dangled down along one wall and live under-mutton wriggled on each end. Big under-mutton. They caught the light, a proper white. But who put under-mutton on a meat hook? He took a step closer, then vomited again. It was mostly water this time; it hit the floor like he'd emptied a bucket. They weren't under-mutton with tails flapping. It must have been meat, but there were hungry-brides crawling all over it, so many he couldn't see what they were eating. It was their fat white bodies that he'd mistaken for fur. Bloated as they were, he couldn't make out where one ended and another began. They pulsed on top of each other.

Bryn ran out of the shed and went straight into the main building. There he finally took a breath. Travis and the Lieutenant looked up from the table.

'Horrible,' he said. He shook his head.

The Lieutenant got up. 'We need that shed clear.'

'Make Travis do it.' Bryn pointed at the little man. 'He goes in there every day.'

'No I don't.'

'But the oatmeal?'

Travis looked up to the ceiling. 'That shed is no good for keepin'.'

'Yet,' the Lieutenant said. He looked set on Bryn doing the job. Latrines were better.

Bryn sighed and went over to his blankets. He wanted to check on the cheese; after seeing the shed he didn't think any food could last in Fort Wilson. What was more, he wanted to get into his blankets and sleep until the smell was just a memory. He picked up his rifle. The Lieutenant looked confused, but didn't stop him.

He peered into the food shed. The hungry-brides might have had enough, moved on whilst he was away. That could have happened for another man – Silas, or George maybe. Bryn wasn't so lucky. The brides clung to their scraps of nameless meat.

In the other doorway, a hood hopped into sight. It seemed to taste the air. It found it less of a problem than Bryn had but it wasn't happy. It must have been too much, everything too far gone. It was the first hood he'd seen since he and George had found that big flock: first in the fort, first in the trees, first in the sky, even. He pushed through the specks, not looking at the hungry-brides, towards the other door. The hood took flight. The rest of them were waiting outside. He stopped, one hand on the doorframe, the other gripping his rifle. Hundreds of beady black eyes fixed on him. Not one of them made a sound. It was as if every hood in the hills travelled in that one group. He edged back. They didn't follow and they didn't leave.

He took hold of his rifle, raised it high enough and then stepped towards a meat hook. The muzzle pressed against a hungry-bride. It was too big to crawl down the barrel. He pushed harder. He couldn't look, though he didn't have anything else to bring up. In a quick jerk he pulled the rifle up and away. A few brides flew across the room. He needed to go deeper. He tried again until he was sure he'd hit the metal hook. He flicked again, and pulled the trigger. The hungry-brides exploded in every direction, some whole, some in pieces. Bryn ducked, but it was too late: he was covered. He tried to brush everywhere at once – if one bride made it to his skin, he'd never sleep again. They were in his hair and he ripped at his scalp. Tearing all his hair out would be worth it. He checked himself over twice, three times. He'd have to explain why he'd fired his rifle, admit to the Lieutenant that it had been an accident. But at least the meat hook was free, if a little bent. He took up the rifle again and shivered as he approached the next one. He ran his hand through his hair to be sure, then once more he pressed the muzzle into the brides. They seemed to have no idea what had happened. He flicked. There was another gunshot – but he hadn't reloaded. He pulled back his rifle and looked at it. Another shot. More. Someone was shouting.

Bryn ran to the door then ducked back. Red-coats.

2 : 2

'Red-coats.' He said it out loud. There were so many – he'd only glimpsed the yard and it was crawling with them. His rifle was spent. He heard a scream, over and over. That wasn't the sound of a man being shot. Bryn knew that sound, and it was quick. They were doing something to him.

He moved back, bumping into a crate. With shaking hands, he lifted it, and the one underneath. He ignored the huntsman and carri-clickies that went scrambling and lay down and pulled sacks over himself. They were wet and heavy. He was wedged between the wall and the stack of crates he had made. The bottom crate had cracked, the side panel sheared in two. Inside were blackened stalks of hay and a harvesting sickle. He took hold of the sickle's wooden handle. The blade was flecked with rust, but looked solid. His eyes were running from the stench, but he was glad he'd been sick so much already.

Someone came to the door. They spat, but did not vomit. Bryn felt shame at that. They stepped into the shed. Bryn pulled the sickle to his chest, careful and slow. The red-coat

111

sniffed. Sniffed, in that place, like hungry-brides and specks and a life's worth of rot were nothing to him. What kind of men did they raise in the south?

Between the sacks Bryn saw the man's boots. They were scuffed and marked and one of the soles was coming loose. He was standing in front of the crates. Bryn heard a lid slap against the floor. He held his breath. Then the crate went. The red-coat wasn't going away. He'd root around until he found what he was after. Bryn wasn't going to wait.

He pushed the sack above his head and swung the sickle. He aimed above the boot and caught just below the knee. The red-coat grunted. Bryn pulled as hard as he could. The man went down. Bryn roared silently and was on top of him. He steadied the sickle with a hand on the back of the half-circle blade. He slammed the tip down into the one bit of skin he could see. And again. A third time, until there was nothing left of the man's throat. He had a black beard, now washed red. He didn't look surprised, like he always knew Bryn was there, that he wouldn't walk out of the shed.

Bryn was sitting astride the red-coat. The moments between his breaths felt long enough for him to choke. The sounds from outside the shed – the gunfire, the shouts, the thumps of courser hooves – were far away. He dropped the sickle. The red-coat's eyes were open, looking out of the open door, towards the waiting hoods. Hundreds of hoods. More patient and more respectful than Bryn had thought birds could be.

'Jackson?' a man called outside.

This looked like he might be Jackson. The beard was right for a Jackson. So were waning cheeks on a heavyset man. Bryn took hold of the red-coat and dragged him towards the sacks. His arms trembled and he had to stop every foot or so, as if it was a mile. Dead, the man weighed more than ten of his fellow red-coats. Bryn packed the body as best he could under the rotten canvas.

The head was still in the middle of the floor. He'd hacked straight through skin and bone and flesh, a circle of white surrounded by ragged red. Bryn's throat burned from the bile he was fighting back. He focused on Jackson's eyes. They were almost normal, just tired. Jackson hadn't slept in days, that was all. Bryn crawled forward and took the head in both his hands. He cradled it to his chest. The man's eyelids fell shut. Bryn shuffled back to the crates on his knees and hid.

Once again Bryn could see the door opposite through a gap between a crate and the sacks. Out there the hoods were waiting – waiting for the red-coats to leave, he realised. It would be easier on them then. The same single hood stepped forward into the doorway.

'Jackson?' a man said. He was standing a few feet from where Bryn was lying. The hood looked up at the sound but didn't fly off. It blinked at the red-coat.

The red-coat spat, cleared his throat and spat again. Bryn had almost become used to the smell of the food shed after one morning. The hood eyed the room again but didn't come inside. It ruffled its feathers, picking at itself with its beak. Bryn clutched at a sack above him. He could feel his nails on his palm through the weave. He waited for the pull. The hood flew back to the others. And there was quiet.

2 : 3

Thomas hit the stake twice and then stepped back. He closed the one eye he still could and tried to line the stake up with the next along, but it was impossible to tell if they were the same height. Even over a short distance the eyes played tricks. He sighed and dropped the mallet, which made a satisfying thud on the damp ground. He hadn't thought of this problem. He'd cut the stakes the same length and assumed that if he dug them in at the same depth it would be fine. He'd forgotten that the ground wasn't flat. How had he forgotten that, on a mountain? *Because he was a dullard and a fool.* He could hear his mother say the words. The only consolation was that she had known even less about house building than he did. There had to be a way of lining up the stakes so the floor of their home would be flat, or close to it. He stood staring at the stakes until Sarah shouted that lunch was ready.

He wanted to stay with his problem but his wife preferred that they eat together. He stopped at the tent and checked on Mary. She was still asleep, though her brow was dry. It was only a day of fever. *Only a day.* He sat down with Sarah. Only a day, even if it was mostly his fault.

Sarah was serving up soup for two. She put a little in a bowl for Mary. She was using bowls: her father's proper porcelain bowls that they had packed up and brought all the way from Barkley. They were mostly blue, with a white line than ran around their middle. Very old.

'Mary looks better.'

Sarah blew on the soup. 'It's good it didn't last.'

'Have you looked at her leg?' he said.

She took a tentative sip. 'I changed the bandage. It looks angry.'

'It didn't look so bad when she did it.'

'That's what worries me,' she said. She tilted the bowl away from her. That was how soup should be eaten – another hand-me-down from her father. She looked silly, like she was going to spill it. 'What are you grinning at?' she said. She'd long stopped wincing when he smiled, at what it did to his face.

'You've just helped me with a problem.'

'More than one, I should think.'

He picked up Mary's bowl and patted Sarah on the shoulder. She could finish her lunch alone this time.

His daughter woke long enough for him to feed her. She was almost as pale as he was, but it was a different kind of pale: the fleeting lack of colour of the sick; with its memory of what it was like to look healthy and fresh. Wet. Ill or well, she looked wet. She didn't say anything, just accepted a few spoonfuls of thin soup and then slumped back on her pillow. He watched her for a while. Her wavy dark hair was pressed against her skin. It used to be blonde, like her mother's, but that had changed, as had so many things. Was it at Marsdenville? Or Leigh Creek? Or West Kennington? Every town was difficult enough. It wasn't Barkley; he knew that. She had left there in her blonde braids. He couldn't remember a morning when she came to breakfast and the yellow was gone. Perhaps Sarah could. The dark colour made her look older, somehow. She wasn't the Mary he remembered – not from before he died, or after. This fever would change her again. And this mountain. How could they not? Sarah wouldn't say so, but it was his fault.

He took the bowl when he left the tent and rinsed it in a bucket of water. He scooped out enough water to meet the white line around the bowl. Back at the stakes he placed a long plank between two, measured to the middle of the plank and carefully placed the bowl there. He figured the stakes to be pretty level, but the bowl tipped further than Sarah would dare with her soup. He took off the bowl, then the plank, and hammered down one stake. Plank back on. Bowl back on. Less of a tilt this time, but still the water stretched up the side of the bowl. Again he took off his level test, hit the stake and then put it all back on. He went slowly, but even still he went too far with the one stake and the water started to lean the other way. He stood with his hand cupping his belly, over his bayonet wound, thinking. He could go at the other stake, but then he might go too far

117

with that one too and he'd end up with two stakes flat to the ground and no foundations. He could try and wrestle the first stake upwards a little, but that wouldn't make for a good solid base. It would slump back down at the first sign of weight.

'Does it matter that the wood is sagging?' Sarah said. She was standing next to him.

'What do you mean?'

'In the middle. Your plank isn't a flat line,' she said.

He patted his belly, making hollow sounds with his hole. 'I don't think it matters,' he said, but he went over and lifted beneath the bowl until he judged it would be level: levelling his level test. The water didn't visibly move.

'We're making this up as we go, aren't we?' she said.

'Has it ever been any different?'

She looked down, at his wound or his feet, it didn't matter. 'I do appreciate what you do for us,' she said. 'You know that, don't you?'

'I want you to be happy,' he said.

'We can try,' she said. 'I want to try.'

Bryn didn't trust the silence. Men could be quiet if they wanted to, even red-coats. He waited until the light went, until he was almost hungry enough to lick the sacks next to him. He could already taste them, sweet and rancid. His stomach made noises like thunder and he waited some more.

The moon was large in the sky. He could see it through the

doorway – the lower half. It hung like a great gut. Jackson was starting to smell bad. It was a different kind of rot to the sacks of vegetables: a man's rot. Bryn inched further away from the red-coat. His arm caught on a crate and he wrestled to get it free, to be out from under the sacks, to be away from the man he killed. He stood in the middle of the shed, panting. The top of Jackson's head was clear of the sacks – the hair looked like a blackened vegetable. It wouldn't have been hard to spot him, had the other red-coat come into the shed. Bryn moved to the door. It looked like the red-coats were really gone. The courtyard ground was churned and broken. He could tell the difference between hooves and boots. There must have been a lot of them. Why didn't they burn the fort down? Or just move in themselves?

There was a light in the main building.

Bryn ducked back inside. He took three breaths and looked again. It was still there: a candle flickering. He picked up his rifle. It was empty, but whoever was in there didn't know that. He glanced at the other door. He could slip out – he could drop his uniform in the trees and come out a different person. He wouldn't be the first – maybe that's what the soldiers of Fort Wilson did before he even got there? Maybe they were wandering the hills in their vests and boots? Words like 'honour' were for bigger men, he knew that: men with titles and coursers and houses. But he wouldn't run away. He'd hidden himself whilst others died. He'd carry that. It was why he was still alive. Leaving was different.

He ran to the main building as quietly as he could. He plunged into the light and blinked against the glare. His mouth watered; his tongue was thick against his teeth. The room was empty. He checked along the bedrolls. They'd been kicked around, their things looked through, but there was nobody there. At the stairs he looked upwards – then he saw someone sitting at the table: the back of a man, his hair blond, no coat.

'Hey!' he shouted.

The man didn't look round and Bryn stepped closer, edging his way clear of the table. There was a blue jacket on it.

'Lieutenant?'

The Lieutenant shook his head. 'Not any more.'

'What happened?' Bryn said.

'You were there,' the Lieutenant whispered.

'Red-coats – too many of them – but how did you survive?'

The Lieutenant pointed at his jacket. There was a hole in it, under the breast. It was stained with blood.

2 : 4

Bryn stared at the Lieutenant. He'd never seen him without his jacket on. He had pale, bony shoulders. He wasn't a hairy man. His vest had the same flowering of blood as the jacket, dried brown.

'There were a lot of people here once,' the Lieutenant said.

'In Fort Wilson?' Bryn said.

'From the coast to beyond these mountains; you couldn't move for people. And then something happened. No one knows what, not really, but now there're fewer people. Fewer people – and the Walkin'. Are we wrong, do you think, Bryn?'

The Lieutenant was about to cry; Bryn could tell. He'd seen Gloria look that way before, when she'd fallen from a tree. There was a moment of calm as it bubbled up inside her, then the tears had come.

'My dad used to say right and wrong were easy to spot, but he lied, I think.'

'There's nothing *right* here,' the Lieutenant said, punching his chest. 'Are you going to shoot me, Bryn? If you do, aim high.'

Bryn had forgotten the rifle. He dropped it, now in a hurry to be rid of it, as empty and useless as it was.

'Why would I shoot you, Lieutenant?'

'Because I'm not your Lieutenant any more, am I?' He gestured to the jacket again.

Bryn sat down. 'I don't understand.'

The Lieutenant leaned over and grabbed his hand. Bryn tried to jerk away, but the Lieutenant's grip was too strong. He could only watch as his hand was pulled closer to the Lieutenant's chest. His forefinger was singled out. He tried to curl his hand into a fist, but the Lieutenant stopped him.

'Stop,' Bryn said. His finger disappeared into the Lieutenant's wound. He looked away, but he couldn't shut out the feeling. Dry leaves.

'You can't look at me, can you?'

'I shouldn't. It's rude to stare.'

'That's how it will be: I am now something that can only be stared at,' the Lieutenant said.

'Did it hurt?' Bryn said.

'I can't remember. But it didn't take long. One shot, right in here.' The Lieutenant twisted Bryn's finger. 'I was awake again before I even hit the ground, or so it felt. The man was coming towards me to see if his shot was enough. I closed my eyes and pretended myself dead.'

He let go of Bryn's hand. Bryn rubbed his wrist, which was red and throbbing, and then his finger. He wanted rid of the feeling. 'But why did they leave?' he said.

The Lieutenant shrugged. 'They appeared to be in a hurry

to get somewhere. They didn't set fire to the fort, or leave a few men here. I would have. They must have had their reasons, but I gave up trying to understand the southern man.'

'I killed one.'

'One more than me.'

'He's in the food shed, rotting with the rest of it,' Bryn said. 'He won't be coming back.'

They said nothing for a while. Bryn watched the candle, his eyes gritty. He'd been awake for a long time. The flame grew bigger, pulsing, then shrank, and the shadows threatened to wash over him.

'With your permission, I'll get some sleep,' Bryn said.

'No permission necessary. No sleep necessary,' the Lieutenant said.

Bryn was too tired to ask any more questions. He got to his feet, using the chair back to pull himself upright. He took small steps to his bedroll. The others were empty, but he wouldn't sleep on another man's sheets. Where were the others? He opened his mouth, but his head hit the pillow and he couldn't form the words. Before he fell asleep, he noticed the grain-thief had taken the food he'd set out.

Bryn woke to a loud thump. George was gazing right at him, his jaw cocked at a strange angle, as if he'd been punched and it had stuck. He was only a few feet away, lying on the next bedroll.

The Lieutenant stood over him, wiping his hands on his vest. 'They feel so wet,' he said.

Bryn sat up. Travis, Silas, and John were on their rolls too: lumps of torn uniforms.

'Best not look too closely,' the Lieutenant said.

'What are you doing?'

'They might wake up.'

'How do you know?' Bryn said.

'I don't.'

'What if they don't wake up?'

'They'll start to smell.' The Lieutenant turned away.

Bryn scrambled out of his bed. 'Should we just let them come back?' He blinked at the soft sunlight. The day had the heaviness of late afternoon.

'I'm not going to stop them, are you?'

'But shouldn't we, as soldiers? Aren't we meant to?' Bryn said.

'You're the only soldier here.' The Lieutenant went outside and walked out of the fort.

Thomas crouched at the corner and sighted along the frame he'd just finished pegging into place. It looked straight and even to him, but who knew when he'd be able to tell if he was right or not? Would it become clear as he laid the first floorboards? Or when he put up the first walls? Or as his wife tripped every time she moved from one room to the other? He could only hope.

It started to rain, large drops which hit his hands and face.

And then the drops were everywhere and he couldn't tell them apart. Rain was falling through his floor – through his house. It didn't matter, not yet, but it was strange to see the water finding the gaps between the bones of the building. He knew what that was like. The hills closed in around him, the grey fading out the horizon.

Mary opened the tent flap. She was still wrapped in blankets. She looked worse through the rain; it drained her of the little colour she had left.

'You should be keeping warm,' he said, wandering over to her.

She coughed. 'I needed some fresh air.'

'How is your leg?'

'It hurts,' she said.

'I'm sorry.'

'This is the first time it's rained since we got here. I thought it would rain more.'

'It will,' he said. He wanted to hug her, to comfort her, but he couldn't: cold bones and dead skin were no comfort to anyone. Warmth was the key to contact – he understood that, now it was gone. 'Your mother is looking for mint. She said mint would help.' He toyed absently with his hand. Water was already swelling the gaps, making his flesh bulge in odd places. He pressed a little pocket with a finger and the water streamed out. He did it just to see it happen.

'The house is looking good,' she said.

He laughed. 'Not yet. But it will. Don't get cold,' he said.

'I'll watch for a bit.'

He went back to checking his work. It still looked straight. He checked from every corner, and then he did it again. He'd never be certain, he knew that, but he could say he'd done his best. He got ready to lay the first plank.

'Hello?'

Someone was standing a way off, little more than a dark shape in the rain.

'Who's there?' Thomas called. His mallet was by his feet. The figure came closer. It was a man, young, with dark hair plastered down either side of his brow. The house was between Thomas and the man.

'I'm looking for work, only asking for food.'

'In these hills?' Thomas said.

'I've come a long way.'

Thomas nudged the mallet with his toe. It was reassuringly heavy. He picked it up and backed closer to the tent. There would be more of them out there.

'You're alone?'

'Yes.'

'Are you lying?' Thomas said.

'How could you know?' He was close to the tent now.

Thomas looked at Mary, who had been listening the whole time. She stared past him. She didn't seem surprised to see the man.

'Maybe you should be going on your way?'

'I can help here.' The man touched the frame. 'You're building a house. I've done the same myself. You'll be keeping woollies. It's the only thing you can do in hills like these.'

'And neats.'

'Yes, the grass is good enough.'

'If you're here to steal our animals, we don't have any,' Thomas said.

'Where would I take them?'

'He's not here to hurt us,' Mary said quietly.

'How can you know?'

She didn't reply.

'I see planks and untended logs. Let me finish them for you?' the man said.

'And give you an axe?' Thomas said.

'I have my own.' He dropped a large leather bag on the ground. 'Please. I will work for the food.'

Sarah appeared out of the gloom, carrying a basket full of green leaves. She saw the man and stopped. Her clothes and hair were flat and heavy with water.

'Thomas, who is this?'

'My name is Callum, ma'am.'

She carefully put the basket down. 'What do you want?'

'Just work.'

'There's no work here,' she said.

Callum gestured to the empty frame of the house.

Thomas went over to his wife. She didn't take her eyes off the man as he said, 'I don't like it either.'

'Is he alone?' she said.

'Says he is.'

'You could use the help,' she whispered. 'That's the truth of it, isn't it?'

'Have you forgotten what our daughter has been through?'

Her eyes narrowed. 'Of course not.'

'It's too dangerous.'

'Not if he's alone.' She squared her shoulders. She looked as strong as ever.

He touched her arm. 'So he says. Why take the risk?' he said.

'With his help, the house will be ready sooner. And the farm. You hoped you could run it just with me and Mary, but with her ill, that might not work. This isn't the biggest risk we've taken.'

'I'll have to watch him,' Thomas said.

'Even when he's sleeping.'

'She's not well.'

'I know,' she said.

2 : 5

That afternoon the rain turned to a light drizzle. Thomas sat on a foundation post and watched Callum at work. They both had an axe in their hand, but Thomas felt sure he could handle the man. Now he was closer, he took a better look at Callum.

'McDermott?' Callum said. 'I recognise the name, though I can't remember where.'

'How old are you?' Thomas said.

'Nineteen. Twenty this summer.'

He looked older; in the rain Thomas had taken him for a man in his forties.

'What's a youngster like you doing out here?'

'Looking for work. And old friends. I've been trying to find them for a long time,' Callum said. He held his own axe, a small hatchet, in a familiar way. He stripped the logs like a carpenter might: clean, easy motions with no waste.

'You a deserter?'

'No, you?'

'In a way.'

129

'What happened to your jacket?' Callum said, sniffing.

'There was a fire.'

'Couldn't have been much of a fire.'

Callum carried on stripping the logs. He didn't speak unless Thomas said something. After a while Thomas began to feel foolish watching another man work. He took some planks to the other side of the frame and started to lay them down; he was careful not to turn his back on Callum. But the man seemed content cutting the wood. The planks were long enough to make it to the middle beam. He left a gap every other one, so the water wouldn't build up. It would be enough of a floor to work with until they got around to the roof.

They. He was already counting on the help from Callum.

'You have a plane to finish these?' Callum said. He eased himself upright, rubbing at his back. Thomas took him over to the crate where he kept his tools. The plane still had a scrap of thin wood in it from yesterday's work.

'You're young to feel it in your back, aren't you?' Thomas said.

'A lot of nights sleeping on rocks.' Callum rolled a shoulder.

'Why not go home?'

'As I said, I'm looking for someone,' he said. 'Can't go back until I find them.'

'How long have you been looking?'

'Eight years, near enough.' Callum took the plane and went back to the logs.

Thomas followed him. Eight years of wandering? He'd been a boy when he started. Thomas hefted the mallet in his hand. He stared at the back of Callum's head, his dark curls bobbing as he worked. He gripped the wooden handle. He could hit the boy. Once or twice, and that would be that. They could burn the body and no one would know. No one would come looking, if Callum's story was true. He must have run away – what kind of parents would let their son go roaming the wilderness? Mary had been young, but not alone. What kind of parent would cave in the boy's skull just to be clear of the worry?

Once again, Thomas found himself watching Callum work, as if he might be able to see who the boy was, or get a better understanding of him. So he knew his way around an axe and a plane? He'd not lied about being helpful; that didn't mean he could be trusted. He had seen Mary earlier: Mary wrapped in blankets with shadows under her eyes and in her cheeks. Thomas had seen men react to his daughter when she was in a worse state than that. Callum had remained cold and pleading. Mary normally brought out the pride in a man. They lifted things; puffed out their chests; talked loudly. It would take just one strike with the mallet. 'Why take the risk?' he'd told Sarah. Why, indeed.

'How are you fixing the roof?' Callum said, looking round.

Thomas placed the mallet on the frame. 'A friend suggested a simple slant, one wall taller than the other.'

'That's how I'd do it. Where's this friend?'

'Marsdenville. Know it?' Thomas said.

'Know of it. Too big for me.'

'For us too,' Thomas said. Sarah was coming out of the tent. 'Finish those, then come and eat.'

Callum smiled at the promise of food. It looked like it had been days since he last ate.

The sun was setting over the tree-line, a damp haze of orange with rings of purple. Thomas had lost track of the day, what with the rain and the new arrival. He stopped by what would be the front of the house and admired the view sweeping down the hills and out to the world: enough green that the colours from before were easy to forget. The yellow of the Badlands. The grey of the cities. The red of his jacket.

Sarah was standing at the cooking pot. He hugged her from behind and she stopped for a moment and rubbed his arms.

'Callum seems a solid worker,' he said.

'That's good,' she said.

'Younger than I first thought.'

'Thomas, stop.'

'What?' he said.

'You know what. We've talked about this before.'

'This is nothing like—'

'You have a daughter,' Sarah said. 'That should be enough.'

He turned her around, causing her to drop the spoon into the pot. 'He came looking for us, not the other way around. We need the help, but I'm not happy about it.'

'"Looking for us." That's what you just said.'

'I did?'

132

'Is that what you think? That this boy was looking for us out here?' she said.

'I don't know why he's here. Not really. And that worries me.'

She waited until he let her go.

'That smells wonderful, Mrs McDermott,' Callum said, sitting a little way off from the fire. He'd left his axe and his bag by the house.

'It's only soup.'

Thomas sat down. The two men watched Sarah chop and sprinkle things into the pot as they would an alchemist. She tasted it once. From her pocket she pulled out a little box. She opened the lid with all her concentration. A pinch, and the box was safely stowed.

'I'll take Mary her bowl. You'll have to forgive our daughter; she isn't well,' Sarah said.

Callum waved away the apology.

When Sarah returned, she placed a bowl before the boy and then sat opposite. She held out her hands.

'We say a prayer before every meal,' she said.

'My parents did the same.'

They lowered their eyes. Sarah began to speak. Thomas looked at her, but Mary was not with them so there wouldn't be any complaints, no broken crockery.

' . . . and for our guest. "I will fetch a morsel of bread, and comfort your heart." Amen.'

'Amen,' they said. It felt good to say after so long. Good to say, and good to hear.

2 : 6

It was raining outside. Like a set of curtains pulled over the windows and the open door. It didn't make a sound; not on the roof and not on the ground outside. It was the kind of rain that didn't fall in big blobs but in thin sheets. Bryn shifted on his chair. His stomach growled, and not for the first time. He was watching their bodies.

He didn't know what he was looking for. Things were either rotten or they weren't. Like in the shed. He'd never seen something rot before, never sat there as it happened. How long would it take? Would he notice the smell first, as the Lieutenant had said? Or would the hungry-brides make it obvious?

If they woke up, well, that would be obvious enough. He wasn't sure how he felt about that. He thought the army was supposed to stop it happening; both sides agreed on that. Can't have a war where everyone gets back up after a battle. There'd be more Walkin' in the country than normal folk. Both sides agreed, but the red-coats hadn't stayed long enough to build a pyre-pit. What was their hurry? Were they going over the mountains, or coming back? There wasn't anything out there, as far as he knew. Still, he'd seen a pyre-pit before. That's what he should be doing: digging a pit, lining it with wood and setting them on fire. But a pit hadn't stopped Mr McDermott. Bryn scratched his chin. It had been itchy ever since he'd spent the night in the shed, like something was crawling on him.

His stomach made more noises and this time there was a sharp pain. He needed to eat. He stood up slowly, like an old man. In the back room he found oats and water and raisins. He didn't bother to heat the water. He ignored the slimy way it went down and ate two bowlfuls, barely taking a breath. Two bowlfuls: that was two days' rations. He hefted the sack of oats. There was more than half left, and maybe there was more somewhere. Travis and the Lieutenant would know. He was the only one who would need any of it. He dug out a handful of raisins. He spilt some, but didn't bother to pick them up.

At the bedrolls he popped a raisin into his mouth. It was still raining. They were still dead. He didn't smell anything nasty, except himself. He needed to wash. There was a river nearby, apparently – or there was the rain. No one would see him. He threw the rest of the raisins into his mouth, missing some. He took off his jacket, then his vest, his baggy trousers, his underwear. He put his boots back on and stepped naked into the rain.

The shock of it made him shiver: it was heavier than he'd thought. He was drenched in moments. He didn't have any soap, but he made sure the water reached every part of him. He ran his hands through his hair, enjoying how slick it was, and the drops of water that ran down onto his neck. He wandered further into the middle of the courtyard and started laughing. He spread his arms and turned to every corner of the fort. He was here: the only one. He was glad he wasn't lying in there on a bedroll, rotting or not. He stopped laughing, but he was still shaking. He went back inside. Nothing had changed.

Shivering, he moved closer to them. He hadn't really looked at any of them, not since waking up next to George. He didn't know how they'd died. That was important and it shouldn't have been left this long. He checked on George first. His jaw was broken, Bryn remembered that. There was a long wound across his chest – not the kind made by lead shot, more like a sabre, like those the mounted officers had. So George had faced up to an officer. Bryn patted the man's foot. Travis and John had both been shot: that was clear enough from the holes in their chests. Travis had taken another to the leg, by the looks of it – the shin was all bloodied and open. Water dripped from Bryn as he leaned over to look at it.

The Lieutenant had dropped Silas onto the bedroll face-down. Bryn rolled him over, then he stepped back, his porridge threatening to resurface. They'd butchered Silas. Bryn couldn't see signs of a shot or stab, but there were cuts lining his cheeks like the bars of a cage. One of his hands was all twisted, each finger snapped into a strange angle. His ears were gone. Bryn remembered the screams he had heard from inside the shed. From his hiding place. *Silas'* screams. Bryn looked hard at the man's broken face so he wouldn't forget, and then he covered him with the sheet.

'Don't wake up, Silas.'

Bryn stood in the middle of the four dead bodies, wearing just his boots, water dripping from every part of him, his shivering getting worse. They'd all suffered – some more than others. But for now it was over for them. Maybe they had it best.

'Don't wake up,' he said.

He stood at the bottom of the stairs for longer than he should. The Lieutenant had left the fort. He'd started the Walk – that's how people talked about it, as if it was something they all had to do when they came back. He'd ask Mr McDermott next time he saw him, unless one of the others woke up and wanted to talk about it. Either way, there was no reason he shouldn't go upstairs into the Lieutenant's quarters. No reason at all.

He kept an eye on the door of the building as he took each step. He'd get caught – he always had as a child, so much that Wesley would just blame him and everyone would believe it. He'd get mad at Wesley, but not for long.

The Lieutenant's quarters were very different from what he was expecting. There was a small bed, neatly made, but no fur quilt or big pillows. The floor was bare. He had a few crates piled in one corner and a coal burner in another.

There were sacks against one wall: the same kind of sacks as in the food shed. He gagged at the memory of their sweet sickliness. With his hand over his mouth he looked inside one of them. Fruit. He looked away and held his breath, but it wasn't rotting. He picked up an apple and turned it around in front of his face, waiting for something to crawl out of it. He bit into it and checked again. It was painfully sharp, like fire between his teeth. His eyes screwed up and there was nothing he could do about it. He ate the rest of the apple, wincing the whole time.

There was a folded towel at the end of the bed. It looked so clean it could be new. He took it and dried himself. His skin bristled blue and felt thin to him, but the shivering stopped. In one of the crates he found spare uniforms. He put on a vest and some trousers, and they fitted better than his own, which was surprising. He thought the Lieutenant was a bigger man. He didn't put on a jacket – they were heavy with stripes. He moved the crate with the clothes in and tried to open the one underneath, but it was nailed shut. Dry and clothed, he left everything the same way he found it, even folding the towel, putting the crate back. He couldn't put the clothes or the apple back, but he didn't think the Lieutenant would care. Wherever he was.

Bryn went downstairs for some water. He sat at the table and uncorked a water-skin. He took two gulps before noticing that someone was missing. There were three bodies lying on the floor. John wasn't there. Bryn got up and went over to John's bedroll. The sheet had been tossed to one side.

2 : 7

'It doesn't work,' John said. He was standing in the doorway. He didn't have any trousers on. 'I can't piss. I thought I needed to go. I always need to go when I wake up.' In the rain he looked completely grey, a man of no colour, fading into the background. He held his prick in his hand, delicate, like it was broken glass.

'You should sit down, John.'

'Why?'

'You need to look at yourself,' Bryn said.

John stared down his front. He seemed to ignore the hole in his gut. 'I can't even get it hard.'

'Sit down.'

'Shut up!' John punched the doorframe. The wall shook. 'There's something wrong with it – wrong with *me*.'

Bryn let him calm down a little. There wasn't an easy way to tell it. Someone like the Lieutenant might know fancy words that would make it sound better.

'You died,' Bryn said. 'Don't you remember? The red-coats?'

'Died? But I was just sleeping, wasn't I?'

'Look at your gut.'

John blinked. He stopped cradling his prick and touched the hole. Bryn's finger ghosted along with John's. He was back at the table, his hand gripped by the Lieutenant, feeling the dry crackle of dead skin and rubbery muscle.

John slumped against the frame. 'There were lots of them, right? Too many. And we weren't ready. We weren't ready. I'm going to sit down now.' He didn't seem to notice he wasn't wearing trousers.

Bryn sat by him.

'Did they get you too?'

Bryn shook his head.

'That's good. The others?'

'All of them. The Lieutenant . . . he's out there,' Bryn waved towards the hills. 'The others haven't come back yet.'

'My mum used to claim we had it in us, when she'd had a few drinks. She wouldn't say it out right, just hint. No wonder I don't need to piss.'

'Won't need to ever again,' Bryn said, smiling, and they laughed at that.

But then John stopped. 'Won't tumble any dresses again, neither.'

'No.'

'What's the point then?' he said. He stood up and wandered over to the others. He spent some time in front of each of them. 'Shouldn't there be a pit?'

'The Lieutenant didn't give the order.'

'Should we dig one any way?' Something in the way John asked sounded strange, as if he really wasn't sure. But more, he thought Bryn might know the answer – that Bryn was the one to make the decision.

'No pit.'

'Is that Silas under there? Why is he covered?'

'You don't want to see,' Bryn said.

John pulled back the cover. 'Christ. They spent some time on Silas, didn't they? He won't be happy.' John came back to the table. 'I left my trousers out by the privy,' he said, noticing his nakedness for the first time.

Bryn shrugged.

'What now?' John said.

'I don't know. Wait for the others to wake up, maybe. Bury the ones that don't.'

'I never thought about what to do, if it happened. I should have made plans. Decided things with the wife.'

Bryn scratched his chin. 'Will you go back?'

'I don't know. There's not much for Walkin' where I'm from.' John held his head in his hands. He looked frail to Bryn then; not the same man. There weren't any jokes. There'd be no more wishing away his hours thinking about women. He'd asked Bryn: 'What's the point, then?' Bryn didn't know what the point was *before* you died; you just got on with things as they happened. Because you were there. There wasn't much of choice in it. But as the Lieutenant said, John wasn't a soldier any more; he might not be a husband or a father. What was he to do? John had been

143

desperate enough to ask him but he didn't know a thing about it. He wasn't married, had no children. He hadn't died and come back.

So they waited, into the night. The rain didn't stop, it just turned from grey to black. Bryn left food under the wall for the grain-thief. He hoped it was doing all right. Hoods were the only birds he'd seen since arriving at the fort and they didn't eat grain-thieves. But there might be all kinds of things out in the woods. He left double. It was bad to name animals; that was a quick lesson on the farm. But next time he saw the thief he'd think of a name.

He lit a candle and went up to the Lieutenant's room. He found some dried meat in one of the sacks. He chewed on it, took another apple and went back downstairs. He wasn't really hungry. Not like before. Bryn ate and John watched. They didn't speak much. Bryn tried, but there was little to say.

They were both staring at the flame of the candle when someone groaned.

2 : 8

Mary was tired of hearing the rain, which pounded on the tent like it was the skin of a drum. It matched the pounding in her ears and across her forehead and her leg. She didn't look when her mother replaced the bandage, but she could smell it: a spongy wet smell that filled the tent. They took it in turns to gag. Her mother cried more often than she did.

Sarah was still asleep. She was tossing and turning and gripping the blankets. She was worried about Mary – or maybe it was the boy. They'd made him set up his tent on the other side of their half-built house. It was just two poles and a treated canvas; a month ago he would have frozen to death. But Mary didn't doubt her father was watching him as much as he was working.

She could still taste the smoke. Thick in her throat but burning hot, like boiling water. Her room was black with it. She had to crawl to reach the door, all the time coughing until phlegm hit the floorboards. Sarah was on the landing, gripping the banister rails. Her face was black with soot, except for two wet streaks. She looked through Mary. She shook her mother, who just nodded when Mary shouted in her face; dragging her down the stairs wasn't easy. The heat pushed Mary against the wall and she heard the flames before she saw them: the crack of wood being eaten up. She placed her hand carefully on the next step, ready for it to go from under her, but it didn't. The fire was in the back of the house. It chased them to the front door.

On the street, Mary searched the shocked faces: people gawping at the smoke and flames, and the few with buckets. She searched for her father, but he wasn't there. Benjamin Ryland was. He saw her. He spat on the ground and he walked off. There was a vase of flowers in the front window of the house, their petals on fire. They were from Benjamin. Her mother had insisted on putting them in the vase, putting them in the window.

She hadn't thought about Benjamin since. He hadn't been the first to get a taste and then want to keep it – keep her. He wasn't the last to take it badly. There was a moment when their face twisted and – no matter how old they were – they looked like a child losing for the first time. The flowers were desperate – and public. It didn't work that way. He was a long way behind them now, a long time behind. Her parents were wary since Benjamin, since the fire, since Marsdenville. But it was hard to set fires in the rain.

The noise on the canvas was lighter now and she reached for her coat, careful not to wake her mother. Sarah looked as if she was in pain, her teeth bared and knuckles white against the blanket. She hid these feelings every day – some days better than others – and that must be difficult.

Outside, the first trickle of light was stretching across the grasslands below, creeping towards them in plain sight. Her father was working on the house. His head and shoulders peeked out from behind the first wall. He was knocking a plank into place. He looked calm, happy even.

'You should be resting,' he said.

'I wanted to see the sunrise.'

'Come and see it from the window.' He waved her forward. 'How it will be every morning.'

She had to limp, her leg not up to taking her weight yet. She gritted her teeth against the stabs that ran down to her foot; it would do no good for him to see her in pain; she'd never be allowed to leave the tent. He pulled her up onto what would be the porch. She didn't like houses with porches – wooden houses with porches and whitewashed walls and screen doors – and the people who protected them.

'Would you look at that? Worth a few weeks in a wagon, isn't it?' he said.

'If that was all it took.'

She noticed their guest stirring under his canvas. Callum. He was more animated now than he had been at the pool, his cold eyes on her cold skin. And now he was helping them build something here, in the mountains. Something else to burn.

'He works hard,' Thomas said.

'I'm sure.'

'Your mother isn't so worried. She says not all men are bad. But you be careful.'

Thomas didn't flinch from her gaze. She dared him to explain, to talk to her about men. To find words that she didn't already know, hadn't already felt the heat of, that hadn't already gripped her hair. He couldn't, but he wasn't a coward; he didn't try to hide it. He stared right back.

'Morning,' Callum said.

'We were just admiring the sunrise.'

'A wonder, isn't it? But not the only view to be found in these hills.'

Her father introduced her formally to the young man. He was different from before: more his age – her age. He smiled, and it covered the whole of his face. His curly hair bounced when he moved, not like the stony frame she remembered. He went straight to work, handing her father more wood for the wall. She left them to it.

She hoped he wasn't watching her now as she hobbled to the tent, but she didn't look back to check. She cursed under her breath at the mountains and the cold and the army crate that had cut her.

Travis got off his bedroll and came towards them. The short man stretched his back, rubbed his nose, and then sat down at the table. John's mouth was open wide enough to catch specks. Not that there were many specks about.

'Just like that, is it?' John said.

'What?' Travis said.

'You were dead.'

'Figured as much.' Travis pulled at his jacket, straightening out the blackened and bloodied hole in it.

'Well . . . Well, you can't piss no more!'

'Right.'

'And you can't eat no more,' John said. He was getting louder. Bryn shrank back and glanced to the men still asleep – but they weren't asleep. It wouldn't really be waking up, that was just how he thought of it.

'Right.'

'And you can't *fuck* no more!'

Travis shrugged. 'Wasn't doing much of that before.' He turned to Bryn. 'Didn't get you then?'

Bryn struggled to reply. What could he say to a man who'd stood before the red-coats and accepted his share of lead shot? His chest felt tight, as if a crate was pressing down on him.

'Right,' Travis said.

'Stop saying that,' John shouted.

'What else is there to say?'

'I always knew there was something wrong with you. Too quiet. Too short. You just die and come back and you're ready to make breakfast?'

'I don't feel too hungry,' Travis said, his hands flat on the table.

'And you never will. Bryn here is starving.'

Bryn squirmed. 'No I'm not,' he said.

'He's right. I should be getting on with it.' Travis stood up.

'That's not what I said!'

Bryn's chest grew tighter. It was difficult to breathe. He could taste them on the air, like burning coals. But there hadn't been a pyre-pit. He stumbled to the door. The rain was weaker now, little more than a mist, and it felt good on his face. It was so dry inside. He opened his mouth to let it in. He left the sounds of the other two arguing and ploughed through puddles, welcoming the splashes that covered his shins.

At the food shed he stopped by the door before entering. The smell of the place came at him again. He ducked his head outside and breathed out hard through his nose. The mist wetted his face. He turned back and held his breath until he could make out the shape of Jackson, lying underneath the sacks. The others wouldn't see him – they wouldn't go into the food shed – so Bryn could leave him there to the hungry-brides.

He wandered back into the courtyard and went to the other sheds. There were marks of the red-coats' passage: wallboards splintered, black smudges of powder, puddles in the craters left by courser hooves. The woodshed was untouched, except for a trail of footprints in the sawdust that covered the floor and the stacks of crates. They circled the middle of the room and then came back out. The red-coats hadn't bothered to open more than a single crate; it was pretty obvious what was inside the others and they didn't want any of it. They weren't building anything.

The final shed was different. The lock on the door had been smashed off and was lying half-buried in the mud. Bryn knelt down and touched its rusty arm. The door was hanging on one hinge so he was careful not to move it too much as he squeezed inside. In the middle of the floor was a pile of empty crates, their lids tossed to one side. This was what the red-coats had wanted: rifles, pistols, dynamite, and enough lead shot to bury a regiment. It wasn't just the supplies Bryn had used as a seat during the weeks in the wagon. There were older crates, marked differently: weapons from the squad posted here before them, and going further back too – the bottom crates were falling apart and stained with dust. He kicked at them and his boot went clear through one side. How long had it taken the red-coats to load them all? An hour? Two? Bryn could only remember the taste of rotten fruit in his mouth and the feel of wet sackcloth. Of course it had been worth stopping at Fort Wilson. He kicked again at the crates, sending the top one crashing into the wall. But not for Jackson. One man knew Jackson was missing, but they hadn't stayed to search for him. *He* wasn't worth it. One man set against rifles and ammunition. Even if they tallied a man the same as a rifle – and Bryn had seen nothing to suggest men rated so highly – then the red-coats had come out better off.

When he left he saw two hoods flapping down between the shed and the main building. They were fighting before they even touched the ground. It was difficult to tell which feathers were attached and which had been pulled loose. He was ignored as they stabbed at each other with their beaks. One picked up something from the ground and tried to take flight. The other grabbed at its leg, jerking it down. They juggled the prize between them. Bryn squinted against the rain. It looked like a piece of bread. He stepped closer and they still paid him no attention. It wasn't bread. The colour was wrong, too pink.

Bryn ran at the birds, clapping his hands and yelling. He was almost on top of them before they stopped fighting and they skidded as much as flew away. He reached down and pulled the ear out of the mud.

2 : 9

Bryn ignored the cold. The rain had gone and the sky was clear enough to see patches of stars. He clamped his mouth so his teeth wouldn't chatter. He was sitting on the wall they'd built between two of the sheds. A completely useless wall. A waste of days. He was sitting looking in when he should have been standing and looking out. He rubbed the ear between two fingers. It felt like his own ear. His frozen fingers struggled to tell the difference.

The food shed was off to his right. It sat there, fat with rotting meat and fruit. He couldn't leave a man inside there, no matter the colour of his coat. But there wasn't much point dragging him into the main building. Jackson didn't need a bedroll to wake up on. The back of the sickle had left marks on Bryn's hand and he pressed at it until the red skin turned white. His arms were heavy. He'd used the sickle like the tip of a knife and somehow cut right through; there was no waking up from that. He would have to bury the man. It wasn't about *owing* anything, just, he'd want someone to do the same for him. And he'd understand if they took their time doing it.

His hands came together and plunged down, over and over. He started to cry, big body-shuddering sobs that were half lost in his shivering. He kicked the wall with his heel, but he didn't have the energy to break it. The wall was new. The wall was theirs. He laughed at that, through the spittle and tears. This useless wall was *theirs*.

Someone was at the door: someone large, blocking the yellow light that spilled from the main building. John was looking for him. He peered one way, then the other, and all the while Bryn was right opposite. Bryn wiped his face with his sleeve. Perhaps John's eyes were struggling in the dark. That would be some blessing. There wasn't a good thing to see here. Or anywhere.

'Bryn! You'd better come in.'

There was a loud crash. John turned to look back at the raised voices. Bryn jumped down from the wall. His feet sank in the mud and he had to pull them free. He couldn't run, but he stepped as quickly as he could.

The table was on its side and Travis was picking up the candles. Silas had a chair in his hands. He threw it at no one and it hit the stairs but didn't break.

'Not bones,' Silas shouted. 'I won't be a bag o' bones.'

'Calm down,' John said. He stepped closer to Silas.

'Calm? Is that what you said?'

Bryn winced at how loud he was.

'It's got most of us,' Travis said.

'What?' Silas picked up another chair. 'Say that again!'

'Most of us have come back.'

Silas threw the chair at the smaller man. Travis shrugged it off.

'It's okay to be afraid,' John said.

'What the hell has praying got to do with it?'

'That's not what I said.'

'Why are you all whispering?' Silas said, his voice still raised.

John put his hands down and shook his head. Travis took his time picking up the chair that had bounced off him.

'He doesn't know?' Bryn said quietly. They wouldn't look him in the eye. He called them every name he knew as he went upstairs, taking the steps two at a time. Beside the bed was a little stand and on the top was the Lieutenant's hand-mirror. Blond hair was caught in its edges.

'Bryn, don't,' John said, but he didn't move to stop him.

Bryn handed the mirror to Silas.

He stared at the imperfect glass for a minute. No one said a thing. They waited. He raised a hand to the side of his head, but didn't actually touch it. He tongued his cheek, making the ribbons that remained bulge out and the gaps between grow wider. He dropped the mirror and cast around, but there was nothing else to break, nothing to throw.

Then he walked out of the building.

They set the table right, putting the candles back and lighting those that had gone out. Bryn retrieved the chair from next to the stairs. He set it down, but one of the legs was cracked and it didn't stand right. One day it would break.

'I should have stopped him,' John said.

'Why?' Bryn closed the door. It was raining again, getting heavy. He got himself a handful of raisins. He needed to keep eating. It would be easy to forget. They used to eat together and only together; now he could eat when he wanted. He was in charge of the food.

'We should clear these away,' John said, standing by the bedrolls. 'We only need one.'

Bryn packed up Silas' bedding. The others did their own, taking their time. They were saying goodbye to something they'd known a long time. Bryn said goodbye to Silas. He'd miss the Lieutenant.

'Only George left,' Bryn said. They stood in front of the dead soldier.

Travis knelt down. 'I don't think he's coming back.'

'We should bury him,' John said.

'No!' Bryn swallowed hard. 'We should wait another day.' They should wait before they buried things, until it was final and all was accounted for.

Thomas stood on the ladder and hammered the first roof board into place. The others watched from inside the shell of the house. Soon it wouldn't just be a shell. Callum clapped and Sarah looked around the house as if seeing it for the first time. She seemed to like what she saw. Thomas gave a mock bow.

'We really could live here,' she said.

'And we will.'

She smiled at him.

Callum passed him the next plank. With the walls up and the roof going on, the end was in sight. He'd got a feel of what kind of house it was going to be: three rooms, all a good size and shape. He didn't like thin rooms. They pressed in on him and he found it difficult to breathe – back when he did breathe. Now a thin room made him fidget. The stove would heat the whole house – but it would be cold until he found somewhere to buy windows. He chuckled at the idea of shops; they seemed very far away from the mountains, a different life completely.

Mary was still limping. Though it was not so bad now, he shared the pain of every awkward footfall. Mary busied herself with preparing lunch while Sarah headed off to fetch more water. They always needed more water. He should have built right on top of the stream. It wasn't easy to admit, but he'd forgotten to think of it. He focused on the best pasture he could see, ground that was as close to level as he'd find in these hills, and near enough to the forest so he wouldn't have to carry wood so far. And instead they carried water. No place was perfect.

'Thomas?'

He stopped, the hammer halfway to the nail. 'Lost in my thoughts. Happens to us old folks.' He grinned, but Callum didn't seem to find it funny. He held out the hammer. 'Knock that peg a little further in from your side.'

'Sure,' Callum said. He took the hammer by the head and

wiped the handle on his shirt. He hit the peg a few times and passed the hammer back.

Thomas stared at the boy.

'What?'

'Nothing,' Thomas said.

'Do you think we'll get the roof on today?'

'The first layer.' Thomas took the next board. 'Then it's the slats. It will be a day or two before we can take down the tent.'

Callum nodded and looked over at his makeshift shelter.

'But you could have the tent,' Thomas said.

'No. That's yours.'

'I don't use it.'

Thomas climbed down the ladder and then moved it inside. He was nailing down the highest end of the roof first and once the planks were all in place he'd do the same along the low side.

Callum stood on the bottom rung. 'You don't sleep, do you?' he said.

'No. I keep working. And watching.'

'Do you miss it?'

Thomas shifted the ladder again. 'I try not to think about it. There's a lot I miss, but I'm grateful for what I have.'

'Your daughter,' Callum said.

'Yes, my family.'

2 : 10

My beloved spoke and said to me,
'Arise, my darling, my beautiful one,
come with me.'

Song of Songs

BOOK 3

3 : 1

Bryn barely slept that night. He took his bedroll upstairs and put it down next to the Lieutenant's empty bed. He tossed and turned, either too hot or too cold. Bryn couldn't let go of the moment Silas saw himself in the mirror. What happened to him – how could a man live with that? Silas was right to be angry. He'd have been angry if he'd come back just like the rest of them, but as he was ... He was right to be angry. The pulling tight of a strip of his cheek with the blackened tongue behind – Bryn shuddered. He was sweating enough for five soldiers.

There was a gap between the bed and the floor and light from downstairs flickered on the banister, like it was on fire. Maybe that was why he was so hot? The building was burning down. A pyre had been set for them. It was right he'd burn with the others – he should be dead too, like them. But there wasn't any smoke – no fire without smoke. Wesley used to set fire to dry grass in the summer. There was so much smoke Bryn was sure they'd be caught, but they never were. Wesley would laugh at Bryn's nerves, but mostly he'd watch the flames. He'd set them in a circle if he could and watch it spread and then die.

The candles burned throughout the night. Bryn slept fitfully; when he woke he saw the yellow light and felt hot, then he fell asleep again. By the morning, his bedroll stank. It hadn't been clean before, but that had been a general dirt: the earthy smell of months of sleep. This was sharp and sat on his lips. He rolled it up, determined to clean it today.

Travis and John were sitting at the table. They were wrestling, their arms locked together. Travis' arm was slightly closer to the table.

'We've been doing this half the night,' John said. 'I win, right?'

'I won't budge.'

'But I'm winning, see?'

'I haven't lost,' Travis said.

George was still on his bedroll and Bryn couldn't deny it any longer: George was rotting. He could tell that with most of the building between them. Closer, he would be certain. He kept his distance.

'I'm going to the river,' Bryn said.

'What for?' John said.

'To wash and get water.'

'Use the well.'

'I could use the walk,' Bryn said. In truth, he'd forgotten the well. It was behind the main building, out of sight. He'd been drinking from waterskins no doubt filled from the well.

'Oh. But I'm winning. You see it, don't you, Bryn?'

He checked on the grain-thief. He'd left plenty of food, but George and the others might have put the little thief off. Having moved the bedrolls it was difficult to tell just where the usual spot was. On his hands and knees, he shuffled along the wall, ignoring John's questions and ignoring George. He pressed his face against the floor and saw little paws and a nose and a fat, round body. It seemed to be stroking the chunks of food, not eating them. Wesley: that was his name. Always taking what Bryn offered him.

'I'm coming back,' Bryn said from the door. 'Don't worry.'

'We won't,' John said.

It had stopped raining some time during the night, but it was cold. Bryn turned the collar up on his jacket and blew into his hands, then he wedged the bedroll in his armpit. The ground in the fort had turned frosty-hard and flakes of mud crunched under his boots. He paused at the edge of the main building where a gate would be, if the fort had had such a thing. He was coming back. No one could accuse him of being a deserter. His sister had said it: he was getting in the way. His father was angry to see him idle and without a farm to work. Maybe something similar kept Travis and John at the fort, more than waiting for George: a sense of duty that wasn't speared by a bayonet or shattered by lead shot. But the Lieutenant had left.

Bryn stopped halfway across the track. The grass was thicker there, even though the track looked like it was rarely used. He had planned on going to the river, seeing the

McDermotts, but the way the weak sunlight slanted across the hills stopped him. He remembered the black line he'd noticed on the first day at Fort Wilson, and thinking on what might be beyond the mountains. He glanced back into the fort and waited three breaths for someone to come out and stop him. Then he started walking up the track towards the mountain peaks, towards the black line.

The going was steady: not steep, but enough work to get him sweating. He kept to where the grass was shorter and avoided stepping on any rocks. He passed the bedroll from one arm to the other when it became uncomfortable. Then he started to count his paces. He held the bedroll for one hundred and then swapped arms. Next time he aimed for one hundred and fifty, and it was a relief to move the roll. As he was counting he watched his feet. The toes of his boots were rough and flaking in places, like bad skin. He stopped to pull some of it off and it coloured his fingers brown-grey. Straightening, the black line didn't look any closer. Or bigger.

He pushed to one hundred and seventy-six paces before the bedroll slipped from underneath his arm. He rubbed at his shoulder where it ached and stopped counting. It was getting warmer as the sun got higher. It was beyond the peaks now – there was something nice about that. He looked back at the fort. He could see bits of it, though it was more like a gap in the trees than a proper building. The sheds weren't there. Only the very top of the two-storey building peeked out between the green. It was a shadow – a smudge. A mistake. He was between two black marks on the mountain.

He pressed on up the track. Again he watched his flaking boots, but now when he glanced up the black line was getting bigger, like someone was drawing more lines on top of it: one new line for each time he looked up. He tried to count how many steps between, but he couldn't concentrate on the numbers. What if he was going to the edge of the map? Is that what the lines were? But some of the mountains looked further away . . . He was sure he didn't need to worry – he could stop before he came to the edge. He'd just stop walking. He wouldn't fall off. It could be a wall – the lines could be a wall like they were building at the fort, to stop people walking over the edge. Or just to stop people.

Bryn stood still and listened. He couldn't hear anything, no men talking, no thumping of courser hooves. There wasn't a cloud of dust coming down the track.

It might not be a red-coat wall. It might not be a wall.

He hurried on, almost running, swinging the bedroll in his arms. He was getting closer now. The big black shape was bending.

His boot kicked something – a rock – and it flew across the track like a swooping hood. A black rock. Bryn tossed the bedroll to the ground, rested his hands on his knees and breathed hard. A black rock. He picked it up, took one look and then hurled it into the trees. Blacktop. It was only blacktop. The whole time it had been nothing but blacktop: useless stuff left over from who-knew-when.

'But what's it doing here?' he said between breaths. 'What's its business with mountains?'

He cast around for another piece, which didn't take much finding. The sun caught all the little shiny shapes inside the black as he turned it. It was like any blacktop he'd ever seen. Ploughing the bottom of one of his father's fields always turned up some blacktop. It was a pain the way it snagged.

Up ahead, all the black lines? They were blacktop, a lot of it. A whole track of it – and how far did it go? Right off the map. He slung the bedroll over his shoulder.

The further he went, the more blacktop there was. The pieces got bigger, like puddles when it rained, flat and spreading. He kept to the grass, but there wasn't much of it left now, because the whole track was covered in blacktop. He started skipping between patches of green, and then there were none. He had to turn back or scramble along the rocky sides – or walk on the blacktop like he was someone from history. He put one foot down gently, but it didn't ripple like water or squash down like grass. It was solid, as if he was stepping on one big, almost flat stone. He'd only ever seen blacktop in handfuls and now here he was, tiptoeing on it like it was a neighbour's best carpet. He expected to ruin it any moment. Or be told to get off. The blacktop didn't seem to notice. He put his whole foot down. The blacktop was so heavy beneath him that he felt it pressing down on his shoulders.

Parts of the blacktop were frayed and ragged, with tufts of grass poking through like spiky explosions against a starless night. The blacktop curved gently up the mountain. Bryn couldn't see the track behind him any more. He couldn't see the fort either. Trees and mountains and the yellow horizon were a long way away.

How far should he go? The sun wasn't even in the middle of the sky yet. He could follow the blacktop for a while. No one would be missing him. Travis and John wouldn't care, or care what he'd found. They weren't interested men, like Bryn and the Lieutenant; they only knew what was in front of them – usually their bellies or their pricks. He wiped his brow with his sleeve and caught the smell of himself. It made his nose tickle and he snorted. He needed a wash, but there was still plenty of the day for that. The blacktop rounded another corner.

Bryn dropped into a crouch. He held the bedroll like a rifle. He wished it was.

There was a building.

3 : 2

Bryn listened hard in the quiet. Twenty or so paces away the blacktop branched towards a building, but the building wasn't the end of it: it carried on up the mountain too. A drip of sweat ran over his lips. He kept his tongue in his mouth. He was trying to breathe like Travis and John, how they didn't at all.

The building was big, stretching out over the trees. It was more than two storeys high, and a funny shape, curved like a fruit at the top – or it would have been if it wasn't in such a bad way. The roof had collapsed and like the blacktop, the edges were jagged where the stone had fallen through. It had to be stone – it was too thick for slate and it definitely wasn't wood.

He'd heard nothing the whole time he'd been staring at the old building. If anyone was making repairs he'd know; building walls at Fort Wilson made all kinds of noises. A bird called out from somewhere in the trees: a lonely sound for a lonely place. Bryn's knees were starting to ache so he stood and went slowly towards the building. He had to take a look – he *had* to. He couldn't go back and tell the others – if they would even care – without having some understanding of what was inside.

He followed the blacktop as it turned towards the building. The trees were clear around it. On one side was a tiny square shed, only as tall as his middle, about right for a child. The little door was solid enough. He pulled at the lock. It was brown all over, but it didn't budge. He couldn't think what would be in something so small, but it was worth locking away. If he'd had his rifle he could bash at it or even shoot it off. Instead, he tried his boot.

He stopped at his own noise. The lock slapped against the door but still didn't break. He looked everywhere at once, expecting someone to come yelling at him – a red-coat, or a man as old as the building, pale as the stone and with all the same holes. But only a Walkin' could be that old.

No one came. He kicked the lock again and the heel of his boot caught the lock just right, but it swayed and laughed at him for trying. These old folks: their buildings might not stay in one piece but their locks sure did. Bryn licked his lips and started towards the building proper. There wasn't a door as such, but where a door should have been was a hole big enough to drive a wagon through.

The gap in the roof let in light enough to bathe the middle of the large room, but the edges were dark. He stood still until his eyes made sense of things. There were shapes and shadows, but nothing moving. His boots made crackling sounds as he took a few steps inside. The floor was covered in something that sparkled like stars in the sunlight. He didn't want to crush them so he kept to the darker parts of the room. There were stairs along one wall, thin metal steps, and some were missing. He couldn't see where they led and he wasn't fool enough to try them. They could keep their secrets.

He stumbled into some ancient crates and steadied himself against the wall, which was dry against his hand. His sweaty fingers left wet marks. He shifted one of the crates with the toe of his boot. It was light, taller than it was wide, and with thin sides. It was empty, which was just as well – you couldn't keep much in a crate like that. If you filled it with tools or even fruit it would bottom out, no doubt about it.

Bryn put his hands on his hips. He wasn't one to dwell on historical matters – he normally didn't have to – but this kind of place made the front of his head hurt. He wished he'd listened more when his father talked about the old times. As far as Bryn was concerned, it was right that times moved on – look how badly people used to make even a simple thing like a crate. And choosing silly round shapes for a roof? No wonder it fell in. He sighed at all the rubble that was scattered across the floor. Anywhere else that stone would have been put to good use. Here on the mountain, it was wasted.

He wandered into a patch of sunlight. It was warm on his face and he closed his eyes. All the fuzz and strangeness of the place drained from him and he relaxed; he'd been

173

bunching his shoulders at his neck without realising. He imagined the floor clean and polished, and the people who had used this building – looking like him but dressed in old-fashioned clothes. He struggled to picture what they'd be doing: sitting at tables, maybe. That was something people did no matter what part of history it was. A man would be carrying one of the top-heavy crates, careful not to spill whatever was inside. He was taking it to the little shed outside for safekeeping. And then he'd have some food, a meal prepared by a woman upstairs. They had to grow their own food on the mountain – she took care of that. They were a family. It was their job to watch for their kind of red-coats. And when they saw, they had to leave. The woman with wavy dark hair—

A noise made him open his eyes, wide. It was the kind of noise all old buildings made as they fell apart: one small bit of stone hitting the floor. And then it was lost amongst all the other stones. He breathed out slowly in the silence. He noticed a corridor leading off from the main room. The noise might have come from there. It was properly dark, but despite not having his rifle he started walking towards it. A family used to live here. This was just one corridor between rooms for them.

He stood at the opening, waiting for the darkness to fade away. There were steps leading down. He kicked a stone and it bounced from step to step, sounding a bit like the noise he'd heard. There was a clang as the stone hit something metal. Bryn took the steps one at a time. They were stone, but that didn't mean they were safe. He tensed, ready for his footing to go. It didn't take long for him to reach the bottom – it wasn't a proper set of stairs. In front of him was a metal door. It had the feeling of weight to it, like a hundred men and shaggies would strain to get it open; he could tell just by looking at it. There were marks and soot covering the bottom of the door and when Bryn ran a finger along it, it came away black.

'They tried more than a boot to get it open.'

Bryn turned. The Lieutenant was standing at the top of the stairs.

'Who?' Bryn said.

'Red-coats, I'd say.'

'Is this where you've been?'

'Here, and other places,' the Lieutenant said.

'You could live here. The building feels right for Walkin'.'

'I don't need to live anywhere.'

'What do red-coats want with this place?' Bryn said.

'What did you want with that little shed? Sometimes we just want to know things.'

Bryn wiped his finger on his trousers. 'They haven't got it open.'

'I doubt they ever will. The walls are just as strong as that door.'

'But they keep coming back?'

'I'll show you why.' The Lieutenant turned and was gone from the opening. Bryn followed.

The Lieutenant didn't look any different from the man

who had walked out of Fort Wilson. A little calmer, maybe. He wasn't wearing his jacket.

'These broken old stairs won't take us both,' the Lieutenant said. 'Go close to the wall, where they're strongest.' He led the way up, taking his time where a step was missing, but it was no great stretch. The stairs wound their way around the building. Bryn hadn't realised how high they went. He lost sight of the Lieutenant. There was a partial ceiling; Bryn put his foot on the first step, and then he stopped and waited. The building was so quiet. A speck landed on his shoulder, then off again. It danced a merry circle and then flew away silently – even specks had respect for this place. Even specks – but not red-coats. Their explosions must have made the walls and floor tremble.

'Come on up,' the Lieutenant called.

Bryn took the stairs at a slower pace than the Lieutenant, testing each one, putting his foot down and gradually easing his weight onto it. There was a handrail for most of the way, though parts of it had snapped. He made sure to avoid the jagged brown-red teeth of the metal. He'd met soldiers with that kind of smile and all of them were mean. He didn't look down or out at the room. He got a sense of getting higher and swallowed hard. Only a little further.

The Lieutenant was standing at the top with his hand outstretched. Bryn took it. His fingers felt dry, like the stone wall of the building. He was glad to let go of it, and glad to be off the stairs. They were on a semi-solid floor. Big arms of metal jutted out below – he could see them through hundreds of tiny strips. Metal for a floor. He hoped it was as strong as the door downstairs. Beyond, the room yawned up at him. The sunlight made everything seem sharp. He started towards it but the Lieutenant caught his arm.

'Stay close to the walls.'

Bryn stared down at the Lieutenant's dusty hand.

The Lieutenant led him to a gap in the wall and Bryn squinted at being outside again, his eyes watering at the brightness of it. He blinked and wiped at them with his sleeve. The sky was almost one perfect colour, with two little clouds drifting in the blue like lost woollies. They were standing on more of the metal that was barely there. Outside it was worse – in the gaps he could see the grass below.

'You asked "why?". There it is,' the Lieutenant said.

'More blacktop?' There was plenty of it. A wide track stretching off as far as Bryn could see.

'No, beyond.'

Past the blacktop there were only trees – lots of trees. But now he really looked at them he could see they were different from the trees around the fort or those around the old building. They didn't have spiky tops like mountains; they were round and difficult to tell apart, except for being all kinds of green. That wasn't normal. Trees that grew together should look the same. And these were slick with a warm wetness.

'That's not on the maps,' Bryn said.

'No.'

'And the red-coats know?'

'As far as I can tell,' the Lieutenant said.

'What's out there?'

'The past. Or the future, maybe. I don't know.'

Bryn understood: the trees didn't look like they belonged in this time. They both watched the green expanse as the sun climbed higher and still the strange trees didn't lose their sheen.

'Keep this to yourself,' the Lieutenant said.

Bryn was the first back on the stairs. Going down was even slower. He leaned on the railings more than he should have and one came away in his hand. He pressed against the wall to steady himself. If the Lieutenant heard the clatter of crumbling metal, he didn't call out. Bryn waited at the bottom. He waited a long time, shifting from one foot to the other, sometimes leaning, but always looking up the stairs. He waited longer than it should have taken the Lieutenant. Much longer. And then he left.

3 : 3

Bryn headed into the hills. It was good to have grass underfoot again. The blacktop was barren and hopeless, but here, things grew freely. There were patches of spindly plants he didn't recognise, looking more like tiny trees than grass and ending in a fan of small leaves. And the colour: a rusty red against the green. They couldn't be that colour all year round – did the summer sun turn them a darker red? Things usually became brighter in summer, more extreme, like golden crops in the good years. He stopped often to pick out new plants and flowers. It might not be a verdant meadow or even a field on his father's farm but it was good to be amongst things that were growing.

It was easier to breathe out here than under the stone of the old building. The air swirled about him and he pulled in great gulps. The freshness made him sneeze and chased away the smells of dry walls and the damp of the fort. He upped his pace, taking long strides, smiling at how he must look.

He was now following the same route he and the Lieutenant had taken when they visited the McDermotts. If

Mr McDermott had managed to set up their farm, Bryn could help – not like a hand, but in offering passing advice, resting his foot on a fence as he considered one important issue or another. Mr McDermott said he'd been a farmer a long time ago. He might have forgotten.

When the McDermott plot came into view he was a little disappointed to see the work was still focused on the house, but it did look fine: a solid cabin, simple but well-made, as far as he could tell. There was more than one man working. Bryn slowed. The other was smaller and slighter than Mr McDermott, with a thin waist. Dark hair. He steadied the ladder as Mr McDermott worked.

Bryn waved and called from a good distance, so not to startle them. Mr McDermott waved back. He finished hammering on the roof and then came down the ladder to meet him. The young dark-haired man waited behind.

'Out on your own today?' Mr McDermott said.

'I'm the only–' He stopped. These men weren't soldiers; they didn't need to know what had happened. 'I'm only heading to the river.'

'This is Callum. He's helping us with the house.'

Callum shook his hand.

'While you're here, any chance you could help with something?' Mr McDermott said. 'It's the stove again.' They headed over to the stove, which was still in its crate. 'Needs to be in the house, but Callum and me, we can't shift it.'

'Between the three of us we'll manage,' Bryn said.

They took a side each and lifted. It wasn't so heavy with all of them. Bryn took small steps towards the house. The crate moved a little as the stove slid to one side, but they caught it. Bryn felt something on his hand and when he looked down he saw Callum's hand was covering his own. He was concentrating on the crate; maybe he hadn't noticed. He didn't notice the whole time. They eased the crate down in one of the square rooms.

'Thanks, Bryn. You'll stay for lunch?' Mr McDermott said.

'No, thank you.' The bare room made him think of the sheds at the fort: one filled with rotting food, another with unused lumber, the last with empty ammunitions crates. 'I should be getting to the river.'

'There's a pool not too far up, good for washing,' Callum said.

'That's right; I think Sarah and Mary use it,' Thomas said.

Bryn dipped his head and retrieved his bedroll. He got to the tree-line and then glanced back. Callum was on the porch watching him. The back of his hand felt hot.

Between the trees the air was warmer and thicker. He stepped on moss and fallen leaves; the ground was too soft – too soft and too spongy. He rested against a tree. How long would it take for the memories to fade? He'd never forget the sickle, or Jackson's beard, but what about the smells? The feel of sickly sugar. How long before he could eat fruit again?

He found the river, and as he followed it the rushing roar of the water made everything else go away. The white foam crashed over rocks, as clean as a summer cloud. He dipped a hand in those quick waters and felt the tug between his fingers. The water had no taste beyond cold. But once he was at the pool, all was quiet. The river could have been miles rather than feet away.

He took off his jacket and vest and splashed water under his arms and over his shoulders. The hair on his body stood up like flagpoles. He was covered in tiny bumps, more hills than the entire world. The water stung his cheeks and ears, and for that he was grateful.

'Why is everyone whispering?' he said, remembering Silas in that moment of quiet.

He unrolled his bedding. There was a noise behind him. He looked around but couldn't see anyone. A branch fell from a tree and he checked it over, looking as high up the tree as he could, not sure who he expected to see. The Lieutenant? Silas? A red-coat? Or Callum?

Another noise, this time on the other side of the pool, and again there was nothing to see. He lifted his bedroll into the water and scrubbed as quickly as he could without looking like he was hurrying. That was important: he didn't want to appear spooked, especially as nothing was there. He was just being silly. The forest made all kinds of noises when no one was around to hear. He wrung out the bedding a little, then put his jacket back on, forgetting to put the vest on first. He left the pool with the bedroll under one arm and his vest under the other.

It was getting dark when Bryn got back to the fort. He almost didn't see the Lieutenant in the fading light. He was sitting on the bank opposite the main building, the track between him and, it seemed to Bryn, many troubles. The Lieutenant still wasn't wearing his jacket.

Bryn sat down next to him. A yellow glow tumbled out of the building, out of the door and through the cracks in the walls. The fort seemed further away than he knew it was – miles away, but not the kind of miles you could measure.

'How many?' the Lieutenant said.

'Only George left.'

'That's something.'

'I didn't think you'd abandon us,' Bryn said.

'Where could I go?'

'Anywhere. That building. Those trees.'

The Lieutenant nodded. 'How did Silas take it?'

'Bad.'

'Only one to bury. It's been worse.' The Lieutenant stood up and brushed off his trousers. His boots were covered in dried mud. His arms were thin and pale. Without his jacket or his hat or his courser he was just a man – not even that.

The others didn't seem surprised to see the Lieutenant. Bryn had wondered if they'd still be at the table, arms locked, waiting for one of them to be declared winner.

'We gave up,' John said when he asked.

'Where's Silas?' the Lieutenant said.

'We don't know.'

They didn't question where the Lieutenant had been. Would he even be able to tell them? Say any more than: the forest or the hills, wandering and thinking?

Bryn was hungry. He hadn't eaten all day. He left them sitting at the table in silence, staring at the wall or the candles or their laps. What did they have to say to each other? What did the Walkin' ever have to say? Bryn hoped he wouldn't come back when he died. It seemed to be harder. He opened the food sacks, but the sight of dried meat made his tongue feel fat against his teeth. He mixed oats and water in a pot, this time taking it downstairs to heat up. He had to wait for the fire but it was worth it. The sack of raisins was still half full – he'd eaten more than he should have yesterday, but no one else was going to eat them. All these sacks were for him now – they'd rot before other soldiers came along. He took two handfuls to add to his porridge. If he felt like meat afterwards he could always come back.

He took his bowl to the table and ate with them watching, too hungry to care. They all had the same small frown and pinched foreheads.

'George needs to be buried,' the Lieutenant said.

'Tonight? Shouldn't we wait for daylight?' Bryn said.

'We have candles.'

'But he might—'

'He's not coming back.'

'How do you know? How do you know how long it takes?' Bryn said.

'I still have a nose.'

John sniffed and grimaced.

Travis stood. 'I'll get him ready.'

'No,' the Lieutenant said. 'It should be me.'

Travis didn't argue, but they all went to the far side of the building. As Bryn came close it was impossible to ignore the smell. It was different to the food shed, but not by much. There was a thickness to it, like an old latrine. Waste: that's what it was: under it all it was the same, the smell of wasted food or wasted life. Bryn covered his mouth. The others didn't flinch, just stared grimly. There weren't any hungry-brides making a feast of George, which was a relief. His jaw was still crooked, but it sagged. The Lieutenant took a clean white sheet and wrapped the body starting from the feet. Bryn thought he'd run out of sheet before reaching the head, but he didn't. He'd done this before.

Bryn felt stupid and young and suddenly aware of his heartbeat. He'd wanted to be a lieutenant, thinking if he just watched and copied everything there was nothing to say he couldn't; making decisions, riding a courser, carrying a pistol rather than a rifle – there was little more to it. He'd been wrong; he realised that as he watched the Lieutenant wrap the body of his soldier with gentle hands, more gentle than Bryn's mother had ever been. But it wasn't his fault, not really. Bryn opened his mouth, but it didn't seem like a time for words. That would come later. The Lieutenant closed George's eyes before wrapping his head.

They moved him to the table, all four of them taking some of the load. The table was only just long enough.

The Lieutenant stood at George's head. 'Does anyone want to say anything?'

'He was the best of us,' John said. There was nothing to

add to that. They waited for more than a minute in silence. Travis left to get shovels.

'Wait!' Bryn said. 'There's— There's someone else.'

'Someone else?'

Bryn led them out of the building and into the food shed. He had to steel himself against the smattering of hungry-brides across the floor and the specks that filled the air. With a hand over his mouth, he picked up one sack at a time. They made wet, slapping sounds as he dropped them against the other wall. Bryn moved the crates of tools and dead seeds until Jackson's body was fully in view.

'You did this?' the Lieutenant said.

'You hacked his head off?' John said. 'With what?'

Bryn found the sickle. Only the tip showed any signs of blood.

'He wasn't a small man.' John started to drag the body away.

'He didn't know I was there,' Bryn said, as if apologising.

The Lieutenant picked up the head. 'At least he won't be coming back. That could have been difficult.'

'And to think out of all of us, it was Bryn who got one back.'

Travis came in holding a shovel in each hand. He looked at the body and then at Bryn. In fact, they were all looking at him: John with his grip on Jackson's shins, the Lieutenant clutching Jackson's scalp.

3 : 4

The Lieutenant wrapped Jackson's body the same way he had George's. Bryn couldn't watch without feeling sick, so he stood outside with Travis and the shovels. The little man was staring at him.

'What?' Bryn said.

'Didn't think you had it in you.'

'It just happened.'

They brought George out first, all of them carrying him to the back of the ammunitions shed. There was a good size space between the shed and the forest, and the ammunitions shed had no back door. One day, the graveyard they were starting would be outside the fort walls, as it should be. There had been other soldiers stationed here, and not just the men that they were supposed to relieve. If any of them had died there should be a mark somewhere, but Bryn had seen none and when he asked the others, they shook their heads. They were starting something new at Fort Wilson. Something it needed.

They laid George in the grass and went back for Jackson.

Bryn made sure he was near the feet, because even in the wrapping the head seemed too loose. Despite everything, he wanted to say sorry to the man. He'd had no choice.

Behind the shed, still carrying Jackson's body, they stopped.

'He shouldn't be near George,' John said.

'Why not?' Bryn tried to push the body forward, but the other soldiers wouldn't move.

'Because.'

'Because he was a red-coat?'

'It'll be unmarked,' Travis said.

'No! He was called Jackson.'

'You ask his name while cutting his throat?' John said.

'Someone called for him. After I . . .'

'They should be buried side by side,' the Lieutenant said. 'It wouldn't be right to have two graves far apart. Wouldn't look right.'

'He's lucky we're burying him at all!' John said. 'None of us would have died if it hadn't been for him.'

'It's not that simple.'

'Seems simple enough to me: Southerners come in and shoot us all.' John let go of the body, but the others held on.

'You're still thinking of them as Southerners? Are you still a Northerner?' the Lieutenant said. He was asking all of them.

'Of course I am,' John said, and Travis agreed. 'This,' John pulled at his jacket, at the hole in his chest, 'this doesn't change that.'

'I haven't changed,' Bryn said, but it didn't feel true.

'Give it time. Side by side.'

'Is that an order?' John said.

'I don't give orders any more.'

A hood landed on the shed roof. It cawed twice. And then hundreds of them appeared out of the trees. They covered the roofs of the shed and the main building, but none of them made a sound beyond the beating of wings. It was as if they were there to pay their respects.

'Fine,' John said. 'Let's just get it over with.'

They finally put Jackson's body down. Travis handed John a shovel and they both got to work on separate graves. They were nearly two foot deep when the Lieutenant called them to stop.

'Our turn,' he said.

'Why bother? I'm not tired,' John said.

'You won't be. But it's important we all do this.'

'Suit yourselves,' John said. He stepped out of the hole and gave the shovel to Bryn.

The earth was wet and heavy. He used his boot to plunge the blade deep and then struggled to lift the dirt clear, but it wasn't long before he started to feel it in his back and arms. He dug smaller amounts each time. Every so often he'd glance at the silent hoods: the beady-eyed congregation. They wore the right colour for mourning, which was more than could be said for him and the others. When John suggested they swap back Bryn had added barely a foot. The Lieutenant had done better.

John offered him a hand out. 'Isn't this a merry jig?' he said. He wasn't smiling.

By the time the graves were shoulder-deep they'd all taken a turn in each one. They eased George and Jackson down. They shovelled in the dirt; once again taking turns, and the sound of mud hitting the clean white sheets echoed around the trees like gunfire. Bryn flinched with every shovel-full.

'Now can I go and get the wood for the markers? Or should we all go and hold hands along the way?' John said.

The Lieutenant didn't reply, so John headed to the tool shed. They stood with their hands clasped in front of them, each holding his own vigil. Bryn hadn't been at his father's funeral. He'd died when Bryn was far away. He couldn't remember which fort it was or which battle or if he'd been on the road; it was hard to say exactly when things happened. But he was sorry he didn't know, and sorry he hadn't been there.

John had already knocked together the markers: two bits of wood nailed in the middle to form a cross. He also brought a knife.

'Who wants to carve? I've never had a steady hand,' he said.

'I'll do it,' Travis said. The little man took the markers and the knife and sat down. He bit his lip as he concentrated on the letters. 'What was the rest of his name?'

'I don't know,' John said, and Bryn didn't either.

'George Frederick Palmer,' the Lieutenant said, still staring at the grave.

'How'd you know that?' Travis said.

'I know all your names, where you were born and when, the date you joined the army.'

'I can only fit George Palmer. Or should we get a bigger piece of wood?'

'That'll be fine.'

Travis went at it with the knife again, rubbing at the letters with his thumb, smoothing them out and taking off one or two splinters. He handed the finished item to John. Bryn could make out the name clearly enough.

'And this fella?' Travis said.

'Jackson. That's all I know.'

3 : 5

The McDermotts moved into the house as soon as the roof was finished. It hadn't taken Thomas and Callum long to put the layer of slats on. The boy was a hard worker; he kept his concentration on the job at hand. At the end of each day Callum wanted to keep going, but Thomas insisted he stopped. He ate his food steadily, and there was never anything left in the bowl. On that last day Thomas stepped back and admired his new house. He put a hand on Callum's shoulder and thanked him. The boy shook his head and said it was nothing, but he was smiling.

There wasn't much to bring in from the tent: some clothes and two sets of bedding. Sarah put one in each of the bedrooms. Thomas heard her laughing.

'What is it?' he said.

'It looks silly: blankets in a bare room.'

'They won't be bare for long.'

Sarah wiped her eyes.

They stacked the crates of tools, everything except what Sarah would need for cooking, in their room, out of the way.

193

Mary tried to help them but Sarah shooed her away and she spent the morning sitting on the porch idling, swinging her good leg over the edge.

Thomas started pulling the pegs out from the tent. Sarah hurried over to stop him. 'I thought Callum could use it. That is, if he's staying.'

'Why would he stay?' Thomas said.

'I don't think he has anywhere else to go.' Sarah took the peg from his hand and rammed it back into the ground.

'Isn't he supposed to be looking for his friends?' Thomas said.

'Hasn't he found some?'

'Maybe he has,' he said.

'I understand why you don't trust him, but he's worked hard on our house. We owe him that much.'

'We owe him nothing. You feed him every day. And it won't last.'

'I know. That's why he should go with you,' Sarah said.

'Go? Where?'

'We talked about this.'

Thomas looked back at the house. 'When did we talk?'

'Once the house was done you would buy some animals; woollies and milking neats to start with. We looked at the map, remember?' she said.

'Something Market?'

'Par Market, that's right.'

Thomas sighed. 'And you think Callum should go with me?'

'If you don't trust him, would you rather leave him here?'

'I'd rather he was gone completely.'

'Thomas.'

'We'd be six, maybe seven days. How long will the food last?' he said.

'Mary and I can manage. If you don't go there won't be any more food.'

Sarah was thin – thin and tired. He hadn't seen it until now. She was too good at hiding it.

'You'll stay tonight, though? Our first in the house?' she said.

'Of course.'

Mary watched her parents talk. She couldn't hear the words but their bodies made it clear they were deciding something. Her father was putting the pegs back into the ground, so the tent would stay. Which meant the boy would stay. She hadn't settled on how she felt about that. She'd seen him working on the house, being careful that he didn't see her. He never looked around, so if he felt her watching, and she couldn't imagine that he hadn't, he didn't care. She could feel when people were looking at her: it was like an extra layer of clothing that pressed down on all of you, even your face and hands. At the pool it was the only thing she wore. He was strong beneath his shirt. His shoulders were broad and she could make out the knotty muscles there. She'd gripped smaller backs before and felt nothing but bones.

'Can I join you?' Callum said.

She shrugged. He sat down close enough that she could smell the morning's work on him. The solid taste of worked wood mixed with a body well used. It was not unpleasant.

'They seem to think you'll be staying.'

Callum cleared his throat. 'Would that be a problem?'

'Don't you have somewhere else to go?'

'Not really.'

'Aren't you looking for your friends?' she said.

'I have been for a while. Helping build your house was a welcome change.'

'There are lots of people out there. Why keep looking?'

'They were important to my father,' he said.

'You shouldn't stay here. Nothing good will happen.'

'The house looks good.'

'They all start that way,' she said.

'Are you always like this? Or are you in pain?' He motioned to her leg.

'I just don't like to pretend.'

'Then why stay with them?' he said.

'She tries. She really tries.'

'I found this in the forest. Is it yours?' He passed her a battered copy of the Good Book. She took it and flicked through the pages. The words blurred into one long mass of lies.

'I don't want it.'

'You should keep it.'

'You take it,' she said.

'I don't need it.'

'You know what it is?'

'I've seen it before,' he said.

She put the book down between them. 'It sucks the life out of people. It tells them who they ought to be, rather than let them decide for themselves. It's a book that makes you blind.'

'Your parents don't seem to think so.'

'That's their choice,' she said.

'Did you grow up with the book?'

'Isn't that obvious?'

'It must have been difficult,' he said, picking it up. He hefted it for its weight.

'You have no idea.'

Her father noticed the two of them talking. He came over, leaving her mother mid-sentence. 'Callum, I'll help you move your things into the tent,' he said.

Mary was left alone on the porch with the Good Book next to her. Her leg burned from the heat of it, as if the lines on the pages were the lines of her red scar. She remembered the Pastor, his thick, curly hair like a bonfire. He read from the book without reading because he knew the words like they were his own. Was he the reason the Good Book was always so hot? The colour and the passion? It couldn't be that simple, but that was how she remembered it: a little girl terrified of a man.

Mary was sitting on her blankets, combing her hair, pulling at the knots and enjoying how they snapped away. Her comb was missing a lot of teeth. She had no mirror, so she was going by repetition and patience. There would be no way for her to see the results.

She could hear her parents through the wall, having one of their rare arguments. Their voices ebbed and flowed, starting quietly and growing louder until they reached a point short of shouting, then they'd stop and begin again. They did this for her. If they'd asked her, she would have told them to shout and scream all they wanted. That would be healthier. More honest.

It didn't matter what they were arguing about. It might be something different on the surface but underneath it was the same thing: it was his fault. Having to come out to these nowhere mountains: his fault. Leaving Barkley: his fault. Sarah's shop failing in West Kennington: his fault. The fire in Marsdenville. The cut on Mary's leg. Callum. Thomas created problems and Sarah tried to fix them. At least, that was how she saw it. Most of the time Sarah was happy enough to play the game, but Mary was tired of it and she didn't understand why they weren't. Why did they insist on trying again? If she had thought it was for her benefit she would have told them to stop a long time ago. No, the truth was they didn't know any other way, and neither did she.

She changed into her nightdress, the same kind of nightdress she had worn as a child. If there was any other kind, she had never seen it. They just changed in size. She opened her door. The hinges were brand-new and shone silver with the moon. She could have flapped the door and it wouldn't have made a sound. The embers in the stove glowed. In the dim light she had to step through a maze of cooking pots and pans and knives and plates, their shapes changing as their shadows flickered. Her nightdress caught on a metal kettle, but she felt the tug and turned in time to see it overbalancing on its base, ready to fall. She knelt and carefully set it down. She knew how to ignore the pounding of her blood in her ears and listen. Her parents were building up to another peak. She held the kettle and considered throwing it across the room, but that would be a different kind of night. There were better ways to make a point.

The front door was locked. How paranoid and blinkered when there weren't any windows. That was her father. Sarah trusted Callum now, and she'd either forgotten the soldiers or didn't want to think about them. The youngest, Bryn, was the only one to come by, and he was clearly harmless. The key was still in the lock. Mary turned it, the loud clunk lost in a crescendo of shouting. She ignored the words that came in snatches.

It was cold outside. Her arms turned to goosebumps and her scar ached. She stepped down from the porch and onto the grass, which felt like ice between her toes. She moved awkwardly towards the tent. She knew where the fastenings were without looking. As she started from the bottom she heard his even breathing. Asleep already, like a good boy. She slipped inside.

'Mary?'

In the darkness she could only see his outline. She got

underneath his blanket. She lay with her back to him. He was warm. He didn't touch her.

She waited a moment and then reached behind. She rolled her nightdress up to the small of her back then undid his trousers. His prick was hard in her hand. She rolled on her hips and he was inside her. She rocked back and forth. He didn't move – he didn't even make a sound. She moved harder, slapping against him, and as she started to shudder he finished. She stayed there until he shrank and was gone. She left without pegging up the tent. The wetness of him slid warm down her thighs.

3 : 6

The next morning she could still smell him. The air between her sheets was thick and she wafted it around the room. She heard her parents clinking plates and moving pots and stoking the fire. Her mother knocked.

'Yes?' Mary said.

Sarah ducked her head in. 'Breakfast is ready. The last of the eggs, I'm afraid.' She shut the door.

Mary dressed despite needing to wash. Later she would go to the pool and come away clean.

She took the plate from her mother. 'Only one?'

'Sorry,' Sarah said.

'There'll be milk and cheese and meat soon enough.' Thomas grinned at her. 'We'll be eating much better when the farm gets going.'

'Take Callum's.' Sarah handed her a bowl of porridge. Mary stared down at her now full hands and opened her mouth, but Sarah had already turned away. She was busy organising one thing or another that didn't need organising.

No one helped Mary with the door; she had to put the bowl down and open it herself.

'Breakfast,' she called from outside the tent and he fumbled with the flap. His fingers looked short and fat when seen on their own.

He stared right at her when she handed him the bowl.

'Thank you,' he said.

She'd expected him to be shy, or embarrassed, but his face was blank.

'It's just porridge.'

He nodded.

Her father came out onto the porch. 'After you've eaten, get your gear together,' he said.

'Callum's leaving?' She couldn't read his dark eyes.

'We both are – we'll bring back a farm, don't worry.' Her father sounded almost excited, as he had when he started the house. As he did when he started anything.

'Will you think about me?' she whispered.

'If you want.'

She was the first to blink. She turned away and went inside the house, the whole way without limping. Her teeth were near bursting from biting down.

Mary and Sarah saw them off. His wife waved, but Mary stood tight-lipped with her arms crossed. She would appreciate the milk and furs. He had left them their one rifle. Sarah knew how to use it – his broken rib was testament to that. But she wouldn't have to. Not out here. They'd already dealt with one traveller; there couldn't be more than that in a season. Or a year.

The two of them held long sticks that Thomas had fashioned in the night. He didn't need one for the journey and he doubted a youngster like Callum did either, but they'd be useful once there were woollies to think about. And a stick was a kind of comfort in itself: it occupied the hands and gave a man a sense of being prepared. He'd promised woollies and neats and all they brought; he'd promised these on the back of friendly advice. A man could purchase these things at Par Market, he'd been assured. *A man* . . .

'What do you know about buying livestock?' he said.

'Not a thing.'

'We have a couple of days.'

They'd been fortunate with the weather. The cold night had hardened the ground. There were clouds on the horizon, but they were thin and almost white. Callum seemed happy to travel in silence. The hills were gradual enough for them to walk side by side, though Thomas could look across and over Callum's head. He did so often: the landscape didn't change, but it was striking every time, with the green draining to the nothing-colour of rock. It sloped gently, so much so that he thought perhaps he could roll the whole way. His eyes lied to him, of course: he would survive such a tumble but he might not be able to use his legs or arms and what good would he be then?

'It's strange what goes through your head sometimes,'

Thomas said. Callum grunted in a way that sounded like agreement. He didn't try for conversation again.

They hiked until midday, as best they could judge. The cloud blocked the sun but the air had a crisp heat and Callum's stomach was making noises, and each time the boy winced, embarrassed. Thomas struggled not to laugh. He stopped them at the top of a rise and sat down, enjoying the view. He wouldn't get tired of looking down at the world. This was how it was supposed to be with mountains: clear views and a giddy sense of perspective. He opened his bag and passed a wrapped parcel to Callum. Sarah had packed it for the boy.

Callum opened it. He stared at the contents for some time.

'It's not much, is it?' Thomas said.

'No.' He took a pinch of bread.

'I'm sorry. She has the two of them to think about.'

'She does good by me,' Callum said.

'We've had some difficult times, but she hasn't stopped helping. Or trusting.'

Callum chewed slowly, eking out the little meal. Before long he wrapped up the parcel, but Thomas didn't take it from the boy.

'I'm not going to decide when you eat,' he said. They sat for a while longer. Callum rubbed his hands and blew into them, and Thomas became aware of the chill in the thin air. But being aware and feeling it weren't the same thing. Was the boy tired? Thomas tried to remember what that was like – and how did someone become tired? Callum wasn't sweating; his face wasn't red beyond a little colour in his cheeks. He was sitting up straight. Thomas watched his chest rise and fall regularly, not quick, nor laboured.

'Ready?' Thomas said.

The boy nodded and they continued on their way.

The landscape changed over the afternoon as the hills flattened out into wide valleys. Thomas watched for any suggestion that Callum was tiring. At the base of the valleys were little streams, small enough to stride over. Callum stopped at each and took a handful of water.

'What does your father do?' Thomas said, as he waited.

Callum wiped water from his mouth. 'He tells people what to do.'

'That's every father.'

'I suppose. I haven't seen him in a long time. He was always busy.'

'Our farm was my father's domain,' Thomas said.

'Will your farm be yours?'

'I doubt it. Sarah is not like my mother. Mary is not like my sisters.'

'We pretend we're nothing like them,' Callum said.

That night they camped at the bottom of a valley that looked like all the others. In the dying light Thomas unrolled his map and tried to judge how far they had come, but it was impossible to say. They needed to continue north until they met a big river, the Par, as it was marked on the map, and they'd follow it all the way to the market. Callum looked at the map with interest.

'Have you been to Par Market?' Thomas said.

'I might have. I didn't know its name but I've passed through a place that might be it.'

'Did you notice the livestock traders?'

Callum shook his head. 'What are these?' He pointed to arrows that marked the bottom and one side of the map.

'Where we used to live.'

'You lived in the south? How far?' Callum said.

'Pierre County. I grew up there.'

'On the farm.'

Callum put up his little lean-to. Thomas had thought about bringing the tent for him, but it would have been too bulky. Callum didn't appear worried. They hadn't brought wood and the valley was bare of trees so there wasn't a fire, but Callum didn't ask about it. He just wrapped himself in his blankets and fell asleep. Thomas sat nearby, close enough to hear the boy's steady breathing. He stared at the water. The moon was almost full, its light shattering on the stream. The map didn't show the Col River, but Thomas never saw a river without thinking about it, the days spent there as a family; the night he waded through it to be with them again. He rolled up his trousers and poked the patch of his leg that he'd lost that night. The skin was still singed and wrinkled from the pyre-pit. Inside, the hole was empty space until he touched bone: a gap in his muscle the size of an egg. He could still walk; he didn't notice it wasn't there. But it would never come back, either. He was used to that feeling by now: the apathy of missing what wasn't needed any more.

He glanced over at Callum. He could suddenly picture the boy in black trousers and a white shirt, imagine him standing outside the church with the rest of the town, his face bearing the fluffy beginnings of the beard of the newly wed. There was a calmness to him that reminded Thomas of Barkley: a calmness of purpose. And his hair – his curly hair, like the Pastor's. Thomas wanted to strangle the boy. His hand lifted without him realising. Callum was trouble. Barkley was trouble. He'd fought for so long to keep his family safe, brought them to the edge of the world, driven them up mountains, and still it wasn't enough.

Callum opened his eyes. 'What are you doing?'

'You were making noises,' Thomas said, pulling back his hand. 'A nightmare, maybe.'

'I don't think so. I don't remember.'

'You're lucky if you only remember the good dreams.'

3 : 7

'What do we do now?' John said.

Bryn looked around the table at every blank face. They'd come back in after burying the two men and simply sat down. He looked at the Lieutenant, but he offered no answers; he was staring at his hands. They sat so long in silence it started to brighten outside. Travis put out the candles and still no one said anything, through John's question hung in the air like a bugle blast.

Bryn started to get hungry. His stomach cramped, but he tried to ignore it, waiting for as long as he could, not wanting to disturb the quiet. But eventually he had to eat. Upstairs, he forced himself to chew dried meat. He'd been avoiding it after too many meals on the road with the dust grating between his teeth and he'd forgotten what the meat tasted like without the dirt. His jaw ached with the work, but he felt better after. A man couldn't live on raisins.

When he returned, the table was still silent, but the Lieutenant cleared his throat. It wasn't a healthy sound, like two rocks rubbing against each other. 'I did some thinking in the days waiting for you all. I could have left these mountains. I wouldn't blame any of you for doing so.' He looked right at Bryn. 'But I didn't. I came here because they sent me, but I'm not leaving this place until it's better off for having me.'

'What does that mean?' John said.

'We started building. I'm going to make sure it's finished. That way, the next sorry souls to be stationed here might have a chance.'

'Have a chance?'

The Lieutenant stood up.

'No, wait right there,' John said. 'There were men here before us, so you said. Before we go thinking about the next relief, what happened to them?'

'What do you think?' the Lieutenant said. He didn't sit down, but he didn't walk out either.

'You mean to say this has happened before?'

'They didn't tell me how many times.'

'And still they only sent six men?' John said.

'None of the soldiers have ever reported back so they don't know what happens here.'

'It's not hard to guess.'

'Shouldn't we send someone?' Bryn said.

The Lieutenant stepped back, his arms open towards the door. No one moved.

'I didn't understand it myself until it happened, until I took some time up there on the mountain,' the Lieutenant said. 'I'm not going back. Once I'm done here I'm done for good.'

He waited for a moment and then went outside. Travis was the first to join him. The little man didn't take long to make the decision. Bryn didn't have much of a choice; he was still in the army. Even if the Lieutenant wasn't in charge any more it made sense to stay at Fort Wilson until he was relieved. Then he could tell someone important about the red-coats and what had happened here. He didn't look at John as he got up. Whatever John wanted to do was fine by him. It must change a man, starting the Walk, change who he was and what he thought.

The Lieutenant and Travis were standing considering the first wall they built.

'I don't see anything wrong with it,' Travis said.

'We just weren't quick enough.'

'Would more really have helped?' Bryn said. So many red-coats; it was hard to imagine what would have stopped them.

'Not likely,' the Lieutenant said, 'but they seemed in a big enough hurry. Maybe with walls they wouldn't waste the time. Either way, that's what we'll do.'

John was in the doorway. 'I've got nowhere to go,' he said.

In other circumstances there might be cheering or pats on the shoulder or smiles.

John shuffled over. The four of them considered the ramshackle fort. 'We could knock it down and start again,' John said. It wasn't a bad idea.

The Lieutenant headed off to the tool shed. They followed, not because he was leading them, but because it was the thing to do. He was just the first to act – maybe that was what made him an officer. If the others abandoned Bryn after their work was done, what would he do? He needed to be ready for that day and the sooner the better. He needed to have it all figured out. A clever man would turn this situation into a good thing, make this the beginning of a career. Someone like Silas.

'What about Silas?' Bryn said.

The Lieutenant stopped and turned around. 'If he comes back he can help. If not . . . ' He shrugged.

'He won't be coming back. Not to help,' John said.

Bryn took up his old position by the cutting blocks. They'd need plenty of planks if they were going to build three more walls. He was relieved to find the back of the shed empty of hoods. He still had one of Silas' ears in his pocket, the one rescued from the birds. If he saw the man again he'd give it back. If it were Bryn's ear he'd rather have it.

The Lieutenant put a hand on Bryn's arm. 'No, Bryn. You need to sleep.'

Bryn blinked and looked up at the light sky. He rubbed his face. It had been a long time since he'd slept. Was it the same day they'd buried George?

'We'll manage. You can help soon.'

'I'll move my bedroll,' Bryn said.

'Use the bed. It's yours now.'

Bryn nodded, knowing he wouldn't. It would be wrong to

disturb the tightly pulled sheets. He hadn't had a mattress beneath him in years. He'd done nothing to earn one.

But he kept the bedroll upstairs. He didn't want the others to see him sleeping as they came in and out of the building. It would only upset them.

The bucket banged against Mary's leg. She'd lost count of how many times it had happened, but at least she made sure it was on her good leg – and it was empty. It would only be worse on the way back. She tried to whistle, but she couldn't manage more than a hiss. People whistled while doing chores but she couldn't. Any noise was swallowed up by the trees.

She stopped by a fallen tree. The river wasn't so far away but there was no hurry. There were only more chores waiting for her back at the house. Building it was her father's job, running it her mother's and they both had a lackey. There must have been a hundred tedious little jobs given to Callum, so her father could concentrate on what was important. But there was a difference: nothing her mother did was so important. She wasted days organising and re-organising, putting things on shelves, then taking them off, moving the shelves, making sure the shelves were straight. And all the while Mary was fetching water, washing clothes, beating rugs, anything that required effort. When her mother was nearby and not completely absorbed in aligning spice pots or the like, Mary would cough; still working, she would cough over and over, and her mother would look up and frown.

213

She kicked out at the bucket. It fell on one side and rolled a little. This was all there would be out here. No parties or dances or drinking into the night. She couldn't remember the smell of whiskey or the way smoke hung beneath a ceiling. In Marsdenville one kind of smoke had brought another, but it was beginning to feel worth it now. Not every town had a Benjamin Ryland. And even here people found you. She scratched her chest, thinking about the soldier and his grip. Callum hadn't touched her at all – not with his hands. She'd done what she'd wanted to do, but it had never been like that before, like he wasn't there. His cold eyes at the pool: that was all she could picture. His eyes must have been the same in the tent. Normally she liked new things—

Something grabbed her: two cold hands around her neck. She choked, trying to breathe, and her body convulsed. She swung her arms, but hit nothing. She tried to stand, but the hands forced her down.

'Where is your father?'

She struggled to form words. Her mouth was wide open, but all that came out were coughing, clucking sounds.

'Where is he?'

'Gone,' she managed to say.

'Where?'

She stopped flailing her arms. They felt so heavy. So did her head. It was dropping forward and she couldn't help it.

The hands let go. She opened her eyes, but there was no one there.

3 : 8

The sky was bloodshot, veined with a red that crackled like lightning across the clouds. Bryn had never seen a sky so angry. It started to rain: large drops that were as red as the clouds they came from. He was standing outside in the downpour, between two of the sheds. He couldn't see a door; the rain was too thick and the light too bad. He tried to get back to the courtyard, but when he got to the end of the sheds there was a wall. It was like the wall they had built before the red-coats had attacked but parts of it were missing: every other upright plank was gone. He couldn't fit through the gaps. He only managed to get an arm through before his body stopped him. It was dark on the other side and he couldn't see trees, or the hills. He turned around and walked away from the wall. The sheds looked bigger than he remembered and he glanced from one side to the other, waiting for them to end in a corner, but instead he found another wall. This one wasn't missing any planks, but there was a flock of hoods manning it. They were facing away from him, watching the outside of the fort. Eyes that missed nothing. He went closer and they turned as one. In each of their mouths was an ear. They cawed and it was thunder to match the rain. The ears fell from their beaks.

Bryn woke. The floor was hard against his joints. He sat up and saw the bed next to him was still pristine. Dust hung in the air above the sheets, caught by rays of sunlight, and stirred at his breath like a swarm of tiny specks – the tiny specks that bit you without you knowing.

He rubbed his head. He remembered snatches of his dream: the rain and the hoods and ears. It was good to see the sun. He stretched and went over to the food sacks. Hot oats would have made a better breakfast, but he couldn't face setting a fire. Instead, he took a handful of raisins and was happy at that.

No one was at the table and the half of the building where they'd had their bedrolls was empty. Squinting, he wandered into the courtyard. The sun was high. He'd slept for a long time. He could feel it: the way his muscles slumped on his shoulders, how his legs were heavy and his head was still on the pillow. It wasn't good to sleep so long.

There was plenty of noise coming from between the sheds. Bryn stopped. The shed walls seemed to lean in on him, their boards bulging under the weight of the sun. It was so different from his dream, but he got the same feeling: he was small. Fort Wilson was bigger than him.

But this wasn't a dream – he could see the others working on the new wall, not more than fifteen feet from where he stood. If he went towards them the corridor between the sheds would not stretch. He was sure of it, but he didn't move. Eventually he was noticed.

The Lieutenant crossed the dried mud expanse between them. 'We're making good progress,' he said.

'You didn't wake me.'

'Why would I?'

'You worked all day and all night?' Bryn said.

'That's right.'

Travis and John were hammering in planks that would form the walkway. They had fallen into a rhythm like the ticking of a clock.

'Working like that you'll be finished in days,' Bryn said.

'It's possible – but there are only three of us.'

'Four.'

'Four,' the Lieutenant said.

'Where can I help?'

The Lieutenant took him by the arm. The first few steps weren't easy. Bryn expected the wall and Travis and John to slide backwards; when he got there they would be gone and a flock of hoods standing in their place. He'd slept too long and that was why the dream was so difficult to shake. If no one was going to tell him when to get up he'd have to take charge of that himself, or every day would be fuzzy with dreams.

The others didn't greet him – they didn't even look up from their work. Bryn climbed the ladder and joined them on the walkway. At the other end, he took a plank and lined it up. The nail danced under his hammer – he was lucky not to hit his own fingers. The noise of his missed blows filled his ears, jarring, out of rhythm with the others, but they didn't seem to notice, or care. He managed to nail down a single board and by that time Travis was next to him and they were almost finished. It was no wonder they'd left him outside the tool shed sawing wood.

Whilst Travis was taking care of the last board, Bryn stared into the forest beyond the wall. It was close here, no more than ten feet before the first tips of the branches. They reached towards him. He gazed deeper into the leaves. He saw their eyes first: glints of sunlight. Then he realised the shadows weren't shadows, they were hoods.

'You've got something of theirs,' Travis said.

'No I don't! It's not theirs.'

'Not what they think.'

'And how do you know that?'

'Obvious,' Travis said.

Bryn hurried down the ladder, away from the eyes in the trees. He checked his pocket. The fleshy nub of Silas' ear was still there. He should find the other – but if the hoods had it, what chance did he have?

'Two down, two to go,' the Lieutenant said.

Travis and John got off the wall. They had buckets full of tools and bits of left-over wood. John held one out, Bryn looked at it and John shook the bucket and pointed at Bryn's hammer. He'd forgotten he was holding it. He dropped it in the bucket and John and Travis shuffled off to build the next wall. They were wearing their jackets, all buttoned up and full of holes. It seemed to take them a long time to reach the courtyard. Their backs stretched away from Bryn. He squeezed his eyes closed, then opened them again. It had been raining in his dream and now it was bright and sunny, but he felt cold and his shoulders drooped as if water-logged.

'Ma?' Mary pointed from the porch.

'I see him.' Her mother hurried inside.

Someone was walking towards their home, plain as day. It was hard to say in the bright sunlight, but it did look like a man – not her father and not Callum; it was too soon for them to be back. This man might have been wearing blue. A soldier from the fort. Not long ago her father had welcomed them to the house, let them help.

Her mother loaded the rifle. 'You should go inside,' she said.

'Why? Would that door stop him?' Mary said.

'He might not go looking for you.'

'He's already seen me.'

The man was now close enough she could be sure of the uniform. His jacket was undone and loose. He didn't hurry across the hill.

'That's close enough, soldier,' Sarah called.

He didn't stop. She raised the rifle to her shoulder and set her feet. Thomas had taught them both how to do it, insisting they both needed to know. Sarah aimed at the sun. The sound was heavy on the porch but grew weaker out in the open air. It didn't seem enough, but the man stopped.

'That's fair warning,' her mother said. She re-loaded the rifle, her hands steady.

'Where's your husband?' His voice was toneless and cold. Mary struggled to swallow and the skin on her neck turned hot. She scratched at it.

'You can't see him.'

'I know he's gone. I want to know where,' the man said.

'What business is it of yours?' The rifle was back at Sarah's shoulder.

'I am making it my business. You might get a shot off before I take you and your daughter. Or one might not be enough.' He took three slow steps closer.

'Par Market, it's called. To the north,' Mary said.

Her mother hissed.

'Long way?'

'He'll be gone a week, maybe more.'

The man started towards the house again and Sarah moved onto the steps, putting herself between the soldier and Mary.

'Any closer and I shoot,' Sarah said.

The man didn't stop. She waited heartbeats longer than she should have, then she fired.

He still didn't stop, though Mary was sure her mother had hit him: his jacket had moved as if struck by the wind. He was close now, close enough to see his face. He had cuts on his cheeks and there were scars where his ears should have been. Twenty paces from the porch he veered away and as he passed, he gave a mock salute.

Sarah dropped the rifle. Her whole body was shaking.

Mary felt his cold, dead hands on her neck.

3 : 9

Thomas let Callum sleep until dawn. When the first light crept over the horizon he shook the boy's shoulder, but he didn't complain. He was packed and ready a few minutes later. He ate a little as they walked. It wasn't enough for a young boy, let alone for travelling. Sarah hadn't planned on feeding a third.

The sky stayed grey, but he was glad it was dry. The ground was solid beneath his stick. The grass had wisps of washed-out yellow running through it: there was enough life left in it for woollies to graze for the last weeks that winter tried to hang on. In summer it would be a different kind of grass for them, a better kind.

They topped a rise and stopped. Below was a wide river, bigger than any they'd seen since leaving the house. It meandered down a valley as far as he could see, not in any rush. On the far bank, less than a mile away, a caravan of some kind had stopped. Shaggies were being led to the water to drink. Big wagons of all kinds of colours waited a little behind and the small shapes of men moved to and fro. After the long days and nights on the mountain with only his family and Callum it was strange to see so many people again. Their voices and noise carried on the wind.

'That must be the Par,' Callum said. 'They must be following it too.'

Thomas couldn't argue. The boy started down the slope towards the river. 'What are you doing?' Thomas said.

'We might go with them.'

'Why?'

'Why not?'

Thomas could think of reasons: because there were more of them; because they had animals; because they shouted and laughed; because they would smell like travelling men; because they would have rifles. All good reasons. But when he came to speak they sounded childish and small. Callum wasn't afraid – when had he become scared of people? He'd lived in cities and towns and managed.

He followed Callum down to the low, placid river and they waved to the men across the water. The men raised their hands. They didn't look enthusiastic.

'I should wait here,' Thomas said.

'If you want.'

'Ask after Par Market. We're looking for livestock – but don't say how much.'

Callum nodded. Using his stick he sounded each footstep across the river. A man in a wide-brimmed hat and brightly coloured trousers came to meet him. They spoke, the man gesturing down the river and then at Thomas. Further up the bank a group of men waited, their arms crossed. If there was going to be trouble it would come from them. Before long, Callum was making his way back over the water.

'He says they're going to Par Market. He can help us.'

'Is he a trader?'

'Exotic animals from beyond the mountains.'

Thomas stared up at the mountains – beyond the mountains. All the maps he'd seen stopped here, using the mountains as a natural edge to the paper. But if this trader had been past them and brought back animals . . .

'We'd better not get too close; I'm bad company for most animals. What did they look like?' Thomas said.

'I didn't see. The wagons were all covered. But there were noises.' Callum looked back over at the caravan. 'I'd be glad to stay over here.'

They waited as the caravan made ready to move. Men milled around busily, hitching shaggies to wagons, carrying buckets from the river, tying down canvas. It was all the more manic when compared to the stillness of the two of them sitting on the bank, Thomas not even breathing and Callum moving only to shift his weight. Some of the wagons were so big they needed a team of shaggies to pull. Thomas couldn't imagine what would take six shaggies to move. Perhaps this trader had brought back part of a mountain. Some stone was worth that kind of effort. But Callum had said animals. An animal that big and heavy would have to be expensive; even if he had no idea what it would be good for. It might be a giant woollie. That he could understand. Its coat would be big enough to cover a house. It would fill jugs of milk every morning.

'I'd like to see those animals,' Thomas said.

'I'll arrange something in Par Market.'

Despite his doubts, he was grateful for all the boy had done for him and his family. They'd shared their food with him, as much as they could have. He'd worked hard. And he was considerate. Thomas had lied to his wife when he said he hadn't thought about it. Callum would have made a good son.

Mary closed the door on her mother's singing. From out on the porch it was like a lone worker buzzing in there, a long way from its hive. She wondered if her mother would follow her out. She was a curious old woman. But the door stayed shut. Mary took the bucket and hobbled towards the river. This morning her leg was bad and each step sent sharp pains up her hip and along the bottom of her back. She didn't let her mother see it. There would be no end to her smothering then.

Mary was barely at the trees when he stepped out in front of her.

He took her jaw in his hand.

She blinked and took a deep, shuddering breath. It burned like smoke. His face was ruined. His cheeks were slashed up and down so she could see his yellow teeth and fat tongue. She raised her hand, but he didn't move away.

'Who—?' She coughed. 'Who was so cruel to you, Silas?'

He flinched at his name. But she stroked the strips of skin that were still clinging to his bones.

'You're not scared of me?' he said.

She shook her head. 'You've seen my father.' He turned his head to one side and she saw the hole. She gasped, not at the sight of the lumpy red ring of flesh, but at the act of it. The pain must have been terrible.

'You didn't go to find my father?' she said.

'I'll wait for him.'

'Have the other soldiers started the Walk?'

'You make it sound grand.' He went to spit, but couldn't. He grimaced. 'Some have. None of them like this.' He gestured to his face. He pulled away from her. 'I only wanted to talk to him. He seems to be living normally.'

'He's made mistakes,' she said. 'But I can help you.' She picked up her bucket. 'If you fetch water for me, I'll fetch you answers.'

'What answers?'

'Can you read?'

'Of course I can!'

'Then I'll come back to the forest. You'll find me, I'm sure.'

She left him holding the empty bucket. She was careful to hide her limp. Perhaps she could get Silas to fetch her water every day. And firewood. Even clean their clothes. That was how things worked this far north. Lots of houses had Walkin' doing chores.

Her mother was in the big room, sitting on the floor with planks of wood spread around her. She had her sleeves rolled up and her hair tied back. At the corner of her mouth was a nail.

'Hold this,' she said when she saw Mary.

Mary knelt down and held the two planks of wood. Sarah steadied the hammer in her hand and then swung. The wood shook and a nail sunk further in.

'There was a time I couldn't do this,' Sarah said, taking the other nail from her mouth. 'And it shamed me. Here, you try.'

Mary took the hammer. Sarah pointed to where the nail was to go.

'Pinch the nail between your fingers. And aim carefully.'

Mary brought down the hammer. It tapped the nail.

'You hit it, that's good. Now harder.'

She did and the nail went into the wood. Her mother smiled. Mary passed back the hammer. She was almost in her room when Sarah said, 'Weren't you fetching water?'

'I just wanted to get something first.'

'What?'

'I thought I'd read at the pool. From the Good Book.'

'Really?' Sarah said.

Mary grabbed her pair of old scissors and battered book. She stuffed the scissors in her pocket and came out wielding the Good Book.

'Just don't take all day.'

'Yes, Mother.'

Mary closed the door behind her. At the back of the house, she cut out the first twenty pages of the Good Book, following the margin. She folded the pages and put them in her pocket with the scissors. She hid the book under the house – the grass was dry; if it rained she could rescue it.

He might not ask for more, but Mary doubted it: she knew the pull of the Good Book. Silas lacked a church and a preacher to give it a voice but he had something far more important: want. He was desperate for answers, it was clear in his voice and the dark shade that covered his eyes. They were lies, but they were answers too. That's what faith was.

It didn't take long for Silas to find her. The bucket was only three-quarters full. His wet trousers explained why.

'You'll have to be more careful next time,' she said.

He dropped the bucket. 'Next time?'

She held out the pages. 'It's a start. Don't read them too quickly. Give them time to sink in. It needs understanding.'

'What is this?' He snatched the folded paper from her.

'Just read them. They'll help. My father would tell you to do the same.'

Silas squinted at the pages. He held them close to his face, almost touching his nose.

'Me and the bucket will be here tomorrow. With more pages.'

'I know how this kind of thing works,' he said.

She didn't doubt it. He seemed the kind of man that had been trading with women his whole life, one way or another. He wandered off, barely looking where he was going, and was soon lost in the trees.

3 : 10

the mountains saw you and writhed.
Torrents of water swept by;
the deep roared and lifted its waves on high.

Habakkuk

BOOK 4

BOOK 4

4 : 1

The caravan began to move. Thomas was eager to keep pace, but after a few hundred yards it became clear that would not be a problem. In fact, the two of them had to check their stride or be in danger of leaving the caravan behind. The huge wagons made a lot of noise, with the creaking and groaning and cracking of seasoned wood heard even above the rumbling of the wheels. Trumpets and snorts came from underneath the coloured canvases. Thomas grinned. It was hard not to get caught up in the spectacle of it, once he was over the initial shock of seeing people again.

They followed the riverbank for a mile or more and then the caravan turned away as a new valley opened up. The river was low and rocky here and Thomas hopped from one slick rock to the other, using his stick to steady himself. He didn't want to risk the water; the last time he'd waded through a river it had taken a part of him. He had no idea how much of his leg he needed to keep it working, but now was not the time to try any theories. He doubted there would ever be such a time. Callum preferred to go through the water after testing his footing on one of the stones. The river barely came above his ankles and he was confused by Thomas' decision.

Once across the river they slowed their pace again to match the caravan. The ground was churned up by the wagons and the hooves of so many shaggies. The biggest wagons were easiest to follow, because they carved deep, clean troughs in the mud. Thomas was able to walk comfortably in the space gouged out by a single wheel. But the destruction wrought by the caravan extended only so far. They were ploughing a temporary river of mud; on either side the grass was oblivious to the passage of wagon or animal.

The day was getting warmer. The clouds still hid the sun, but Callum must have judged it midday as he took out his meagre meal. He allowed himself three pinches of bread.

'We'll get you some food at the market,' Thomas said.

'I've lived on less.' The boy took his time chewing the tiny portions.

'You're helping my family. It's the least I can offer in return.'

Callum waved away the thought.

At the end of the valley the caravan turned again and followed the bank of another river, this one wide and deep. It looked even slower than its smaller cousins, but such rivers were liars: currents swirled underneath the surface ready to pull down the unwary – ready to pull away a piece of a Walkin'. He was glad they wouldn't have to cross it.

'Blood and bones!' Callum said. He tried to swat at the swarm of specks that suddenly descended on him. Slow rivers were perfect for specks.

'You shouldn't curse over something so small,' Thomas said. The specks avoided him.

'You sound like my father.'

'Walk closer to me. They won't like that.'

Callum came shoulder-to-shoulder with him and his presence did provide some respite. If so many specks were bothering a single man, Thomas thought, the caravan ahead must have been covered in them. He felt for the animals. Perhaps they didn't have specks over the mountains. The nasty little bites would be some welcome.

The first sign of Par Market was the smoke. Even in the daylight plumes were rising into the sky, black against grey. The land had flattened out; they were no longer following the bottoms of wide valleys. But the grass continued to the horizon. The parched yellow lands were to the south, a world away. Small houses were scattered here and there, and walled-off areas of ground suggested farms, though none of them were particularly big, about the same size as the farm he'd grown up on. In this lush, richly coloured land that struck him as strange. But he'd learned over the years that no two places were the same; you could walk a mile and face very different customs. And Barkley was a particularly poor point of comparison.

The caravan kept to the riverbank, where there was more

space. Houses started to cover the ground for a mile in both directions: single houses at first, standing alone. But the further they went the denser the buildings became, and tall, too, some three or four storeys. He'd seen places that big in Marsdenville but they still didn't look right to him. Top-heavy; they should have fallen over. What if a storm blew in? And some were even made of stone – as if that was a proper thing to build houses with. They made him feel small.

Moving along the river, it was clear they'd not entered Par Market by the usual route because the houses and shops faced away from them. Thomas looked in through back windows into kitchens and parlours. There were rooms full of men and women at work. They sat at contraptions Thomas didn't recognise, some with threads dangling from them, others like enormous bowls. Even the buildings that were obviously homes were different, full of furniture – more than just a table and chairs and a stove and some shelves. There were dressers and soft seats and bookcases, and more small tables than a family could need.

'There's money in Par Market,' he said.

Callum didn't seem interested in the houses. He ignored the windows, and the people behind them.

There was a bridge over the river, with big pillars sunk into the water and low stone walls. Thomas could see people from the waist up, going in both directions, moving at the pace of a crowd: a careful, respectful shuffle. But that changed with the arrival of the caravan. A lot of men in bright trousers formed a line at the start of the bridge. Their thick arms and bare chests stopped the crowd. There were murmurs, and one or two raised voices. But by then it was too late and the bigger wagons were already on the thoroughfare. No one wanted to get too near them, so people waited.

Thomas and Callum followed in the wake of the caravan, but soon enough they were pressed together by the sheer number of people. There were all kinds of faces in the crowd, man and Walkin'. Thomas tried to catch the eye of some who were more obviously Walkin', but they ignored his smiles and ducked their heads. No one seemed to avoid being near him, but he had room in front of him the whole way along the street. There was food cooking on either side, soups, meats, nuts, corn, with men standing behind big pots and trays.

Thomas leaned over to the boy. 'You should eat.'

'After,' Callum said, motioning to the caravan. They could still make out the big canvas tops above the crowd but they were falling behind. Callum pressed his way through the river of shoulders and Thomas followed in his wake, apologising whenever a head turned around. Mostly they shrank away from him, some with wide eyes, others holding hands to their mouths.

A young boy appeared out of the crowd and stood in front of Thomas. The boy had black matted hair that clung to his forehead. His trousers didn't reach below the knee. His shirt was missing buttons and when he held out his hand, he only had three fingers.

'Pennies for the poor?' the boy said.

'I can't spare them.'

The boy's expression was pitiful. And rehearsed. 'I just need—'

Thomas tried to push past the boy, but he caught hold of Thomas' hand.

'Help,' the boy screamed. 'Get off me, bones, get off me!'

'What are you doing?' Thomas said, trying to shake the boy loose, but his meatless arms were stronger than they looked.

'Get it off of me!'

There was a loud whistle that blew again and again, and a man in a tall hat came pushing his way through the crowd. They parted as much for the noise as for him. He marched right up to Thomas and blew his whistle.

'Let go of that boy, you worthless, worm-eaten bag o' bones.'

The boy let go.

'He– he—' The boy sniffed and tears started to roll down his face. 'He tried to take me away. To his home.'

'Not true,' Thomas said. 'This boy is a beggar and a liar.'

The man took the cudgel that was hanging at his belt and pressed the end of it to Thomas' chest. 'Be careful what you call people, bones.'

'But—'

'You better come with me,' the man said.

'Why? Where?'

'Where you can't be bothering innocent little boys, that's

where.' Behind the man, the little boy smirked through his tears. He rubbed his fingers together.

Thomas nodded and the man took hold of his arm.

'Uncle William, is it really you?' The boy wiped his face and stared up at Thomas. 'But it's been years and years.'

The man turned. 'What's that?'

'Is it really you, Uncle William? Back from the war? We thought you were dead?'

'I am – I mean, I was. I did die,' Thomas said.

The man looked at them both. 'You know this bag o' bones?'

'It's Uncle William, I'm sure of it now. I just didn't recognise him.'

'Well, don't you go grabbing people before they know who you are,' the man said, hooking his cudgel back in place. He took a long look at the boy and then nodded to himself. He walked away through the crowd. He wasn't wearing any shoes.

'That's three pennies then,' the boy said.

'Three?'

'You want to be Uncle William or not?'

Thomas was careful to keep his coin bag in his pocket as he took out three pennies. As soon as they were in the boy's hand he was gone. He wondered if the boy would even get to keep two.

Thomas had lost sight of Callum, but halfway down the thoroughfare the caravan was turning off through a big broken gate. He pushed his way to the wall and once again waited at a distance whilst Callum talked to the men – to one man in particular. He was wearing a plain shirt and fanned himself, though it was not that hot.

Callum came back. 'They can arrange for you to see some woollies. For a price.'

Thomas nodded, taking out a small purse. 'And neats?'

'That will take longer. He suggests an inn; we stay there tonight and see the woollies tomorrow.'

'Fine.'

'He thinks I own the farm and you're the farmer.'

Thomas put the purse in Callum's hand. 'I hope this inn isn't too expensive.'

'It won't be.'

Callum spoke with the caravan owner again to get directions to the inn, then led Thomas there through the crowded streets. Away from the main thoroughfares, Par Market meandered and twisted. The houses were packed close together and the gutters ran ripe. They were careful to stick to the middle of the narrow alleys now the sky was growing dark. There had been no break in the clouds all day. Windows were starting to glow with the light of candles that were too bright to Thomas' eyes.

The inn was no bigger than the houses around it but there was a sign above the door with a faded picture of a shaggie, no words. It was quiet inside and the air was heavy with smoke. A few men sat at tables, pipes resting in their mouths. The floor was covered in old sawdust. The room was smaller than the cabin he'd built. A middle-aged woman standing behind the bar put down her cloth as they came in.

'Do you have any rooms?' Callum said.

'Plenty.' The woman's voice was hoarse and deep. 'And there's a shack out back for his kind,' she said, nodding at Thomas.

'I won't need a room.'

'Par Market has a curfew.'

'A what?' Thomas said.

'No Walkin' on the streets at night, that's what.'

'That'll be fine,' Callum said. 'I'll take a meal as well.'

'Sit yourself down then. The shack is through there.'

Callum said he would be fine, so Thomas went out the room and into a small yard. There was a door that looked like a privy and opposite the inn was an open set of double doors, like a barn. The woman had called it a shack, which described the state of it well enough: the walls were wonky and the roof didn't fit. He stepped inside and peered into the gloom. There was no candle light, but gradually he could make out the shapes of other people, other Walkin', both men and women, sitting on the floor, leaning against the walls or lying down.

'Hello,' he said. No one answered. As his eyes adjusted he could see there were more than twenty or so Walkin' in the shack. Their clothes were grubby and threadbare and many of the men were topless. Their skin was pale, easy to see even in the darkness. He settled down in an empty spot against the wall, next to two men, one with a thick red ring around

243

his neck and the other missing an arm. They were playing some kind of game. Thomas watched them for a long time. When he was in the Protectorate men used to play games with cards. He never had a knack for it. As they finished a hand he introduced himself.

'Jones,' the hanged man said. 'This is Saul.'

They dealt him in without his asking.

'I'm here to buy livestock,' Thomas said.

'That a fact?'

'No Walkin' can buy stock,' Saul snorted.

'My son is in there.' The lie came easily.

They made noises of understanding. That was different. That made sense. If they had sons, it would be the same.

'You not from around here?' Jones said.

'South of here. A long way.'

'It's tough in the south,' Saul said. He wiggled the stump of his arm. 'Real tough.'

Jones started wheezing. He was laughing.

Someone was singing, softly at first: a woman singing low notes. The woman she was next to told her to shut up and she stopped.

'They don't have high-class places like this in the south,' Jones said.

'I went somewhere once,' Thomas said. 'It was supposed to be good for Walkin'. Like a home.'

'No such thing.'

'No, there wasn't.'

'Isn't that a tough one to swallow?' Jones said, laughing again.

'I still have a family.'

'So you said.'

'A wife and a daughter too,' Thomas said, putting a card down.

'Still living?'

'Yes.'

'Isn't that something!' Jones cupped a hand to his mouth. 'Hey, Rusty. This fella has a living wife.'

'What the hell for?' a voice called back. Some Walkin' laughed, others called for them all to shut up. That was something that happened a lot. It was a long time until dawn.

4 : 2

Behind the house Mary scanned the hills and the tree-line. She held her hand to her eyes against the sun's glare. The Walkin' was probably watching her. If he wasn't he was a fool. No matter – even two days of not having to fetch water was worth her copy of the Good Book. But maybe he believed her when she said it took time to read. To understand. Maybe he had a sense of honour for a trade buried under that thin skin and wasted muscle. Starting the Walk changed people. She wouldn't speculate on a man she barely knew, just enjoy it for as long as it lasted. And find more for him to do.

She flicked through the pages, making sure to cut out only twenty. Constancy, tradition, symbols – they were all part of the Good Book. She laughed – she was giving sermons – but the laughter tasted bitter.

The walk to the forest was painful and she had to stop barely fifty paces from the house. The throbbing in her thigh was too much. She closed her eyes, and when she opened them, there were black smudges at the corners of her vision. No matter where she looked the smudges were there. She tried to calm herself, taking slow, measured breaths. Gradually the black faded. It took her much longer to reach the trees. Every part of her ached. She sat at the base of a tree and leaned back.

'You look ill,' Silas said, looming over her.

'That so?'

'I read your fancy words.' He tossed the pages into her lap. 'There's nothing there.'

'What did you expect? Did you think it would be so easy?'

'Those pages have nothing on the Walk.'

'You have to read between the words,' she said. 'The meanings are there.'

'You calling me slow, girl?'

'No. Just keep reading.'

'You have more pages?'

'Water first,' she said.

'What's to stop me taking them? Taking all of them?'

'Nothing.' She stared blankly up at him.

He growled and snatched the bucket.

The next morning there was a bucket of water on the porch. Mary went to the back of the house. The Good Book wasn't there. She checked behind all the pillars; it hadn't rolled away. She shielded her eyes as she looked to the forest but she couldn't see Silas.

Bryn knelt down and counted the planks of wood. Six left, and a pile of odds and ends in the corner – the remains of boards that had been trimmed or cut to size. He hefted the remaining wood under his arm.

Travis, John and the Lieutenant were working on the third wall. Like before, they had silently fallen into the same rhythm. When he was working with them he forgot it after a while, but going to and from the tool shed made the strangeness of it jar. He dropped the wood on the ground.

'This is the last of it,' he said.

Only the Lieutenant stopped working. 'What do you mean?'

'There's no more wood.'

'We'll get more.' The Lieutenant took the last six planks and soon they were lost in the wall. It was only as tall as Bryn. The hammers fell silent and all of them stared at the wall. Did they see hoods there too, clutching at a regiment's worth of ears? They didn't sleep and they didn't dream, but maybe they saw things at night when they were working. Bryn couldn't look at even an unfinished wall without seeing the hoods with their open beaks, or hearing the heavy patter as the ears hit the wood.

'Scrounge what wood we can from the fort,' the Lieutenant said. 'Then we'll go to the forest.'

Without a word they split up, heading to the four corners of the fort. Bryn went to the main building. The table and chairs could be used. He picked up a chair. There was nothing else in the room – nothing else in the other room either, just blank walls and this table. It didn't seem right to get rid of it. The Lieutenant wanted to better the fort, not gut it. The soldiers who came next would need somewhere to sit and eat, somewhere to talk. That kind of thing was important. He put the chair back. Upstairs, he stared at the bed for some time. There was wood there and no one was using it. But the next Lieutenant would. If they took the bed an officer would have to sleep on the floor with his men. That wouldn't make it a better fort. Instead, Bryn took all the food and tools out of their crates and stacked them by the wall. The crates he took out to the courtyard.

There was a shout. It wasn't a word, not that Bryn could tell. Travis and the Lieutenant appeared out of the sheds and the three of them ran towards the sound, towards the far end of the fort where they'd buried George and Jackson.

John was standing by the graves. He turned to them. 'Who did this?' He pointed at a third cross in the ground.

No one answered. 'John' was carved on the cross.

'Who did this?' he screamed.

The Lieutenant moved slowly, his hands raised. 'We didn't put it there, John.'

'How do you know?'

'We've been with you all the time.'

'Not him!' John said, jabbing a finger at Bryn.

'Why would Bryn do this?'

'I don't know. He's – he's gone strange.'

'It wasn't me!' Bryn said.

The Lieutenant walked over to the cross.

'Don't touch it,' John said. 'Don't move it. Bad luck.'

'You want it left there?'

John growled. 'Just don't touch it.' He shouldered past Bryn and Travis.

Bryn stood in front of the cross. He tested the ground with his toe. It was solid. It didn't look like anyone had been digging. Was that worse? A marked grave waiting to be dug.

'It wasn't me,' Bryn said again.

'I know.' The Lieutenant stood beside him. 'And so does John.'

'But then who put it here?'

'Maybe he did.'

Bryn glanced at the Lieutenant. He wasn't joking.

'I've heard people do all kinds of things when they start the Walk.'

'The letters are carved different,' Travis said, peering at the crosses. 'I don't figure that was me.' He nodded to himself and left the little graveyard.

The two of them stayed there longer than they should have. It was quiet. Bryn could hear his own breathing and could see his own breath in the fading light. He wrapped his arms around himself. The Lieutenant paced from John's empty grave to the other two and back. Something moved in the trees, high in the branches, and Bryn saw a black glint.

'Why do they come here?' he said.

The Lieutenant looked up into the trees. 'Do they bother you?'

'They're always there, even when I'm sleeping.'

'Birds can be good or bad luck, depending on who you ask.

Blightbirds are supposed to see death coming days before. I don't know any stories about hoods.'

'They weren't welcome on our farm,' Bryn said. 'We dressed up straw to scare them off.'

'These don't seem too scared. Not even of me.'

'I think they've seen this all before – seen it here, at Fort Wilson. Nothing seems to surprise them.' Bryn rubbed his arms.

'I was in charge of sixty men and none of them got a grave like this,' the Lieutenant said. 'Sixty was a small part of that battle. They dug pits and set them alight.'

Bryn looked up to the hoods again. It felt like the Lieutenant's story was as much for them as it was for him.

'Somehow they blamed me, said I didn't follow orders.'

'Doesn't sound like you.'

'It wasn't,' the Lieutenant said. 'I followed my orders and my men still died. I wasn't to blame, but I was responsible. You'd think losing four would be easier than sixty.'

'Is that why they sent you to Fort Wilson?'

'Punishment? Maybe they do know what's happening here.'

'But then why send us? What did I do wrong?' Bryn said.

'They don't care.'

Bryn went back to the main building. It was dark, but he didn't light a candle: the door was open and the moonlight was enough to go by. John was sitting at the table. Bryn opened his mouth, but closed it again. He'd already said it wasn't him. Instead, he took some food to the gap under the wall and got down on his hands and knees. The floor was so cold it burned his cheek. Wesley was there: the small, fat shape of him was black against the grey-washed ground. Bryn pushed the food through the gap. But the grain-thief didn't move. Bryn pushed it further towards Wesley, but still nothing. Bryn pulled back his finger. There was something on the edge of his nail: a smear of mud or muck. He brought it closer to his face. It was dark red.

He rushed outside and ran his hand along the wall, feeling the wet roughness of the wood. Now he was looking for it, he couldn't miss it. The metal knife caught the light for only an inch.

Kneeling down, he pulled the knife clear. The grain-thief was barely bigger than the blade. He'd been cut almost in two. Bryn cradled it in his palm, pressing its sides together. In his other palm he held the knife. He took them both to the table. He placed them carefully side by side.

'You didn't have to do that,' Bryn said. He didn't wait for a reply. He went upstairs and dropped into his blankets.

'Fire!'

Bryn's eyes snapped open. He was facing the stairs. He could see Travis' head in the gap between the bed and the floor.

'Fire,' the little man said, and then he was gone. Bryn ran after him, not waiting to put on his boots. The ground was hard beneath his feet. He didn't feel hot, and the air was clear. The main building was quiet and empty.

He took a few steps into the courtyard and saw the blaze: the old ammunitions shed was as bright as dawn. Thick smoke billowed upwards. Now his cheeks and hands were tingling with the heat. Twenty paces of dark earth were between him and the fire. Something cracked and broke – a wooden sound, like the McDermott wagon had made when they first met. There was a gust of air and the fire flashed yellow-white. Bryn covered his face.

The Lieutenant and Travis appeared, carrying buckets, and ran to the side of the shed. They tossed the water, but missed, hitting the new wall instead.

'What are you doing?' Bryn shouted.

They were already on their way back to the well. 'Stop it spreading.'

Bryn moved closer.

'Don't,' the Lieutenant said.

The window was still intact, but the glass was black and moving, like a river at night. His eyes started to water and his skin dried out as flakes of glowing wood swirled in front of him. He knocked them away. He covered his mouth but that didn't stop the coughing. He glanced back, but the others were gone. Pushing forward he could feel the heat on his tongue and in his nose. Another step and it was in his throat. His eyes kept streaming, but the tears didn't make it to his cheeks.

He was close enough now to see through the glass. There was a pile of crates stacked in the middle of the floor and

John was on top of them. Flames gnawed at him but his eyes were closed. His arms were crossed.

The Lieutenant and Travis came back and tossed their water on wood that wasn't burning.

'John is inside,' Bryn screamed.

They didn't stop.

He stumbled towards the door. It was locked, the broken, rusty padlock bent and twisted. He pulled at it, but snatched his hand away, crying out: his fingertips were wrinkled by blisters, but he couldn't feel his own pain.

Bryn staggered back and ran to the well. The further he got from the fire the more he felt it, behind his knees and under his arms and his elbows, all cracked and stinging. It was raw to breathe. He clutched at his hand. The skin was falling off in slow sheets, like porridge from a spoon. Travis was working the winch. Bryn shoved the Lieutenant aside and held a bucket in his good hand whilst Travis filled it. There was a hole along the bottom rim and water seeped out. He covered it as best he could and hurried to the shed. He threw the water and the fire spat and hissed, and then it burned on. He went back and forth to the well, sometimes working the winch on his own, until his feet were numb. One hand was useless, and every time he got to the shed, there was a little less of John inside.

He caught hold of the Lieutenant.

'Stop it! You have to help him,' Bryn shouted, but the Lieutenant shrugged him off and looked at the fire.

'It's not on the wall,' Travis said.

'Forget the wall!'

'We can't save the shed,' the Lieutenant said.

'John is *in* there.'

'We can't save John.'

Bryn turned away. He took his bucket and tossed the water onto the shed. He'd empty the well if he had to. The others joined him and they worked through the night. Bryn slowed, putting less and less water in each time. Before dawn he couldn't lift half a bucketful. He sat down, his hand in water, watching the new skin form. It was a darker red than the fire.

Travis and the Lieutenant didn't stop and by the time the sun was fully up the fire was out. All three of them were covered in soot and ash and stained by smoke.

'Did we save him?' Bryn said.

'There's nothing left.'

'Was it him? Did he start it?'

The Lieutenant squatted down beside him. 'The door was locked from the outside.'

'Then who?' Bryn looked from one to the other.

Travis shook his head.

4 : 3

Mary opened the door. There was someone sitting on their porch – a soldier – and next to him was a full bucket of water.

'You have the whole book. I don't have anything else,' she said.

The soldier turned his head. It wasn't Silas but the young one. He looked awful. His face was smeared with black muck. His uniform was burnt and singed – though she'd seen worse. His eyes were red and his skin was flaking.

'Is your father here?' he said.

'Why do you soldiers always want to talk to him? Is it because he was a soldier too?' She sat beside him on the porch steps. He shifted away so they weren't touching.

'He's . . . he knows things, having been one for a while.' The boy was holding his hand. His fingers weren't right, but she couldn't see why – he hid them when he noticed her looking.

'Been a Walkin', you mean?'

'That's right.' He paused long enough for Mary's backside

257

to fall asleep. She fidgeted, trying to get comfortable. 'Do you think they have souls?'

She started to laugh. But he looked so earnest. 'I didn't realise every soldier had a spiritual side.'

'What do you mean?'

'I don't have my copy of the Good Book – that's the place to look for souls. But if you're asking me? No, they don't have souls and neither do we.'

'But where do we go? After?' he said.

'How would I know?'

'We're dying at the fort. One by one.'

'Everyone dies,' she said.

'You'll come back, right? Because your father did.'

'Seems likely.'

'I'm not sure I will. I don't think—'

The front door banged open. Sarah was standing there with a rifle aimed at the boy. In the silence the clank of the hammer seemed to roll around the hills.

'What are you doing here?' Sarah said.

'Again, Mother?'

'This one bleeds. What do you want, soldier?'

He stood up slowly. He raised his hands: one flat, the other curled into a claw. 'I just wanted to talk – to see people. That's all.'

'Get inside, Mary.'

'But—?'

'Now!' Sarah stepped aside, motioning with the rifle.

She stayed by the door, her mother between her and the

boy, and crossed her arms. What difference did it make if she was inside or not? Sarah had the rifle.

'What are you talking about, "see people"?' Sarah said. 'You've got more soldiers in that fort, don't you?'

'They're all . . . ' The boy's eyes rolled back. Like a felled tree he stiffly dropped off the porch.

'Oh no you don't,' Sarah said. She kept the rifle trained on him as she nudged him with her foot. 'Get up.'

'I think he's fainted.'

'I'm not falling for that one. Get up.' She kicked him. He didn't move.

Mary knelt down and put a hand on his chest. 'He's still alive.'

'Of course he's alive.'

'We should take him inside.'

'I bet he'd like that!'

Mary picked up the boy's ankles. 'He's obviously hurt and he needs our help. He's our neighbour. The Good Book has a lot to say about that.'

'Don't lecture me on faith,' Sarah said. She put down the rifle and took up his shoulders. Between them they managed to half drag, half carry him inside.

'He can have my bed,' Mary said.

'He won't have *any* bed.'

'We can't just put him on the floor.'

Sarah sighed. 'Fine. He'll rest in mine.' She angled the body towards her room. She didn't pull back the sheets, instead just dumped the boy on the bed and hurried out.

Mary went to take off his boots, then realised he wasn't wearing any. His feet were black with patches of blood. Sarah returned, still carrying the rifle, and dragged the room's single chair to face the bed.

'Look at him,' Mary said. 'What happened at that fort?'

'Who's to say? But those sheets will need cleaning.' Sarah rested the rifle on her lap.

'He's so young.'

'They start them that way. Your father wasn't much older. I doubt he feels young, the things he must have seen.'

The boy stirred, but didn't wake. He was clutching his hurt hand.

Mary gently took it. Three of his fingers were a tender pink. New skin, raw and smooth, went from the tips down to the second knuckle, stretched over the muscle and bone. Though she'd wondered aloud what had happened, she recognised the soot stains and the marks on his clothes: there had been a fire and he'd been burned. His hand was how the body was supposed to recover: a delicate, vulnerable new start. She'd held her father's hand like this in those first few days and touched the scorched bone. It had been dry; like hot sand it seemed to suck moisture out of her. The boy's fingers were little bulges of water. If she pressed them, they would pop.

'That probably hurt,' Sarah said.

Mary let go of his hand and he held it close. She brushed the hair from his forehead. It was stuck to his skin by a layer of black dust. The hair left stripes of white behind.

'I'll watch him. You said you'd sweep the porch.'

'Yes, I did.' Mary stood. There was a broom waiting for her, and then shelves to dust. Her mother closed the door behind her.

Bryn felt something soft beneath him. He must have crawled into the Lieutenant's bed. The Lieutenant didn't deserve to have a bed – no officer did, not if they would save a wall before a man. Bryn's eyes were closed and he didn't want to open them. He preferred the dark. If he looked he would only see that image again: John sleeping in the fire. Perhaps if he waited long enough it would happen to him too. He could just go to sleep and it would all be over. No more dreams. No more hoods fighting over severed ears. No more being a soldier.

'I can tell you're awake from the way you're breathing.'

Bryn was still dreaming; there was a woman talking to him. She sounded old. Her voice was rough, and it shuddered at the end of words. His mother would sound like that, if she'd lived to be old.

'You're awake,' the woman said. Something poked his ribs.

He looked down to see a rifle pressing against his side and Mrs McDermott at the other end of it. Her mouth was set in a flat line. She was thinner than he remembered. How long had it been? Days? Weeks? Her cheeks were hollow. The bones at her collar cast shadows. He tried to sit up, but she jabbed him with the rifle.

'Don't move. You're rubbing soot into my sheets.'

'I'm sorry. I didn't mean to come here,' he said. He had to speak slowly – his lips were cracked and it stung to form the sounds, some more than others.

'Then why did you?'

'I had to get out. I had nowhere else.'

'Who started the fire?' she said. 'Red-coats?'

'Not red-coats. They could have but didn't. I don't know who, but John died.'

'Did the whole fort burn down?'

'No.' He sneered. 'They saved it.'

'Fires don't start themselves,' she said.

'It wasn't me.'

The door opened and the daughter came in. She had a cloth in her hand. 'Are you hungry?' she said.

'Mary, no.' Mrs McDermott got up from the chair.

'I shouldn't be here,' he said. He moved his legs out of the bed. The floor was cold under his feet. He tried to stand, but his legs wobbled and he fell back. Mary helped him lie down.

'I'll fetch you some soup,' she said. 'We can spare it.'

His stomach twisted at the mention of food, the thought of a hot meal after weeks on raisins and dried meat and watery oats. But food wasn't the only warmth he'd forgotten. The girl's hand was hot, even through his jacket. Her body was alive with heat – so different to the Lieutenant and Travis. They were cold to the touch. Cold when they were close. Cold in a room. Maybe John wanted to be warm again.

The two women left him and he settled back into the bed.

4 : 4

Thomas lost another hand of cards. Saul and Jones were gracious winners, or they were bored of winning. But they kept playing with their attention only half on the game as they watched and listened to the other Walkin' in the shack. Thomas found himself similarly distracted.

There were all kinds of people. Some bore obvious marks of how they started the Walk, wearing them with pride, choosing to reveal stab wounds and patterns of lead shot rather than cover them up. These were mostly the shirtless men.

The woman sitting next to him didn't show any mark. Her face was a little pale, but otherwise there were no cuts or gaps or clots. In the busy streets of Par Market she might even pass for a normal woman. But she was in a courtyard shack with them. She wore a plain dress that was grubby along the hem and had loose stitching. He stole glances at her over his cards. She stared straight ahead, not talking to anyone. She didn't move. He waited what must have been hours, though there was no way to tell – the games blurred into one.

'You don't even look ill,' he said, eventually.

She turned her head and smiled. Her teeth were crooked. But not a bad colour. 'You're kind to say.'

Saul and Jones studied their hands, obviously listening.

'You don't want to show people how you started?' he said.

'I couldn't, even if I did. I don't know.'

'You don't know?' Saul said. Jones hissed and kicked him.

'I went to bed one night. Woke up the next day like this.'

'You a serving girl?' Saul said, motioning at her dress.

'Was − I tried to pretend nothing had happened, but everyone could tell. Everyone who knew me.'

'Can be a hard thing to hide,' Thomas said.

Saul moved his arm-stump and Jones started laughing.

The woman looked away. 'Is it true you're still married?' she said after a while.

'Yes.'

'She stayed with you even after you died?'

'We have a daughter,' he said.

'I see. It must be difficult.'

'Raising a family is.'

'But there's things you can't do any more,' she said.

Jones shifted so his back was to them and he and Saul stared hard at the cards on the floor.

'True. But there's more to marriage than that. Safety. Comfort. She says those are more important.'

'She's lying,' the woman said, smiling.

'You were married? Before?'

'Engaged. He didn't like it when I wouldn't bruise.'

Thomas coughed.

She rested a hand on his arm. 'I hope your marriage lasts,' she said. 'Just don't stop her when she decides to go.'

'You don't know her.'

'No, I don't.'

The first rays of dawn were slipping under the shack wall, where there was a gap big enough to run his hand under. The light hit the creased cards and they became almost too bright to look at. Saul scooped them up, the dawn his cue. Others were standing without stretching and leaving without goodbyes. The woman in the dress was gone. As the shack emptied, Thomas smiled at anyone who would meet his eye, but no one looked cheered by the starting day. He had no idea where they were going, what they would do once they got there. Not even Saul or Jones had spoken of what they did and he felt foolish for not asking, but now it was too late. To ask now would be prying: they hadn't shared their business, just their cards. None of the Walkin' left through the inn but through a side gate that hung on a single hinge.

'Good luck with your son,' Jones said. 'And your farm.'

'Good luck to you too.'

Jones grunted.

Thomas pushed at the door to the inn, which didn't open. He tried the handle, but it was locked. A wheezing laugh drifted from the courtyard and out to the alley beyond. There were candles lit in the windows, but he couldn't see anyone inside. He banged on the door and when he got no response, went through the gate. The alley was narrow, made more so by banks of dirt and rotting vegetables and broken glass and shattered boxes. There was a thin, snaking path cleared by the feet of Walkin'. He followed their steps.

Before the alley spilled out onto the street he saw a face poking out of the rubbish. He stopped and knelt down. A man with no hair, his cheeks rounded and still red, stared past Thomas. His body was bloated. This man wouldn't start the Walk. He had ended here in an unmarked alley off a street in a small town at the edge of the known world. In the army it was easy to forget that men died out of uniform for no reason. He had seen so many bodies tumbled into pyre-pits – that was how death was. He tried to close the man's eyes, but they were too big now.

The front door to the inn was also locked. He knocked again but there was no answer, so he waited in the sun, enjoying the growing warmth of it.

The landlady opened the heavy door and pinned it into place. The sun was well past the roofs of the terrace. She dragged a mat out onto the top step. Brushing her hands on her apron, she said, 'He's having his breakfast.'

Thomas gained the first step, but the woman didn't move. 'You stay here,' she said. She made a face like she was going to spit, but nothing came. The women of Par Market were an interesting breed.

Callum didn't keep him waiting long. He came out with his pack slung over his shoulder.

'I'm glad you had something to eat,' Thomas said.

Callum grimaced. 'It wasn't good.'

'And the bed?'

'Full of scalp crumbers and sheet-specks.'

Thomas glanced up at the nameless shaggie sign. 'We won't come back here again.'

'No.'

Callum led the way down the street. Signs of the day beginning could be seen in every window and doorway. Curtains were drawn, signs put out, porches brushed. It reminded him of his childhood, following his mother to school each morning, except bigger. They turned onto a thoroughfare, much larger than Barkley's and just one of many. There was a little more room than the day before, but again Thomas found himself alone in the crowd. He kept sight of Callum's back, but it was difficult not to stop and stare at the different stalls and shops opening. It was a far cry from Barkley's general store, barber, and smithy. There were entire shops dedicated to hats, or walking sticks, or carriage cushions, and behind the counters were warm-blooded, smiling faces. For the length of the thoroughfare, more than thirty glass frontages and street-carts, he saw only one other Walkin': a man wearing a black suit and black shoes. His windows were curtained the same colour. He put a sign out – 'Undertaker'. He tipped his hat to Thomas. As he went back inside, Thomas looked past him into the shop to see shelves of urns, some intricately decorated in gold and silver, others plain black. They were all more expensive than the ones Gravekeeper Courie threw back in Barkley.

They turned onto another thoroughfare, similar to the one before. He hadn't appreciated the size of Par Market. It made Marsdenville look small. So many people and shops this close to the edge of the map – so perhaps there were more than just exotic animals beyond the mountains. Something had to draw men and women and Walkin' here. From the maps, he'd assumed Par Market was small, that he was setting up his family a few days from a town the size of Barkley: far enough to be out of its influence and close enough for supplies. But seeing its heavy trade and bustling streets he realised there was little chance of isolation. Callum's appearance started to make sense; it would be only a matter of time until someone from Par Market wandered far enough and found them, maybe looking for another route through the mountains.

Callum stopped at a walled compound. The gate was already open, the ground churned by wagons. But there were strange prints in the mud: big prints that made a shaggie's hooves look dainty.

'Do they keep the animals here?' Thomas said.

'I don't know. Wait at the gate.' Callum entered the first building.

There was a loud thud from inside, then another, and another. They came regularly: something was moving between the buildings. Through a small gap he saw an enormous eye – it had the same watery blankness of a shaggie's

– and then a wall of grey that kept moving. The noise became faint, but when he knelt and touched the ground he could feel each step the animal took as it moved away from him. He wouldn't get to see it, not properly. That was no surprise. He understood the effect he had on animals big and small.

The door opened and Callum waved him forward.

'They're ready for us now.'

Thomas followed the boy through dark corridors where the smell of animal dripped from the walls: manure and straw and unwashed skin. Callum sneezed. They passed empty cages, their thin bars coated in rust, with stone floors scrubbed but not clean. Thin windows near the ceiling let in a little light, revealing flaking paint and scuff marks at roughly waist height. They might have kept woollies in the cages, but not for long, he hoped.

The corridor opened out into a large room big enough for whatever was in the wagons – whatever he had felt walking. Like the cages, the floor was made of stone. Callum didn't stop but headed straight towards a group of men. One came to meet him – the man who had been fanning himself in the street. He didn't have a fan now.

'Callum,' the man said. 'Your friend is just as you described.'

Thomas held out his hand, but the man ignored it. He was tanned and had wrinkles at his eyes and mouth. His loose shirt hung on his wiry frame. Thomas could imagine him whipping wild animals under a hot sun. He wouldn't be gentle.

'Is everything ready?' Callum said.

'Woollies are most important, but it would be good to have a couple of milk-neats,' Thomas said, but the man looked only at Callum.

He clapped his hands and the group behind him drew pistols from their hips. Thomas stepped back and the man clapped again. More men came from the corridor; they had rifles braced against their shoulders.

'What's going on?' Thomas said.

'You come with us.'

'Do as he says, Thomas,' Callum said.

The man led him towards the middle of the room, but Callum didn't follow. He stayed back with the men with rifles.

'Callum? What are you doing?'

The men with pistols spread out, keeping their stubby barrels aimed high – at his head. They knew what he was. As he got closer, he noticed some of them were Walkin' too. There was a plain wooden chair.

'Sit,' the man said. Thomas looked around at Callum and the boy stared back. He didn't look confused or scared. One of the men with pistols pushed Thomas towards the chair and he sat down.

'What's happening?'

The tanned man went over to Callum and held out his hand and Callum dropped the little bag of coins into it. The man counted them. 'This is more than we agreed.'

'It's yours,' Callum said. 'I don't need it.'

'The money is his, isn't it?' He laughed.

'I just wanted to buy some woollies,' Thomas said. 'There's no need for all this.'

Someone pulled his arms back and he struggled to get free. A barrel was pressed against his head. The hammer was pulled back. The sound rang through the side of his face like a slap. He stopped fighting them.

4 : 5

'Nothing personal,' someone whispered in his ear. It was a dry voice. 'I'm sorry for your wife.'

Thomas twisted around to look at the man. A Walkin'. Thomas didn't recognise him, but he could have been in the shack, sitting in the dark, listening to Thomas talk.

They tied his wrists, then his arms, then his legs. The rope was thick, used for bigger animals than him.

Callum watched it all.

'Why are you doing this? We took you in! You helped build my house.'

The men stepped back. Thomas flexed against the ropes but they held firm. He wriggled and pushed until the chair toppled over. They righted him.

'Don't do that again,' the Walkin' said. He tapped Thomas' skull with his pistol.

Callum opened his bag and took something out. He came closer. It was a book.

'What are you doing with my Good Book?' Thomas said.

'It's not yours.'

Callum placed the book on his lap. It was in worse shape than his copy; the cover was battered and creased and the corners of certain pages were folded down.

Callum squatted at his feet. 'I've been with you for a long time.'

'What do you mean?'

'I found your house in Marsdenville. The gap it left. People were happy to talk. I bought needle and thread from your shop in West Kennington. In Leigh Creek I washed windows on the street you lived on.'

'That was years ago – you would have been a child,' Thomas said.

'I would have been, Thomas, but that wasn't allowed.' Callum opened the Good Book. On the inside the cover was written: Obadiah Gray. The letters were small and carefully formed.

'Gray?'

'Yes.'

'But the Pastor didn't have any children.'

'Not with Mrs Gray,' Callum said. 'Not with your sister.'

'You're lying.'

'Why should I? My father gave me a task, to make me a man in the eyes of the Good Lord. He loathes all Walkin'. I only hate one.'

'I thought they stopped looking,' Thomas said.

'I didn't.' He closed the Good Book.

Thomas struggled against the ropes again, but it was no use. 'What are you going to do?'

276

Callum stood and gestured to one of the men who had a bucket in his hands. He poured mucky brown water over Thomas' legs, down his back and over his head. It seeped through the gaps in his skin. It smelled sharp and made his clothes shine in the light.

'Callum? Callum look at me.'

The boy turned.

'Don't hurt my family. Whatever you do to me, leave them alone.'

A man struck a match.

'I only wanted them to be safe. To build somewhere they could be safe.'

'"With the indignation of His anger",' Callum said, his voice flat and even, '"and the flame of a devouring fire. He has made it deep and large."'

The man cradled the match in his hands. He stepped carefully towards Thomas.

'"Its pyre is fire with much wood. The breath of the LORD, like a stream of brimstone, kindles it."'

He tossed the match.

It hit the edge of the Good Book and rolled along his leg. Where it touched him there were flames. The match stopped at his knee. Half had already turned to black where the little spark was eating up the wood.

He stared down at his lap on fire. He knew there was heat, that his skin and muscles were burning. But there was no pain. Would he understand pain after all his years of the

277

Walk? He would know it as something different – something remembered, but not felt in a long time.

The Good Book caught. The pages shrank back and the cover curled at the corners. A flame no bigger than the match sprang up in its centre. It seemed too round, too perfect, like a child's drawing of fire.

One of the men coughed as they all backed away from Thomas. Except Callum, who came closer. His lips were peeled back. He spread his arms wide, basking in the heat.

'The breath of the LORD,' he said.

'Don't hurt them!'

'The breath of the LORD.'

The flames spread from his legs to his body and down his arms.

Callum repeated the same words. He was looking beyond Thomas and beyond the fire. He was smiling, tears running down his cheeks.

Thomas tried to move his arms. One responded, but the other was completely lost in shades of orange and yellow. Glimpses of scorched bone showed all that was left. But the ropes began to loosen. He wasn't the only thing burning. He pulled an arm clear. His hand was untouched. He reached out to Callum. The boy stepped back.

'Is the pain so great?'

'No.'

Callum frowned.

The ropes around his legs slumped to the floor. He stood. The ashes of the Good Book rained down around his knees.

The fire had reached his face. It was like staring at the dawn. His legs locked in place. He wanted to walk towards the boy, to embrace him before the end.

'Mary,' he said. He forced one foot forward. 'Sarah.'

Then all was black.

4 : 6

Mary inched the door open. The room was dark, but a square of moonlight crept through at the edge of the window. Her mother was asleep in the chair, but the soldier was awake. His eyes caught the light.

'You should be resting,' Mary whispered.

'There's no rest in sleep.'

She sat down on the bed. 'I used to have bad dreams. Not when I was little, after my father came back. I dreamed that I would wake up and be like him, my skin all dried up and my bones sticking through.'

Sarah mumbled in her sleep. The rifle lay across her lap.

'And when I did wake up I had to make sure I was alive.'

'How did you do that?' he said.

'I'll show you.'

She ran a hand up his leg. She could feel his muscles tense. But he didn't stop her. She undid his trousers. He was warm, and he shifted as she touched him.

'What are you doing, Mary?' Sarah said.

She took away her hand.

'He was having a nightmare. I could hear him from my room,' she said.

'He doesn't need your help.'

Mary closed the door quietly behind her.

In the morning, the soldier was gone. Black stains marked her mother's bed sheets and there were smudges on the floorboards. They would be her first chores of the day. There was a fresh bucket of water on the porch.

Bryn stumbled along the hillside. Clumps of wet grass snagged at his feet. He followed the hills as they rolled like waves. He shivered, and wedged his hands under his arms. His burned finger tips throbbed.

He fell. His hands were too slow to catch him and his face hit the ground. The grass tickled his nose and mouth. He curled up and cried. John's calm face; the girl's warm touch: he didn't understand why these things happened. It would be easier to have someone to blame. The door was locked from the outside. He would remember doing that – he'd remember if it was him. It didn't matter that he'd been having dreams; they were just dreams. But if it wasn't him then it was the Lieutenant or Travis or Silas come back, or the red-coats, or somehow John. He needed to get back to the fort.

The sun flooded the hills. The sudden warmth on Bryn's cheek made him shrink back into a ball. He could still feel the fire, the way it dried him out, the tickle of singed hairs. His raw fingers were close to his face. He put out his tongue,

but tasted soot and ash. He'd eaten the McDermotts' soup
and it was the same.

He got up slowly, his legs unsteady. He reached out with
his good hand. The sun cast a harsh glare. The grass caught
the light and fired it at him. He tried to shield his eyes, but
there was nowhere to look. He coughed, and blood and
spittle clung to his lips. He wiped them away. He managed a
hundred paces before falling again, but this time he stopped
on his knees. There was more coughing and more blood.
Black flecks ran through it, like there was something extra
inside him: something trying to change him. People didn't
catch it. They either had it or they didn't. His father didn't
have it, so he wouldn't either. He could die right now and he
wouldn't come back. His sister had said so. He could lie there
and wait until he coughed out all his blood, nasty and all.
But what if being around them changed that? There weren't
any Walkin' on their farm, or the farms nearby – his father
wouldn't have them. His sister, and everyone else, might
have been wrong. He wiped his mouth again and stood.

The fort was quiet. Bryn waited in the entrance, the only
gap left. The Lieutenant wanted gates here to close the fort
up. It wouldn't keep the red-coats out, they all knew that,
but he had his reasons. Bryn glanced up and down the track.
The mountains still loomed over him and the yellowed earth
still spread out far below. It pulled at him, as it seemed to
pull at the fort. Things slipped off these mountains. They
didn't want him there. The red-coats were smart, not trying
to keep Fort Wilson. People weren't supposed to build this

close to the peaks. Things *happened* here. They were all finding that out, the McDermotts too.

Bryn expected to hear the thud and ring of two hammers working in time, or the cutting of wood, but when he coughed, it echoed.

The Lieutenant appeared from behind the food shed. 'You came back,' he said.

'Did you think I would run away?'

'Why didn't you?'

Bryn scratched the back of his head. The mountains asked him the same question.

'I'm still a soldier,' Bryn said.

'No one is keeping you here. And you're no help. Take off the jacket and leave it. Don't you have somewhere you'd rather be?'

'She didn't want me, not without my farm. Gloria laughed at me.'

The Lieutenant sighed. 'There are other girls.'

'I joined up because I had nothing. Has that changed?'

'Maybe you are like us,' the Lieutenant said. He crossed the courtyard to the main building. 'There's food left.'

'I'm not hungry.'

The Lieutenant went inside.

Bryn stood in front of the ammunitions shed. The memory of heat made him swallow hard. There was no roof and the door was gone. The walls were jagged and burned black, like the mountains at night. He touched the wood. It was soft, and came away in his fingers. But he was surprised to find it wet – it didn't look wet. It smelled old, musty. It didn't have the life or sweetness of the food shed, so if this was decay it was a different kind. He stepped through where the door had been. There were ashes, and shards of crate that had somehow escaped the flames. He couldn't see anything of John, no scrap of colour that might have been his uniform, no patches of skin or clumps of hair . . . unless the pale pieces of wood were really bone. John's ashes. They should be buried.

He turned to leave and noticed the padlock. Only the arm stuck out of the ground. He rubbed at his new skin. He knelt down to dig it out, but stopped – he'd touched it so casually before and it had marked him. The same fingers, but he took his time. The tips brushed the metal and he pulled them back, but it was cold. He checked his hand. The skin wasn't peeling off. He wedged two fingers beneath the arm and lifted it from the ground. It was icy in his palm, though it had no business being cold. He gritted his teeth and threw it as hard as he could. It passed beyond the fort wall and into the forest. He didn't hear it land.

The tool shed would have something to hold the ashes. He pushed the door open, glad of its weight. The dust of their work was thick in the air. He waved his hand but the motes danced beyond him, like specks in high summer. There were obvious scars where the piles of wood used to be. Saws and hammers and planes were no longer in crates. Some were piled carefully, others strewn across the floor – by Travis or the Lieutenant? It was difficult to say. Before, he would have denied the carelessness was either of them, but the

Lieutenant was in a hurry now, to improve Fort Wilson before the red-coats came back. Or another man died. Or before more of their own soldiers arrived. Trying to imagine which would worry the Lieutenant more only made Bryn's shoulders slump further.

There were metal bowls and jugs in one corner. The bowls were full of nails. He ran his hand over the surface as if it was water. He took the smallest jug. Inside was a fat-bodied huntsman. It was in the wrong shed – the specks all buzzed around rotting food, not dusty nails. But then, it didn't seem to be doing so bad. He tipped the jug and it came scurrying out. He lost it under the bowls. Huntsmen weren't scary. Gloria had shown him that. When he shied away from one she laughed; she put it in his hand and closed his fingers with hers. The huntsman felt like sand trying to slip through. He'd squirmed, but she wouldn't let go.

He took the jug to the ammunitions shed and cupped the ashes into it. Every handful was a black smudge that made him think of the huntsman. After the first few the jug looked too big. He felt ridiculous. It was for milk or water; there were special things for ashes. Despite going slowly he spilled tiny waterfalls between his fingers. Worse was the ash he couldn't scrape from the ground. He would have to leave some of it behind. He hoped that was the remnants of wood and not John. In the end, there was so much the jug was almost full and it was surprisingly heavy. He carried it out to the graveyard, covering the top, in case there was a gust of wind.

The shovels were still leaning against the fort wall. He stared at the cross with John's name on. It had made him so angry. Bryn would only make the same, only the letters carved a little differently, so there was no point moving it. Next to George was where he belonged. Bryn started to dig, though his arms ached before the first shovel of dirt hit the ground. He pushed on, ignoring the way his thighs shook. It wasn't quick, but there was a hole.

'Let me finish it,' the Lieutenant said. He was holding one of the other shovels. Bryn stepped away.

'Travis should dig some too. Where is he?'

'Chopping down trees.'

'Will you carve his last name?' Bryn said.

'Of course.'

When the hole was finished, Bryn eased the jug down. They took turns to cover it. The Lieutenant added John's full name to the cross. Bryn leaned on his shovel. The sun was sinking towards the trees. There was a thinness to the sky. Veins of orange ran through the grey cloud. The light wasn't strong enough and it was hard to focus: on the Lieutenant's back, on the disturbed mound of dirt, on the cross. They slipped together. The trees pulled forward. He couldn't hear anything but the small splitting of wood and the slickness of the knife. Everything was still.

'Lieutenant?'

Hoods burst from the trees.

4 : 7

The beating of black wings was like a battle line erupting. Bryn ducked as the first of them flew over the graveyard, blocking out the sky. He covered his ears. Feathers brushed against his neck and hands, and then claws. They snagged at him, leaving little cuts like thorns. His knuckles bled. His hair became wet with his blood. He curled tighter into a ball, but the hoods still swarmed. He glanced over towards the Lieutenant. Between the thick lattice of wings and beaks he could see flashes of pale skin. The Lieutenant was standing. The hoods flew round him. As he came towards Bryn they parted for him. He was a stone in a river of birds. The hoods spiralled around them. There were thousands, more than he'd seen at the fort before: a world's worth.

He stood in the Lieutenant's bubble. The Lieutenant's mouth was moving. Bryn took his hands away from his ears, but he couldn't hear words, only the beat of wings. The hoods flocked out of the trees, but they stopped at the fort, wheeled and followed the wall. He couldn't make out individual birds, but the mass of shimmering black feathers had a direction. The Lieutenant took his arm; though Bryn struggled, he couldn't break the grip. The Lieutenant was talking again as he led him in the same direction as the hoods. If he abandoned Bryn now, the birds would leave only ribbons: bloodied ribbons of clothes and bones. Not enough to come up from. They should have been heading towards the trees, where it was safe now, but the Lieutenant wouldn't leave the fort. His slow, steady paces were louder than his lost words. He owned Fort Wilson until he was done with it.

Bryn was stuck between the Lieutenant and the hoods. The flow of wings turned the corner, then they were gone. Bryn swallowed, and his ears popped.

'We have to follow them.'

Bryn shrank away from the Lieutenant's booming voice and dropped to his knees. He rubbed his hands together, trying to dry the blood that ran between his fingers. He flinched at the memory of the brush of feathers on skin. With his nails he scraped the back of his neck until he could only feel it burn, to feel anything other than feathers.

The Lieutenant stooped down. 'Come with me, Bryn.'

'I don't want to see.'

'You have to.'

The Lieutenant dragged him to his feet.

'I couldn't count them,' Bryn said. 'There's a number of birds that are bad luck.'

'That many can't be good. But you know that.'

Bryn tried to turn away, but the Lieutenant stopped him. He pushed and punched the Lieutenant, but it was like hitting the fort wall. The Lieutenant carried him around the corner.

There was a cloud of roiling, writhing hoods on the track. Flashes of light caught on eyes and beaks and claws. A few birds fell out of the group and hit the grass. They struggled to stand, their twig-legs wobbling as if they were drunk and their wings stretched at odd angles. One by one they returned to the cloud, only to be replaced by others who fell and sprawled on the ground. The hoods were mute – not a single caw over the heavy thrum of wings.

The Lieutenant led him towards the birds. He couldn't look away, though the shapes made no sense to him. The cloud was opposite the entrance to the fort. They crossed the track and as they came nearer, the birds started to peel away. Fingers came out of the black mass: grey tips that shone. Every step showed more cold skin. An arm stretched out, and then a nail, fat and square and ugly, driven through the wrist. The head was worn, with little chips along the edges; veins of rust lurked there too. The centre of the nail had been hammered clean to the metal. There wasn't any blood; it looked like the skin had given way willingly. More and more hoods took flight, revealing a bare chest, the ribs clear to see.

The Lieutenant ran forward and the hoods scattered, though they didn't fly high, or to the trees. Their ungainly flapping took them as far as the roofs of the fort, where row after row of birds, arranged neatly up the slanted tiles of the main building, watched them. The lip of the shed was lined with puffed black chests too. They covered the flat roof; Bryn couldn't see but he could feel the weight of them, silent as ever.

The body was Travis. He was stripped to his underclothes and nailed to a big wooden cross, the nails through his wrists and his ankles. The hole where he'd been shot was as dull and colourless as the rest of him, the skin puckered. Bryn felt how smooth it was. Above it a piece of paper was pinned to his chest. It was torn all along the sides and covered in scratches and marks from beaks and claws. Bryn had the same on his hands. He pulled at the paper tearing it off the pin.

Travis' head fell forward. There was a crack as his chin hit his chest and his teeth snapped together. Bryn dropped the page.

A huge purple gash ran from Travis' forehead back to where his crown should have been. It was deep. This was what a man was made of: slick squares piled on top of each other, like tiny soft crates. Inside them had been Travis, his memories, what he thought about, how he saw things. Someone had cut the lid off enough of those crates and he had fallen out.

The Lieutenant knelt and picked up the page. At Travis' feet was a folded uniform. On top of it was an axe.

"'Then he called for a light, and sprang in, and came trembling, and fell down before Paul and Silas, and brought them out, and said, Sirs, what must I do to be saved? And they said, Believe on the Lord, and thou shalt be saved."'

The Lieutenant held out the paper, but Bryn didn't take it. He ran his hand along the handle of the axe. It was rough and cold. The blade was notched and dull. It had dealt with trees as it had dealt with Travis.

'Was it the same with John?' Bryn said. 'Did Silas leave his mark then, too?'

'Not that I found.'

'Are we supposed to fall in front of him and beg to be saved?'

'I don't know what he wants.'

Bryn faced the rows of hoods. 'Is that it, Silas?' he screamed. The birds stared on.

'Someone gave him this from the Good Book,' the Lieutenant said. 'I saw the McDermotts praying when we were with the wagons.'

'Does it matter?'

'I'm trying to understand.'

'What good is understanding?' Bryn snatched the paper. He screwed it into a ball and threw it at the hoods. It was quickly lost in their ranks. 'It's not hard. Look!' He pulled down Travis' arm as far as it would go against the nail. Travis' name was carved on the beam of wood.

They dragged Travis, still on his cross, around the fort to the graveyard, while the hoods watched. Bryn didn't see them move, but they were always facing him. He held the bottom of the cross, careful not to touch Travis' ankles, but it was too heavy. The Lieutenant carried the weight. They laid it down on the grass.

'We can't bury him like that,' Bryn said.

'Then we take him off.'

The Lieutenant grabbed Travis' arm and wrenched it clear. Bryn swallowed back bile at the snapping sound as the nail parted the bone. He looked away as the Lieutenant freed the other arm. The sound of the ankles was too much and he vomited. The puddle he made was thin and clear, as empty as he felt. He spat to clear the taste, but it stayed with him. His teeth were wooden, his tongue ready to splinter.

The shovels still had fresh dirt on them. Bryn took one. It was like moving a boulder. He could barely lift the blade from the ground. His arms failed him. He dropped the shovel.

'I'll manage,' the Lieutenant said.

Bryn ignored the judging eyes of the hoods as he walked back. He fell onto the bed and listened to the steady slap of earth being moved as he fell asleep.

He was hungry. He had forgotten to eat yesterday. Food was difficult. He was used to people telling him when to eat, what to eat. For a long time it had been his father. Plates were put on the table: meat, potatoes and something green, most of the time, and all of it from their own farm. Some nights there was more meat, some more greens. The amounts changed, but the meal didn't. Then the Lieutenant: he decided when the wagon or the marching or the drills stopped. Eating was passing dried meat from hand to hand; plates were a long way away.

Bryn pulled some meat out of the sack. Chewing, he tried to remember what it was like cooked. He could picture juices, but the taste wasn't there.

His stomach complained as he went downstairs. Light streamed in through the doorway and he looked up at the sun. It was bearing down on the mountains. He'd slept for most of the day. He rubbed at his eyes, but it didn't get rid of the hazy feeling behind them. His mouth was sticky-dry and the meat hadn't helped. He smacked his lips and cast around for some water, but there was nothing but burned down candles on the table. He searched for a bucket, but they must have been at the well where they had been left after the fire. How many days had passed? Had he gone without water for so long? The McDermott women gave him water. He scratched the back of his head. He shouldn't have slept so late.

Outside, the shadows were long across the courtyard. The roofs were noticeably bare, which was a relief. He got halfway across the yard before he noticed the Lieutenant, standing in the gap between the main building and the shed: the last gap in Fort Wilson. Instead of a mighty barred gate there was him. His hands were by his side – he was holding his pistol pointed down at the ground. Bryn joined the Lieutenant in staring out at the track. There was a long scar where they'd dragged the cross, running the length of the fort and then around the corner, all because Bryn didn't have the strength to lift a man and his cross. Travis' uniform was still in a pile, together with the axe that killed him. Bryn had forgotten about it and the Lieutenant had buried him without it.

'What are you doing?' Bryn said.

'Waiting.'

'For what?'

'Him,' the Lieutenant said.

'We could go looking?'

'You think we'd find him in the forest? The two of us?'

Bryn headed out of the fort, away from the scar that led to the graveyard. The buckets were scattered around the well. He took one and left the others as they were. Grass was already growing around them, green threads poking through the sagging wooden slats. The winch was stiff. The well was completely dark, but when he sat on the stone wall and peered in he could hear the water sloshing below. The night sky had stars and the moon. Even if there were clouds there was some light. The flock of hoods caught the sun. They weren't like this black. He fought the urge to lean in further and further and then there'd be nothing: no fort, no army, no remembering his family – no Gloria and her laughing face.

'Silas!' The Lieutenant's voice echoed around the trees. A bird took off, but only one.

He waited for the sound of raised voices and gunfire. There was no other way for it now. But the silence of the hills came back: a big open silence that the sounds of the forest were part of. He wanted to hear the noise of people again. He'd hoped to find it at the McDermotts, but they were just two women. He needed the clamour of a town. When he signed up to the army, he'd fallen asleep to the ringing of worked metal and slurred drinking songs.

'Silas!'

The darkness of the well silvered and the handle of the bucket appeared. He changed hands on the winch. The skin on his fingers was a bright pink but it didn't hurt. He poured the water from one bucket to the other. He didn't bother to winch it back down. He gulped handfuls and then swirled water in his mouth, enjoying the feel of it.

He passed the Lieutenant. The bucket was leaking in more than one place and he left a trail across the yard. He put it down on the table and watched as the wood changed colour.

'Silas!'

He was hungry again, so he fetched some raisins. When he scooped them out, his fingernails raked the bottom of the sack. He took a chair and put it in the doorway and sat so he could see the Lieutenant. He ate his raisins one at a time. He had nothing else to do.

When the sun went down it started to rain. There was no misting or spitting; the air was clear, and then it wasn't. There was no wind. The rain fell straight down in one long sheet, and the roar of it was constant. He could still see the Lieutenant – an outline that hadn't moved all afternoon. He called out Silas' name, over and over, nothing else. The name was enough.

The night dragged on. Bryn slept in the chair, his head resting against the doorframe. He woke regularly, sometimes with a start, bumping his head. He didn't hear what woke him, but he figured it was the Lieutenant's shouting. He kept on going all through the night: 'Silas!'

Bryn had his prick in his hand. He was going against the side of the main building. What did it matter? With the rain. With them being dead men any way.

'Silas!'

His stream of piss stopped and then started again. He sat back down in the chair. He got up twice more that night to piss.

'Silas!'

Bryn was staring out at the courtyard as it gradually became lighter. The outlines of the sheds grew out of the darkness, solid in the washed-out grey. It was still raining. Water cascaded off the roof, as constant as a waterfall, but it was colourless. Even with the daylight it stayed clear. He stood underneath the fall with his mouth open and it cut across his face, cold enough to make his cheeks hot and his teeth ache. His throat was numb by the time he'd filled his gut. He rinsed his whole head.

Things were sharper now: the curve of the Lieutenant's shoulders, the scuffs on the barrel of the pistol. Water dripped from his fingers in fat, deliberate drops. Bryn breathed in and out as they formed and fell.

The Lieutenant, the fort, the rain. Things could look constant, even though Bryn knew they weren't. The Lieutenant's body swelled and Bryn mouthed along with him:

'Silas!'

By nightfall Bryn's back was throbbing and his stomach was cramping. He got up from the chair. He moved slowly and there were popping sounds from his knees and ankles. His father had struggled to stand and that had been difficult to watch. That was long before the end. Bryn was tired, despite dozing for most of the day. This wasn't the kind of tired that went away with sleep.

He paced from one end of the building to the other as he ate. He passed the table where they'd sat and talked and told stories as it all happened around them. There were the marks on the floor where Silas had tipped the table over. He ran his hand along the smooth banister. He chewed meat as every step took him to where a different soldier had slept, the bedrolls striping the floor. The ghosts of George, John, Silas and Travis, all lying there. They disappeared as he went by. One at a time. As they woke up. Or didn't. In the far corner there was a puddle, creeping further and further into the room. There were scratches on the bottom of the wall where he'd pushed scraps of food out for the grain-thief. Where it was splintered the wood was stained red, though the rain had washed most of it away.

He stopped where George's bedroll had been. He'd been sorry when George hadn't come back, but he'd been wrong: it was better to go once. There was nothing good to hang on for.

He sat back down on the chair and tossed raisins into his mouth.

There was a bang. It echoed around the fort, rippling along the wooden walls, some of which he'd help build. Bryn hoped for thunder; he looked up for another flash of lightning, but the sky stayed grey.

4 : 8

Sarah balanced the basket of washing against her hip, the weight of it digging into her side. There was a time when she wouldn't have felt it on her bone, but with all the coming and going and the worrying she had lost weight. She'd be sorry for it come winter. It would be very cold on the hills. She'd not leave the stove; Thomas could go out and chop wood and wash the sheets. There would be animals to tend – whatever he'd managed to buy. The wool would be welcome. She hoped there would be enough to line the walls as well as for bedding.

She walked beside the river, deeper into the trees. The river was full to bursting and drowned out all other sound, like the forest was listening to its tantrum. Where it was deeper it was a muddy brown, but even in those places it looked quick. There'd been a lot of rain the last few days – so much rain, more than she'd seen in a whole winter in Barkley. What that town could have done with just a day of that kind of rain. Thomas' woollies would be fat things. His neats would produce enough milk to bathe in. She'd doubted his ideas – mountains weren't for farming. But seeing so much water, she could no longer deny him.

The rain made washing the bedlinen more difficult. Her usual place was a swirling mix of dirt and leaves and branches ripped from trees, but where the river rushed over stones it was clear. Her eyes might lie, but she had little choice: her sheets stank of the boy soldier.

There were good spots where the rapids were white and foamed, but she couldn't reach them because of the thick bushes which blocked the way, their thorns sharp enough to ruin her dress. At other places the bank was too high or too steep. The pool she swam in wasn't far away, but that would be too still, and the wrong colour today.

She stopped to inspect some of the early berries. They were not yet a dusky colour, not yet near ripe. A few months and they'd be good for pies. She shifted the basket to the other side and carried on. After thirty paces the berry bushes stopped and she could see the bank again, now sloping more shallowly down to the river. There was a bend and stones and the water was clear. She hitched up her dress and tied the skirts around her waist before going to the river's edge. Using a corner of a sheet she tested the water: the cloth came out a paler shade, but not muddy. She balled the sheet in her hands and knelt down. She felt a sudden rush of blood to the head and reached out to the basket to steady herself. Breathing deeply, she cursed.

'They won't come clean.'

She turned to see Callum. His face was dirty and his black curls were stuck to his forehead.

She stood and undid the knot in her dress. 'Where's Thomas?' she said.

'I've been trying to understand you.' He took a step closer. 'Why stay with a man after he's died?'

'You wouldn't understand.'

'Does that mean you don't know?' he said.

'We have a family. Where is Thomas?' She backed away, but the river was right there.

'Your daughter is old enough to look after herself.'

'Where is he?'

'Why?' Callum said.

'I love him.'

'Love isn't enough.'

'He came back for us. He could have lived any kind of life, but he chose us. You're too young to know what that means.'

'I know the kind of choices men make,' Callum said.

'Where is Thomas?'

'Gone.'

'You're lying,' she said.

'He wanted you to be safe. He tried so hard, even I could see that.'

'I'm not going to listen to this.' She tried to walk past him, but he grabbed her arm. 'Let go of me.'

'I can't.'

He pulled her back towards the river and she struggled to stay on her feet. She hit out at his shoulder and chest, but he didn't stop. He pushed hard and she fell into the river. Her bed sheets tumbled after her and she saw his face between them. He looked calm. She felt the shock of the water, felt it pulling her. Her head hit something hard and she cried out, but water filled her.

The Lieutenant pitched forward. Bryn ran through the rain, the mud sucking at his feet. He knelt at the Lieutenant's side, his knees sinking into the brown water. The back of the Lieutenant's head was gone. Blond hair ringed the crater. There was no blood, but the rain made it all look wet. There were the same spongy blocks that had been cut away from Travis: the only part that meant anything. Bryn reached out his fingers but didn't touch it. He rolled the Lieutenant onto his back. He tried to wipe away the dirt on the Lieutenant's face, but he only smeared it across the cheeks and forehead. It gathered at the edges and in his hair. The Lieutenant looked calm, no fear or surprise on his face.

Bryn felt along the arm until he got to the pistol. The barrel was cold, the hammer still pulled back. He had to prise the Lieutenant's fingers from the handle – it took both his hands to move one finger. The knuckles wouldn't bend and the middle finger snapped as he pulled at it. When he did manage to get the pistol loose, the Lieutenant was still gripping.

The Lieutenant stared up at the sky, water running over the whites of his eyes, pooling at the corners and then disappearing, lost in the greater downpour. Bryn went to close them, but he couldn't move the eyelids – he'd seen the Lieutenant blink. Or at least, he thought he had. He would have noticed if none of the Walkin' blinked – he'd have noticed that. They wouldn't budge now.

He grabbed the Lieutenant under the arms. He would bury him with the others. He'd have a bigger cross. He'd take time to carve it right: Lieutenant Matthews. It was a shame he didn't know the Lieutenant's first name.

'Silas!'

Bryn dropped the Lieutenant. For a moment he stared at the pale lips, but the voice had come from behind him. He turned to see the silhouette of a man holding a rifle, there on the far wall, standing on the boards they'd put there, under the Lieutenant's orders. They hadn't kept Silas out – what good were they? What good were *any* of them?

Silas jumped down from the wall. Bryn held up the pistol. It was hard to see in the rain; shapes had no proper edges. He squeezed the handle; his new fingertips felt thin against the polished wood. He wiped water from his face. The shape of Silas wasn't getting any bigger. He ran his wrist over his eyes again and Silas was gone.

He moved the pistol left then right, squinting against the rain, and then he ran. There was nowhere to hide. The mud fought him, but he pushed his legs hard. Every time his foot hit the ground he waited for the thunder: the sound that would bring the end. He made it into the main building and kept running.

'Where are you going?' Silas shouted. He was laughing loud enough to hear over the rain.

Bryn took the stairs two at a time. At the top he tripped – he was holding the pistol with both hands and put out his elbows. He felt the shudder up his arms and along his shoulders. He cried out as he twisted his body to face the stairs, then wriggled until he was leaning against the wall, the pistol aiming downwards. His chest was thumping: he couldn't breathe quickly enough. He gulped at the air. Sticky threads of spittle spanned his lips. He couldn't wipe them away. He blinked hard, trying to keep the water off his brow from his eyes.

Silas was at the bottom of the stairs. He was taking them slowly. Bryn pulled the trigger. The crack of the pistol rang in his ears. It smelled of wet burning – like the shed after they'd put the fire out.

Silas didn't stop. 'Higher, Bryn. Higher.'

Bryn's thumbs shook as he pulled at the hammer, but it wouldn't move. Silas was at the top of the stairs now. Bryn squirmed away from the Walkin', but the wall was solid behind him. The puckered red scars on Silas' cheeks shone. He leaned forward and took the pistol.

'Please, don't—' Bryn spluttered.

There was a loud slap.

Bryn closed his eyes and waited for the pain that would start in the chest or the head and grow until there was nothing else, but it didn't come. Silas stood in front of him and between them was a black book. The cover was battered and water-stained.

'"Can you even read?", she said.'

Bryn glanced from the book to the pistol Silas was holding. He put his hands in his pockets and took out Silas' ear. 'I kept this for you.'

'I don't need it.'

'I won't come back,' Bryn said. 'My father didn't.'

Silas grinned. It pulled the ribbons of his cheeks. It looked like the legs of a huntsman.

'You think I'm going to kill you?'

'You nailed Travis to a cross. Shot the Lieutenant. You set the fire for John!'

'Yes, but are you like them?' Silas said. 'You're my witness, Bryn.'

'Witness?'

'"And this gospel of the Kingdom shall be preached in all the world for a witness unto all nations; and then shall the end come."'

'An end to what?' Bryn said.

Silas raised the pistol to his head.

'We became a wicked thing here. Tell them that.'

He fired.

4 : 9

Mary stabbed at the fire and the embers flared in protest. She took two logs from the pile next to the stove and placed them gently inside. Small flames tickled the wood as she closed the stove. Her thigh was bad today: a constant ache. She ran a finger along the scar; she could feel it through her dress. At least there wasn't any pus.

She tied back her hair and looked around the room. There were dishes to wash and the floor needed sweeping. Her mother's bed had been stripped – she'd left before Mary was awake. Sarah was washing out the boy. He had smelled busy and used, like men did. It didn't bother her, but it had been a long time since her mother's bed smelled like that. It was no surprise she was in a hurry to be rid of it.

The front door opened. She had the broom in her hands.

Callum came in.

'Back so soon?' she said.

His clothes were streaked with dirt. His eyes were red, with heavy marks under them. 'I came as quick as I could.' He closed the door.

'Where's my father?'

'I need your help, Mary.' He was holding out his hand and she stared at it. Black mud lined his nails; it was in the cracks of his skin.

He wanted the broom, she realised. She propped it against the wall. 'Why?'

'There was trouble in Par Market. They won't let your father go.'

'Who won't?' she said.

He went over to the stove and warmed his hands. 'There are some very ignorant people in this world.'

'What can I do? What help would I be?'

'I'll take you to them. They'll listen to you,' he said.

Mary glanced around the room. 'My mother – she's out washing.'

'I saw her. She's already on her way. She wanted me to come and get you.'

'But I can't go. I would only slow you down.'

He opened the stove and the light of the fire caught his dark curls. He looked tired, older than she remembered, though it had only been a week or so.

'It's a way off this mountain. I know you want that,' he said.

'How could you know what I want?'

'It's obvious. This is no place for you. Your father came here to run away from people. He wanted to build something safe. But you don't want safe.'

'There's no such thing,' she said.

310

'He needs your help. *I* need your help.'

'I'll pack some things.'

She found a shoulder bag and filled it with enough clothes for a few days. She left space for some food. The room suddenly looked empty. They'd come to the mountains with almost nothing and she'd leave nothing behind. But there was one part of it worth saving. She stuffed the sack-weave doll into the bag. As she pulled the strings together, she could see its emerald button eye.

She closed the front door but didn't lock it. Her parents would be back soon. And who would steal what little they had – the soldiers? They were busy with their fort. The boy didn't seem the thieving kind. Silas had all he needed from them. She hoped he found peace in the Good Book, the way her father did.

Callum drank a handful of water from the full bucket on the porch.

'Another house I've left,' she said.

'I don't like being tied to a place.'

'Tell me again.'

'What?' he said.

'Tell me what you're offering.'

'A way off this mountain.'

'It's not really about my father, is it?' she said.

'That's your decision.'

She gazed at the house her father had built. She'd ruined so many before. Their lives would be easier without her. Her mother could stop worrying, stop hoping, and her father could stop running away. She took the porch steps slowly, but she had less trouble on the grass.

Callum let her set the pace, though it was clear he had to force himself to match her. Before they were far from the house he twice went on ahead without realising. He stopped and waited for her.

She smiled at him, rested her hand on his arm. He took her bag.

'Did you think of me?' she said to his back.

'At times.'

'Good.'

She'd thought of him often. More and more with every day that passed and she didn't bleed.

4 : 10

If either of them falls down,
one can help the other up.
But pity anyone who falls
and has no one to help them up.

Ecclesiastes

EPILOGUE

Her eyes were already open when she woke. It was dark, but the wrong kind of dark: a heavy brown. She was moving, she could feel that much, but she couldn't feel her arms or her legs. She thought hard about lifting each one in turn, tried, but they didn't respond. There was a hollow silence around her. She bumped into something solid and it turned her around, but the view didn't change. It was gone before she could tell what it was. Her mouth was open. She couldn't close it.

There was ground beneath her; it was a darker brown and where the ground should be. Her foot scratched the surface and sent up a spiral like a dust-devil. Again she was spun around. A long time passed. Or not. The light didn't change and she could do nothing but think, and that was difficult. She couldn't remember anything before the brown. All she could do was notice shapes as they passed and try to move her body. She touched the ground every so often. Each time she created a cloud and then bounced up and beyond it.

The colour changed and now she saw white and grey.

There was a lot of noise – not different noises, but a single large sound that filled her ears as something else drained away. Her body was dragged over hard, round shapes that pummelled her back and legs. It didn't hurt, but she knew it wasn't good. Her head was struck and for a moment she couldn't see. When the grey came back she reached out and caught hold of – a rock. Her fingers slipped off and she was moving again, but she was in control of her body now. She closed her mouth, but too hard; her teeth cracked like gunfire. More rocks came and went, until eventually she wrapped two hands around one and held on. Angry water pushed at her, but she pulled herself forward until she was standing, chest-deep, in the river.

She howled silently at the clouds. She worked her mouth, but she couldn't summon the words. Hand over hand she hauled herself towards the riverbank. It was three or four feet above the water. She looked behind her, but she couldn't see if it was lower further down – and she might not be able to stop herself again. The bank didn't look so big, but it felt like a cliff to climb. She grabbed at a bit of earth and it came away in her hand. She slipped and almost lost her footing, but she felt stronger now, able to fight the water. She tried again, aiming for some patches of grass, hoping their roots were deep. Her body felt heavy with water. She reached over the top and searched for something to hold onto. There was only the grass but that was enough.

When her legs were clear of the river she sagged under the sense of freedom.

Sarah slumped on the bank until a spasm caused her to lurch to her knees. Her face was still on the ground. She coughed violently, and muddy water poured out of her. She spluttered, her lips working to get clear of the puddle that was forming. Her arms were useless at her side as her body shook. More water came.

When the shivering stopped she forced herself up and spat until her mouth was dry. There was more inside her; she could tell. She coughed and retched, but it wouldn't come.

The backs of her hands were wrinkled, and so was the skin up her arms. She looked down at her chest and that was the same. Her feet, her legs: all of her was wrinkled and pale, as white as the moon. She felt her face. It was difficult to tell, but she traced the lines there that ran across her cheeks. With different fingers she felt the same: lines as big as valleys.

Her legs wobbled. She could feel the water inside settling high in her chest and low in her gut. She took a step and it sloshed forward and back. A few more paces and the water started into a swaying motion. She stopped and waited for it to be calm again.

A bird called: shrill, too loud. She covered her ears and looked up. The bird was fat and white against the darkening clouds. It was going to rain. The bird knew and that was why it complained. She didn't recognise it: as big as a blightbird, but without the long, bald neck.

The grass was greener than she remembered; the ground

317

flatter. There were more fields, and then something silver in colour. Clouds, but lighter than those carrying rain? The grey broke and the sun came through. The silver turned to gold, so not clouds. She followed the horizon as far as she could in both directions. It was water, not muddy like the river, but water nonetheless. It was too big for a lake – even from this far away she got a sense of its size.

Sarah closed her eyes. She'd seen maps, heard stories. It was the sea. She knew it was, but it couldn't be.

She spun around, desperately searching for high peaks and hills, or yellow crags and bluffs.

The land was green and flat. No mountains.

The End.

Turn over for a sneak peek at

YOUR RESTING PLACE
The Walkin' Book III

Coming November 2015

1 : 1

The summer sun was hotter than a cornered mouser. Ryan pulled his straw hat down till it almost covered his eyes, though the sun still went on through to most of his neck and shoulders; dead-lies and the seasons had eaten away at it. He chewed on a hay stalk like he'd seen the men do, then spat.

Stepping onto the lowest beam of the fence, he looked out across their one field. The hay was getting tall, and no amount of looking would get the harvest done; the army man was late. Crops were being worked all along the low hills. The McGraw fields were already on their second cut. He bounced on the beam, half hoping it would break.

He turned his back on one mess only to face another. Their house squatted at the top of a long slope leading down to the road. Between the road and the house was an old corral that hadn't seen use in years, and a chook house with half the chooks already dead and eaten. They had sold the neats two summers back; fat Simmons, with his sweaty hands and busy eyes, taking pity and paying for what he could've stole.

Ryan headed over to the well, kicking any stones in reach. They rattled across the dry dirt. He glared as one hit the back wall of the house and waited for a shriek, but it didn't come. It wasn't long past noon; she'd still be drunk. At the well he lowered the bucket, rattling it all the way down. It might remind her of what went on outside and piss on her morning.

Despite his racket, today was too peaceful for that. Even the chooks didn't start a fuss when he took them the water. The heat might have slowed their senses, but still he didn't take any chances: they were a malicious bunch. Chooks and mothers were created under the same bad moon – they made soothing sounds, all right, but there was evil in every eye and their claws were knife-sharp. The sickly-warm smell of chook shit, old and new, made Ryan gag. He filled up their water bowl with one hand over his nose.

They would need feeding later, a few handfuls of seed from the bag that sagged against the house. It was half seed, half weevil now, but the chooks weren't worried. Loveless, demon-eyed chooks. He kicked a stone at their house, but even that raised nothing more than a warble from them.

'Ryan!' his ma screamed. She was standing in the doorway glaring out at the world. 'What are you doing out here?' She leaned hard on the frame. She was wearing nothing but a nightdress: a string of bones topped by lank black curls.

'Morning, Ma.'

'Don't you sass me. Where's the—?' She belched and spat onto the porch. 'Where's my eggs?'

'I'll see to them d'rectly, Ma.'

'Well then. Don't go waiting for them to hatch, eh?' She stumbled back into the house.

He took the bucket back to the well. Taking off his hat, he scratched the sore on his head. It was dry today. He checked over the field again. Them soldiers had better come soon or he'd have to watch it all rot, as useless as a bucket full of holes. He took two logs from the woodpile, which left a big empty space where the pile should've been. There weren't any trees worth chopping down on the McDermott farm. At least he now had a reason to be away from the house that night; sometimes his ma thought that was important when she had company; other times she didn't seem to care. First he'd steal the axe and then steal the wood – or maybe just steal the wood, depending on where McGraw chained up his rufts.

'I told you not to move that damn chair,' Ma yelled. She could've been bawling right in his ear, the gaps those walls had. There was a crash, likely the chair hitting the table. Even drunk, she had a wiry strength.

Hefting a log in each hand, just in case, he went round to the front of the house and peered in. Ma was sitting, arms crossed, at the small table, which had been shoved up against the wall. The other chair was lying on the floor. One leg was missing.

'That'll need fixing,' she said. She must have eaten the leg; it was nowhere he could see.

The bedroom door was shut. There were marks on the floor where he'd dragged his pallet out. He remembered kicking at it, just to see the dust cloud up – did he move it last night, or was it the night before? Either way, he'd slept by the cooking fire that he'd managed to keep going on hope and ashes, warmed by the embers, trying not to hear. When he needed to, he went and did his business outside, at the far end of the field, then walked back slowly. His ma wasn't so picky.

He'd swept the floor that morning whilst she was sleeping, but now he was bringing it all back in. There was black stuff between the floorboards; who knew what that was? He opened the stove and shoved one of the logs in.

His ma was drumming her fingers on the table. He washed his hands in the bucket while the pan heated up.

'There any bread?' his ma said.

It was four days old, and mould covered half of it. He hacked off the bad bits, then cut the rest into slices that hissed as he dropped them into the pan.

'I don't want it *cook*ed,' she said.

'You don't want it like rock neither.'

He had broken one of the yokes as he'd broken them into the pan; he put that egg on his plate.

'You eat like a mouse – look at you, all elbows and wrists.' She seized his arm with one of her claws. Her nails were bitten to the quick. 'I am cursed with weak men.'

He'd given her three eggs, taken just one for himself.

Ryan wasted the afternoon hours in the shade behind the house, throwing stones and watching any critter that moved, while his ma sobered up. She found him there as the sun started to get red, all colours of angry. She'd had a wash and her cheeks had a little colour, She'd changed into a flowery cotton dress, not her best but it had only one hole, which she had patched over. She'd used cloth from an old red blouse so the patch looked like a faded bloodstain. She wasn't smiling, but she wasn't glaring either.

'We got washing to do,' she said, and he got up and followed her into the house.

Ma came out of the bedroom with a bundle of sheets. The broken chair was leaning against the wall. Chances were she couldn't remember lunch. He picked up the table, turned it sideways, and started for the back.

'No, Ryan, put it in the sun.'

She was ready with the soap and a small pruning knife that had rusted near the handle. She shaved three slices of soap into the water and started scrubbing. His job was to drape the clean clothes over the fence. Left out overnight they would be icy-cold by morning, but mostly dry. Both of them knew this was a chore that should be done early, and they both knew why it wasn't.

'Someone's coming over tonight,' Ma said into the bucket.

That meant his pallet stayed out. If he got back too early from thieving McGraw's wood he'd have to stuff his head under a pillow if he was to get any sleep.

'An important man.'

He didn't want to hear it.

'You'll like him; he rides a big white courser. Deep pockets.'

He went to the fence and wrung out a pair of cotton trousers, the cloth straining in his fingers. His stomach was bile and his breath was hotter than coals.

He stood for a while, watching her as she fought with a sheet. She'd tied her hair back, but stray curls kept slipping out. Her face looked rounder and her skin warmer as she worked. Her arms were too skinny and the black marks under her eyes never went away, but maybe she was pretty.

She passed him the sheet. It still smelled of men and their business.

ACKNOWLEDGMENTS

I would like to thank the whole team at Jo Fletcher Books for their patience and insight. Thanks to my agent, Sam Copeland, for his constant support. And finally, thank you to Ben Nother for explaining how he would build a house on a remote mountain.

David Towsey is a graduate of the Bath Spa Creative Writing Masters programme. He is continuing his studies as a Ph.D. student at Aberystwyth University, where he lives with his girlfriend and their four cats.

Author photo © Keith Morris

ALSO AVAILABLE

YOUR BROTHER'S BLOOD
David Towsey

Thomas is thirty-two. He comes from the small town of Barkley. He has a wife there, Sarah, and a child, Mary; good solid names from the Good Book. And he is on his way home from the war, where he has been serving as a conscripted soldier.

Thomas is also dead – he is one of the Walkin'.

And Barkley does not suffer the wicked to live.

Jo Fletcher
BOOKS

COMING SOON

YOUR RESTING PLACE
David Towsey

Rumours of the Drowned Woman are rife. She hunts down wanted men but never collects on the bounty. Some say she can't be killed, not in the usual ways – there's talk a man tried to burn her once and the flames died as they touched her. The Drowned Woman is looking for one man in particular: he killed her husband and stole her daughter.

Her family has been wronged.

There will be a reckoning.

Jo Fletcher
BOOKS